"I need the two of you to look into something for me."

Bartenders learned to roll with the punches, but this had caught Teddy off guard. Seth, asking for *their* help?

"An old friend from my boxing days is getting screwed over by his landlord. Bastard's throwing him out, claims he's doing something illegal."

"So what do you want us to do?" Ginny asked.

Seth met her gaze squarely. "I want you to save his dumb ass, before this breaks him so bad I can't put the pieces together again."

"We'll look into it for you," Teddy said. "But"—he held up a finger—"if there's even the slightest hint that your friend is guilty, we're done and you drop it. All right?"

"He's not guilty."

Praise for *COLLARED*

"Charming. . . . Vivid descriptions of Seattle's Ballard neighborhood are a plus in this cozy tale."

—*Publishers Weekly*

"The plot moves quickly, enhanced by smart dialogue and good characterizations. . . . A strong beginning to what should be an entertaining series."

—*Library Journal*

Praise for *FIXED*

"There's really no way to see where this suspense story is going or what the final, action-packed chapters will reveal."

—*BookLoons*

Also by L.A. Kornetsky

Collared
Fixed

DOGHOUSE

A GIN & TONIC MYSTERY

L.A. KORNETSKY

POCKET BOOKS

New York   London   Toronto   Sydney   New Delhi

Pocket Books
A Division of Simon & Schuster, Inc.
1230 Avenue of the Americas
New York, NY 10020

First Pocket Books paperback edition July 2014

POCKET and colophon are registered trademarks of Simon & Schuster, Inc.

For information about special discounts for bulk purchases, please contact Simon & Schuster Special Sales at 1-866-506-1949 or business@simonandschuster.com.

The Simon & Schuster Speakers Bureau can bring authors to your live event. For more information or to book an event contact the Simon & Schuster Speakers Bureau at 1-866-248-3049 or visit our website at www.simonspeakers.com.

Cover design by Richard Yoo

Manufactured in the United States of America

10   9   8   7   6   5   4   3   2   1

ISBN 978-1-4767-5004-0
ISBN 978-1-4767-5005-7 (ebook)

In memory of Mooshu, all fluff and heart

1

Theodore—Teddy to nearly everyone not related by blood—Tonica was king of his domain. Or maybe ringleader was a better description, he thought with a grin, snapping the bar towel in his hand at a patron who tried to reach over the bar and change the music. "Hands off the dial, Joel." The radio was set to a local jazz station, and it didn't get turned up any higher than could be heard at the bar itself. Those were the rules, and everyone knew it.

The joint was jumping—well, jumping for a relatively quiet part of Seattle early on a Thursday evening, anyway. The eleven bar stools were in use, and most of the chairs were taken, too, people settling in to stay for a while. It wasn't the crazed rush of a weekend, but there was enough work to keep both hands busy. Teddy set up two beers and pushed them across the bar with a professional flourish, then paused to check on his waitress.

Stacy was working the floor, moving around the tables with economy, unloading her tray, taking orders, and swiping empties. He'd been worried that once she was boosted up to off-shift bartender she'd not want to waitress anymore, but Stacy seemed to slip between the two roles without hesitation or ego. He suspected that she made more money in tips as a waitress, anyway. The regulars here weren't stingy. You couldn't be, if you wanted to keep coming back week after week. And people did.

The phone in his pocket vibrated slightly, and instinct moved his hand toward it, even though he knew better. The motion was checked when the guy leaning against the bar held up a hand with several bills folded between his fingers. Teddy nodded in the guy's direction, holding up his index finger to say he'd be right there. He fished the phone out of his pocket and checked the number, even though he was pretty sure who was calling. "Not now, people, not now," he muttered, tapping the button to refuse the call, and shoving the phone back into his pocket. His sisters and cousins seemed to think that he needed to be dragged into the latest family flap. He disagreed, vehemently.

This was why he'd *left* the East Coast.

"What can I do for ya?" he asked, finally turning to the new customer. The guy ordered a winter ale and a Pink Squirrel. Because Teddy was a professional, he didn't roll his eyes at the order, even though he wanted to. It embarrassed him that he actually knew how to make a Pink Squirrel. Mary's was a respectable neighborhood bar, a place for draft beers and classy drinks, not foofy sugarbombs. But the customer was always right, so long as they were sober.

He supposed it could have been worse. After a local newspaper did a puff piece on the "crime-solving bartender" and the exotic cat smuggling case they'd worked last year, Patrick, the owner of the bar, had suggested that they create a specialty drink, something cat-related. Teddy had managed to avoid doing it long enough that he hoped that idea had died a natural death. He was a bartender, not a mixologist, or whatever the trendy title was these days. Patrick could run specials like that at his new place when it opened, not here.

"Besides," Teddy said now, lifting his head to look at the top of the shelves behind him, "you're the only cat that this bar needs."

Only the tip of her tail and the edge of one white-dipped paw were visible, but he was pretty sure Penny's whiskers twitched in agreement. Not that an animal could understand the words, but the fact that the little tabby considered Mary's her domain—and Teddy her human—was a fact among the regulars of the bar. Even he'd come to accept it. He laughed at himself now. Who knew letting a bedraggled kitten come in out of the rain would turn him into . . . well, a pet person was overstating the matter, but a specific animal person, anyway.

The front door opened, a burst of wet air rushing in, and someone yelled out a complaint before the door was quickly shut again. Even without looking up, Teddy knew who had come in, because Penny leaped down from her perch, landing gracefully on the back counter. She only ever reacted like that for one visitor.

"One gimlet, just like the lady likes," he said, pulling up the ingredients even as Ginny slid up to the bar. As crowded as it had been, a stool suddenly opened for her, and she took it like a queen accepting her throne.

"One of these days," the blonde said, "I'm going to come in here and order a beer, just to mess with you."

"No you won't."

Ginny laughed. "No, I probably won't. But I might."

She might, he thought, especially if she thought she could catch him out. Ginny Mallard had a streak of mischief a mile wide for all that she looked like butter wouldn't melt in her mouth just then. Either she'd had a good day at the office, or he was about to get hit with the worst joke he'd ever heard. Or, possibly, both.

"And hello to you, too, Mistress Penny," she said to the cat, who gave her a delicate sniff and then leaped down to the floor to visit with the newcomer she was actually interested in, Ginny's shar-pei, Georgie, who was happily settling at her mistress's feet.

Until recently, Georgie, like all other canines whose owners frequented Mary's, had been relegated to the sidewalk outside. There was an unofficial tie-up next to the bike rack where dogs could rest in the shade, out of the way of foot traffic. Since Teddy had become manager, those rules had been loosened, until Georgie now took it as much her right to come inside as it was Ginny's.

One cat and one dog. That was as far as he'd let himself slip.

"Try not to get stepped on," Ginny said to both animals, and then turned her attention back to the human across the bar. "Busy, for a Thursday. Did every other bar in town close?"

"Hah. And actually, yeah. The Fish is having renovations done, so their space is about half the usual." Teddy made a face. "I think we're getting the overflow, based on the level of hipster tonight."

Like most neighborhoods in Seattle, Ballard had an assortment of drinking establishments, each with its own atmosphere and clientele. The nearest competitor, Fish, was upscale, while Nickles, across the avenue, attracted college students. Mary's had intentionally cultivated a "neighborhood joint" feel. It was the place you went to talk your best friend out of a bad idea, or took a date when you were finally ready to introduce her to your friends. There was no jukebox or band, no pool table or dance floor, and only a small bar menu with just enough choices to soak up your beer, not to replace dinner. The only time outsiders showed up in any number was for Trivia Night, which had the reputation as being one of the toughest, most fiercely contested competitions in all of Seattle. The rest of the time, Teddy could identify 90 percent of his customers by name.

He'd worked flavor-of-the-month clubs before. He much preferred this.

He'd met Ginny the first week he'd started here. The curvy blonde had walked in that first Trivia Night, sat down with her team, and helped dismember every opponent—including his own newly joined team—with a combination of razor-sharp mind and good-natured snark.

The two of them hadn't clicked so much as clacked, and it had taken another year for that to ease into a comfortable rivalry.

In fact, it was only in the past year that he could really say that they had become friends, and most of that probably had to do with Georgie. Penny had taken to the shar-pei puppy the very first time they'd met, which gave the two humans more reason to converse. That friendship had only deepened, much to both their surprise, when she'd talked him into working with her. Ginny had taken her real job—personal concierge services—and used it to start a sideline of private investigations, or what she called "researchtigations." It had been against his better judgment, helping her out, and he was still amazed that he had agreed.

Still, he admitted that the challenge of these side jobs had intrigued him enough that he'd said yes not just once, but *four* times.

And that challenge had also gotten him shot at, attacked by a big cat, padlocked to a walk-in freezer, and his family name bandied about. That last had probably bothered him more than anything else, he admitted.

Teddy squinted at her suspiciously now. If she had a new gig, she was on her own. He wasn't going to let her talk him into anything more. But saying that up front would only challenge her.

"You here to drink away your cares, or celebrate your brilliance?" he asked instead, setting a napkin down and placing her drink on top of it with a flourish.

"Neither. Or both. To celebrate my brilliant cares?" She shrugged, and took a sip of her drink. "I made one client deliriously happy with me today, and have two new clients waiting for me to send them contracts, so Georgie gets to keep in kibble for another few months. Life is good." She picked up the wedge of lime and sucked at it delicately.

Every time he saw her do that, he cringed. "Jesus, what're you, at risk for scurvy? At least have the decency to drink tequila if you're going to do that."

"Wuss." She left the rind in her mouth, pressed up against her teeth, and gave him a green smile, making him roll his eyes. Ginny Mallard looked like a classy dame, but some days she had the sophistication of a fifth grader.

"If I can interrupt this group hug?" Stacy came up behind Ginny, sliding her tray onto the bar and ducking quickly to make her greetings to Georgie, who responded with an enthusiastic face-licking, if Stacy's giggle was any guide. The waitress resurfaced, grinning. "Boss, I need three Black and Tans with back, and a glass of the Cabernet. Hi, Ginny. Still up for bowling next weekend?"

Ginny flinched, dropping the lime wedge onto her napkin. "I really agreed to that?"

"You did. And bring the man. I can't believe you've been dating for months and we haven't met him yet."

They hadn't even learned the guy's name yet, for that matter. "She's afraid to bring him here," Teddy said, pulling the first of the beers. "That's assuming he even exists, anyway."

"Don't start," Ginny warned them. "I adhere to the

six-month rule for relationships. Let them get comfortable before you throw them to your friends."

"Yeah, but we're not friends, we're *Mary's*," Stacy protested.

"Yeah, well I don't live here like some people . . ."

"Ginny, you're in four days a week," Teddy said, finishing with the beers and pouring the wine. "If you actually drank worth a damn, we'd engrave your name on one of the stools."

"And on that note, I'm gone." Stacy loaded her tray and disappeared back into the crowd.

"So," he said, leaning forward and waggling his eyebrows like a cut-rate Groucho Marx. "It's *almost* been six months. . . ."

"Don't start," she repeated, her eyes narrowing in clear warning, and he backed off. He could tease her about Georgie, about her endless love of her technology, of her impatience and her lack of schmoozing skills, but not about her personal life. Fair enough. He had no desire to open up about his, either. That thought made him look guiltily at his phone, then he went back to work, leaving her to her drink.

"G'night, Gin," someone called out, and she raised a hand in farewell, even though she hadn't actually talked to him tonight. It had been pretty crackling when she walked in at seven thirty, but the bar was starting to clear out by ten—apparently the overflow from Fish were early-to-bed types. Ginny had switched to ginger ale about an hour ago, as usual, but sitting at the bar people-watching was preferable to going home and trying to do more work, or staring at the television. Rob—the boyfriend of speculation—was heading out on a business trip first thing tomorrow, so she was on her own for the weekend.

Georgie clearly didn't mind hanging out here: the dog was snoring happily at Ginny's feet, Penny curled up between oversized canine paws, also asleep. Ginny looked at the two of them, and shook her head fondly, then pulled out her tablet and snapped a picture and posted it to the bar's Facebook page. Then, unable to help herself, she checked her email. One message was from her mother, which she ignored. The other . . . "Oh, are you kidding me?" She sighed. So much for not working anymore tonight, but if she left it until the morning the client would work himself into a frenzy—and she wouldn't be able to sleep well for worrying.

Grumbling, she started pulling up the information she'd need to put out this particular fire. Fortunately, she'd developed the ability to shut out the ambient noise and movement of the bar around her, and lose herself in the work.

Sometime around ten thirty, an older man wearing cargo pants and a gray sweatshirt under a mostly clean apron came out from the back and sat down next to her, glaring at the thirtysomething couple who had been leaning against the bar waiting for service, until they made room for him. Ginny turned her head and gave him a curious look. A former boxer, Seth was in his sixties, balding and wrinkled, but his body was still strong enough to give would-be troublemakers pause. The older man ran Mary's kitchen, if you could call the galley space behind the bar anything that grand, and he wasn't a fan of Ginny, or Georgie, or Penny, for that matter. In fact, Ginny wasn't sure he was a fan of anything, although Tonica said that he was actually a good guy. For a professional grouch.

When he sat there and didn't say anything, Ginny decided to return the favor. It seemed only polite. After a while, though, it got to be weird, of the creepy-weird variety, and she swiveled around on her stool to look directly at him.

"Kitchen's closed?"

"Stacy knows where to find me, anyone wants to put an order in." He was staring at the mug of coffee in his hands—at least, she thought it was coffee. She'd never actually seen Seth drink alcohol. Not that she spent much time watching him, or anything.

"Uh-huh." She might not have Tonica's people-sense, but something was definitely weird. She looked up, trying to find Tonica, catching his eye and tilting her head to let him know that he was needed down here. Whatever was up, she didn't want to get hit with it alone.

The bartender worked his way back down the bar to the two of them, taking the situation in with a brief glance and absolutely no change of expression. "Top that off for you?" he offered, reaching for the coffeepot, but Seth covered the mug with one hand. "I'm good."

It was coffee, then, or Tonica was hiding something high-test in the pot. That wasn't in character for either one of them, though.

Tonica waited, and Ginny waited, and Seth stared into his coffee mug, his face set in stone. The silence was starting to get to really awkward when he grunted, and finally spoke.

"I gotta talk to you two."

Them, not her. Even in Ginny's relief, she was amused at how those words seemed to move Tonica into "sympathetic bartender" mode without his even noticing. He leaned forward, resting his elbows on the bar top, left hand folding into his right, his expression open and attentive. It worked wonders on the drunks who unburdened themselves to him on a regular basis, but Seth didn't seem to notice.

"Me, too?" Ginny asked, just to make sure.

"Yeah, you, too, Blondie," Seth growled. Whatever it was he wanted to talk about, he wasn't happy about it. "I want to hire you."

It took a lot, at this point in his life, to leave Theodore Johan Tonica dumbfounded. Seth had just managed it. "You want to what?"

The old man growled slightly. "You heard what I said."

"I heard, I just wanted to make sure I heard right. I might have been hallucinating." Teddy realized, even as the words came out of his mouth, that joking wasn't the way to go. The old man looked as unhappy—and as un-comfortable—as he'd ever seen him, and that was saying something. Even Ginny had picked up on it, her profes-sional "I'm trained, I can help you" expression firmly in place, but her hazel eyes widened with shock.

"You mean, as investigators?"

"No, as a bartender. Of course as an investigator." Seth might be uncomfortable, but he wasn't at a loss for snark. "I need the two of you to look into something for me."

"Ah. Um." Bartenders learned to roll with the punches, verbal or otherwise, but this had caught him off guard. Seth, asking for *their* help? "You know we're not licensed, or anything like that, right? I mean, maybe . . ."

"If I wanted to go to someone else—if I *could* go to someone else—I would've. You in, or not?"

"Tell us what this is about, and we can tell you if we can help you."

Teddy noted with relief that Ginny had learned that much at least: she no longer leaped in with a promise to make everything better before she learned what "every-thing" was. That was good, because while every instinct Teddy had was telling him to say yes, that anything that made Seth ask a favor had to be serious, the reality was that anything that drove Seth to ask a favor had to be serious. He'd already said—several times—that he wasn't inter-ested in continuing this "researchtigations" thing Ginny had dragged him into, much less get involved in a friend's problems that required such help. . . .

"I'm asking for a friend," Seth started, and then shot them both a glare. "Shut it. I am."

Both of them kept their expressions serious and intent, although Ginny's lips twitched slightly with repressed laughter, her shock fading to interest.

"And?" she asked.

"A friend of mine, old friend from my boxing days. He's getting screwed over by his landlord. Bastard's throwing him out of the house he was renting, claims he's doing something illegal and that invalidates the lease. Bullshit accusations, but he's . . . Deke's a good guy but he took a few too many hits and not enough mat, if you know what I mean."

"Punch drunk?"

"Whatever they're calling it now. He's a little slow, but he's a good guy, good heart, probably doesn't even jaywalk 'cause he knows it's wrong. But you don't want to put him up against some suit of a lawyer, someone'd make him look like a fool. Deke'd come out badly. And the thing is," Seth hesitated a moment. "Deke *needs* to stay in this house. He's been there for years, it's familiar, and he needs that familiarity. You understand?"

Teddy thought maybe he did. An older man, not entirely there, suddenly homeless? That was a recipe for a fast decline and a bad ending.

"What do you want us to do?" he asked, resigning himself to the inevitable.

"Hell if I know, whatever it is you do. I just want proof the landlord's a lying sack of scum, so we can make him back down."

"What are they accusing him of?" Ginny asked. "The illegal part, I mean."

"Bein' part of a dogfighting ring." Seth blew out a heavy gust of air, smelling slightly of pickles and cigarettes, and his shoulders slumped, just a little. "Of all the hare-assed ideas ever. Deke might've hit a few guys in his time, but he wouldn't ever do that to an animal. And dogfighting? He's not a brainiac, but even he's not that dumb, and he sure as hell isn't that mean."

Before the whole scandal with the sports figure and dogfighting a few years back, Teddy had never given it a thought, never known that that was a thing people *did*. Once he'd seen the photos in the news, he'd been horrified and disgusted, if not terribly surprised: people did horrible and disgusting things, especially to creatures that couldn't fight back. But it was ugly stuff. His first, instinctive reaction was to back away, fast, even as Seth insisted his friend was innocent.

"If you two are half as good as you say you are, should be a piece of cake, right?"

Ginny started to bristle, but Teddy lifted a hand, calming her—for the moment. Seth was even more wound up about this than he'd thought, at first. Whatever was going on, it was important.

"Is there any chance that your friend could be involved—even if by, I don't know, accident?" Teddy held up a hand again when Seth glared at him. "We need to know. People stumble into all kinds of stupid things, especially if they're . . . not the sharpest knives in the drawer."

Seth glared at him some more, then shrugged. "Maybe. I don't know. But he swears he didn't do anything wrong, didn't do anything illegal. And I believe him."

"Why?" Ginny asked. "Why do you believe him? I mean, you know people do dumb things if they need the money, and you said he wasn't, well . . ."

Seth pushed his hands against the bar, but didn't move away. "I can't doubt him," he said quietly, all the anger gone. "You let someone down once, it's human nature. You let 'em down again . . .

"It's not in him. Not that. You gotta trust me on that." Seth normally looked young for his age, but just then, he was an old man.

Ginny looked at Teddy and shrugged, just the slightest lift of one shoulder.

"Is there anything else going on?" Teddy asked. "Maybe a score being settled, he got on the wrong side of his landlord, somehow?"

"Deke swears he didn't do anything to piss the guy off, but, well, he wouldn't mean to, but the guy's got no filter, you know? He thinks it, he says it. Sometimes he says it before he thinks it."

"So what do you want us to do, specifically?" Ginny asked, turning her drink an exact quarter turn, then looking directly at Seth. He'd given her enough shit in the past few years. Teddy couldn't blame her for pushing him, now.

Seth met her gaze squarely. "I want you to prove he didn't do anything wrong. Save his dumb ass, before he's homeless, before this breaks him so bad I can't put the pieces back together again. He's only got a couple more days before he has to get out. He sure as hell can't stay with me, I barely got room to turn around myself, and who'd rent a place to him, in this market, without references? He was barely making ends meet in that piece of shit house, as it was."

Ginny exhaled, a tiny breath through pursed lips. Unlike Teddy, she was a dog person. He could only imagine her reaction to the accusation. But—not for the first time—she surprised him. When she looked at Teddy, her gaze told him that this was his call; that she'd go with whatever he decided.

He'd said no to jobs before, especially after the walk-in freezer incident. He had a full-time job—hell, he had a more-than-full-time job. So did Ginny. Neither of them needed more stress, and it wasn't as though Seth was going to be able to pay them much, considering he knew exactly how much the old man earned. . . . But Seth was a stand-up guy, for a grouch, and he'd asked them for help.

And it sounded like Deke needed somebody on his side.

"All right," Teddy said, like there had ever been any doubt. "We'll look into it for you. But"—he held up a finger when Seth started to mutter what might have been a thank-you—"if there's even the slightest hint that your friend is guilty, we're done and you drop it. All right?"

"He's not guilty."

"All right?"

"All right."

"Finally!" At Ginny's feet, Penny let out a satisfied grunt. Her eyes were half lidded as though she were still asleep, but she had been listening to the humans talking above them. Georgie's wuffling snore rumbled underneath her, and there were other people talking, so she couldn't hear all the words, but she knew the tone in her human's voice, and Georgie's human, too. They were sniffing something new out. Something that needed doing, or fixing. And that meant that things were about to get interesting again.

Penny yawned, her tongue curling against her teeth, and stretched her body out lazily, slowly waking all the way up. She wanted to wake Georgie up, too, but the dog would get too excited and distract the humans. For now, Penny would do what she did best: listen, watch, and learn.

2

The start of a new job was always a tangle of excitement and nerves. Despite her exhaustion, Ginny couldn't fall asleep until well after midnight, nearly an hour after she'd gotten home from Mary's. Part of her brain was whirring excitedly, wanting to fire up the laptop and start doing research. But she knew that starting anything now would mean that she wouldn't get to bed until three at the earliest, and she'd be a wreck all the next day. She wasn't twenty-five anymore, that she could get by on four hours of sleep.

What that meant, though, was that she slept through her alarm, and woke up half an hour late. Georgie was waiting patiently by the side of her bed, paws on the mattress, tattered pink leash in her mouth, large brown eyes doleful. When she saw Ginny was finally awake, she let out a pitiful whine.

"I'm sorry, baby," Ginny said, reaching out. "Gimme a minute, okay?"

A glance at the clock said it was only six forty, so she wasn't too far off schedule. Lucky, otherwise Georgie might have broken training and left a puddle on the floor.

The weather was damp and cool after last night's rain, but the trees were starting to show green, and there was a feel to the air that said it might turn out to be a nice day after all. Ginny nodded a silent hello to the other people walking their dogs, but didn't run into anyone she knew well enough to actually say good morning to. Back in the apartment, she fed Georgie and took her shower. Just because she worked at home now was no reason to fall into bad habits, and her brain worked better once she was washed and dressed.

On the dot of seven thirty, barefoot but otherwise dressed in black slacks and a button-down silk blouse, she walked into the small bedroom she used as an office, pushed a pile of paperwork she'd planned to file off to the side, and opened her laptop. She had until 10 a.m., when Tonica had said that he would pick her up, to do the first strokes of preliminary investigation.

"Residential leases, and Washington State law," she said to herself. "Start there, see what turns up."

An hour and a half later, she left Georgie sleeping under her desk, grabbed her shoes, and went down to the sidewalk with a travel mug of coffee in one hand, timing it so that Tonica's old Saab coupe swung around the corner just as she hit the curb.

She might not be able to organize the entire world, but managing the small things could be deeply satisfying, too.

"Morning," Tonica said as she got into the car. He looked like crap, the skin under his eyes showing a lack of sleep and probably some dehydration. She knew that his normal MO was to sleep through the morning when he worked the closing shift, so he was probably running on less than half his usual shut-eye. Ginny felt a moment of guilt, but only a moment. He'd been the one to agree to take this job, and to meet with Seth and his friend this morning. Hopefully by the time they arrived, his brain cells would have started perking again.

She offered him her coffee but he shook his head, indicating the to-go cup in the cup holder already.

"Did you have breakfast?" she asked.

"Yes, Mom." Which was a laugh, because he was more mother-hennish than she was, ever. "Seth called me this morning; we're supposed to meet them at a place called the Regulator, over in Capitol Hill."

Them being Seth and his friend Deke, their nominal client. Normally a meeting like this would be at Mary's, but Seth wanted to keep his friend in familiar territory. Between that, and the way Seth had seemed convinced the guy would fall apart if he had to move, Ginny wondered what shape this guy was really in, and if that was going to be a problem. But she'd agreed anyway. What else could they do?

"Traffic on 99's not too bad. I told Seth we'd be a little late, figured we could swing by the house first, check it out, and then head over."

"All right." She fastened her seat belt and rested her head against the back of her seat. "Wake me when we get there?"

She had only meant to doze, but she jolted out of a sound sleep when he pulled the car to the curb, and stopped the engine. She wiped at her mouth, afraid that she'd been drooling.

"You're fine," Tonica said. "A little on your chin, but otherwise—"

There was nothing on her chin. She didn't even bother to glare at him, instead looking out the window, matching the street number on the house to the information Seth had given them the night before. The house looked a little battered from the outside, the paint needing a touch-up, but the porch steps looked sturdy, and nothing was warped or sagging. Pretty much standard for the neighborhood, which had managed to avoid both gentrification and a descent into what Realtors would delicately call "fixer-upper status." Someone had been trimming the hedges in front, too.

"Did you get a key?" she asked, wondering what the inside looked like.

"No. I just want to see the place. Get a sense of it."

"Okay." She had already looked the address up on Google Earth that morning, but she supposed he was right: seeing things in person told you more than someone else's photographs.

Ginny extracted herself from the coupe, and looked at the house more carefully from the sidewalk. It was a plain one-story jobber, off-white siding with brown shutters, and what looked like storage or crawl space under the eaves . . . was there a basement? Yeah, she could see windows set in the foundation to the left of the steps, so some kind of basement. Maybe a thousand square feet, plus another five hundred underneath? Ginny drummed her fingers against her thigh, thinking.

"I don't know anything about dogfighting," she said to her companion, "but if Deke was allegedly involved, I mean, doing it here, wouldn't they need more room?"

"You didn't do any research last night?" he asked, surprised.

Ginny shook her head. "Sleep seemed more essential." He winced and nodded. "Anyway," she said, "this morning I focused on renter's rights and lease agreements. That seemed more important, knowing if there was anything we could use to block this right away. I . . ." Her mouth twisted up. "I really didn't want to know, I guess. Anything I looked up online, even with a filter, there were going to be pictures." Just the thought made her stomach curdle, and she wished she hadn't had that bagel for breakfast.

Truth was, her inability to fall asleep last night had probably been more directly tied to unease about this job than anticipation to get started. Somehow, this—the house, the job, the idea of it—just howled bad news all over the place. Then again, their first job had seemed so simple, and it had turned out to be really bad news, so maybe her spidey-sense was off. Or maybe she was getting better at listening to it.

Ginny suspected the latter was more accurate. She didn't say that to her partner, though. No point: they were already here, and committed.

"So." She looked at him, and he shrugged, for once

letting the issue drop rather than ragging on her. Maybe he wasn't feeling good about this, either? Tonica played a tough guy, but she'd seen him with Penny and Georgie, and the animals in the shelter, and she suspected he didn't want to think about animals maybe getting hurt, either.

He'd left his leather jacket in the car, even though it was a cool morning, and for a moment she could see him in the burbs, daddy material, with a partner and 1.5 kids, maybe a dog. . . .

He didn't talk about his past much, where *much* meant at all. She knew that he'd gone to Yale, and that his family was of the established-in-society type. Moneyed. The rest . . . she could learn, easily enough, but she hadn't. Their friendship was the here and now, not who they'd been or what they'd done.

She wondered what Seth had done, that he talked about failing his friend in that tone of voice. But that wasn't her business, either.

"Let's take a look," Tonica said. "Casual-like."

They walked up the front path from the sidewalk, both of them tense, as though expecting someone to shout at them to get off his lawn at any moment. The porch steps were solidly built, the sound of their shoes on the wood echoing oddly, the way sound did when there was nobody home.

"Pretty bare-bones," Tonica said, looking in through the narrow window on one side of the door. "This guy decorates in early basic frat boy. Considering Deke must be Seth's age, or close enough, that's depressing as hell."

"Based on what Seth said, I doubt he can afford much." Ginny looked around the porch, noting the utter lack of anything like a chair, wind chime, or planter to make it feel homey. "Not like you have all that much furniture, either, Tonica," she pointed out. She looked in the other side-panel window, and shuddered a little. "But you're right. Not a lot there, and none of it nice."

"Yeah. At least my stuff doesn't look like it came from Goodwill."

Ginny had seen his apartment once. His furniture was definitely not Goodwill. She'd bet an entire paycheck, in fact, that some of it was antique. She reached out and turned the door handle, not really expecting it to be unlocked. It wasn't.

"You want to go around back, poke around, pretend to be interested new tenants if anyone asks?" Curiosity was gnawing at her now.

Tonica looked tempted for a minute, too, then shook his head, looking at his watch. "We're going to be late, if we don't get going."

"I don't think our client's going to be a stickler for punctuality," Ginny said, but she followed him back down the stairs and to the car without further objection.

As it turned out, Ginny was wrong: Deke Hoban was a stickler for punctuality. He sat at the table in the restaurant they had specified, his hands clenched in front of him, almost white-knuckled, and kept looking up at the clock on the wall. Seth was with him, reading a newspaper as though he had settled in for a long delay.

"We're only five minutes late," Tonica muttered under his breath, while Ginny took in the scene. The Regulator was an old-style burger joint, faded and ragged around the edges. She got the feeling that it—like much of the neighborhood around it—was primed for gentrification, a slow, inevitable creep. It made her uneasy for some reason, as though the steamroller were aiming at them instead of old brick buildings.

"Man's under stress," Ginny retorted, shaking off her own nerves. "You'd be pacing and driving everyone crazy, if it was you."

"I would not."

"Would, too."

He obviously had the urge to stick his tongue out at her, just to see how low they could sink, but they were pretending to be professionals now. They bypassed the hostess, who didn't look too enthusiastic about greeting them anyway, and headed directly for the table. Seth put aside his newspaper and nudged his friend with an elbow.

"Deke, this is Theodore Tonica, the friend I told you about. And Ginny Mallard. They're gonna help you."

Ginny grimaced at the way he made her into an afterthought, but she let it pass.

"You gonna get my house back?"

Deke was built like a bullet: rounded head, rounded shoulders, hands that kept fisting as though the only thing he knew how to do was hit something. But the face that looked up at Ginny had the open hope of a child, set with the wrinkles of a man who had to be at least seventy.

What was it Seth had said? "Too many hits and not enough mat." Ginny didn't like boxing, but she'd followed enough news to hear about the effects of repeated concussions, and brain damage, even more than what they were talking about in the NFL with football. That was why Seth had gotten out when he did, the story went: because he didn't want to end up like Deke.

It explained why he was being so protective of him, too, maybe. Tonica probably knew all that, which was why he'd agreed to take this job, even though she knew he had even more doubts than she did about the, well, the *smartness* of what they were doing.

They weren't professionals. They weren't trained, whatever she might say about being a trained professional problem solver. They'd gotten lucky so far, but—

"We're going to try," Tonica said to Deke. "The most important thing is to make sure that we make sure everyone knows that you didn't do anything wrong. Because you didn't, right?"

"No!" Deke shook his head, then frowned. "No. I didn't do anything bad. I didn't do what Mr. Cooper said I did. I didn't!"

His voice rose with each word, a thread of hysteria creeping in.

"All right, Deke, settle down," Seth said. "We're in your corner, remember? So you gotta stay cool."

Both Seth and Tonica were using soothing, even-toned

voices, almost monotones when talking to Deke. Ginny took note of that, and tried to follow their lead. It was a lot like what her trainer had said to do with Georgie: you couldn't yell, or use baby talk, just keep a steady tone all the time, so the dog didn't get spooked or distracted, and you could keep her focused.

"We need you to tell us what happened, exactly," Tonica said. "What did Mr. Cooper say?"

Deke took a deep breath, his hands trembling. "He came to the house. A week ago, just after I had breakfast. I had cereal, and soy milk. 'Cause I'm not supposed to drink regular milk anymore. And he knocked on the door, and then came in, like he always does. Because it's his house; I just live there."

That had the sound of something he'd been told often enough that it stuck. Ginny already didn't like this Mr. Cooper.

"And he said that I'd done something against the lease, something bad, something illegal. And I had to leave, because he couldn't be responsible, couldn't have that happening in his property, dogs fighting and such. If I left he wouldn't tell no one. But I didn't know what he was talking about. I told him that."

"Easy, Deke. Calm down, breathe out and in." Tonica's voice was slow, soothing, his hand resting on the older man's arm. She'd asked the bartender to help her with the first case she took because his people skills were better than hers, the way he could get people to talk, even when they didn't want to, or were trying to hide something. It looked like he was good at dealing with panic attacks, too.

Ginny pulled her tablet out of her bag and made a note to find out if this had been an actual eviction or a termination of tenancy. She didn't think Deke was in any condition to tell the difference: she had to see the paperwork. By state regs, Deke was supposed to get twenty days' notice, not a week. But if this Cooper was claiming noncompliance with the lease, or being a nuisance . . . No actual charges had been filed or would be filed, it sounded like, no matter what Seth had said about dogfighting. Maybe he'd misunderstood, or misheard?

"Did he tell you what you had done that was so bad?" Tonica asked.

Deke shook his head. "That I'd had dogs on the property. And bad people." His voice lowered, as though telling them a secret. "I know bad people. Very bad people. I would never let them inside the house."

Ginny and Tonica both looked at Seth, who nodded once. Deke did know bad people, and Seth was convinced that he would refuse them entrance. Ginny suspected that Seth knew those bad people, too. Probably, from the way he wasn't meeting their gazes, they'd had something to do with the guilt he'd voiced last night, the failure he was trying to atone for.

Her fingers tapped on the edge of the tablet. She really needed to stick to white-collar crimes. Not that embezzlement had been any safer . . .

"How bad is bad? Seth, if you've gotten us tangled up in anything having to do with the mob . . ." Tonica went from calm to seriously pissed-off without raising his voice. It was a neat trick Ginny wished that she had.

"No. Those guys he knows, they're bad news, but they pick on players their own size. They wouldn't do something like this to Deke. Whatever's going on it's not that. If it were, I wouldn't have asked you."

Either because he knew they couldn't handle it, or because that was something he could handle himself . . . Ginny didn't know and honestly didn't want to know.

"Did he look around the house?" Ginny asked now, turning back to Deke. "Did he go into the basement, or the backyard, looking for dogs?"

"No. He just told me, and then he looked at me a long time, and then he left." Deke hesitated, then added, "There were no dogs in the house. I don't own any dogs; there weren't any in the house."

"And the agreement specifically says no dogs, Deke?" Tonica asked.

"I got a copy of his lease," Seth told them, passing a manila folder across the table. "No pets, no parties, no smoking, that kind of thing. And yeah, looks like he doesn't have to prove it, just claim it, say someone objected to the barking." Seth shrugged. "It's a crap contract, but it's not like Deke had many options. The rent was cheap, and it's a safe neighborhood. Even a crap rental is better than a men's shelter."

There wasn't much they could say to that. Ginny took the folder, but didn't open it yet. There would be time, later, to go over the fine print. "He's gone for the court order?"

"In the folder," Seth said. "Looks like the bastard started the paperwork before he even talked to Deke. It took Deke another day to call me." Seth was upset about that.

"He really should have a lawyer, not us. You know that, right?" Tonica scrubbed his hand against the top of his head, exasperation coming off him in waves.

"I tried that argument already." Seth made a face, like he'd bitten into something sour. "He said no."

Seth had said going into court would hurt Deke, and Ginny, looking at the man, had to agree. She'd seen what could happen, when you got inside the courtroom, and a guy who'd kick an old man out into the street wasn't going to pull punches once you started costing him legal fees, too.

"No lawyers." Deke sounded like a petulant five-year-old. "Don't want 'em, don't trust 'em. They didn't help last time, neither."

"He's got a record?" Tonica's voice, an aside to Seth, was the kind of quiet that wasn't good, like he was trying hard not to yell.

"He spent some time in the system," Seth said. "Nothing criminal, nothing to do with . . . those other people. He took a swing at someone in a homeless shelter, got a couple of weeks to clear his head, no big deal. But he had to stand in front of a judge, and I told you, we try to argue this in court and that will all come up in his brain, and I can't tell you how Deke'll react." Seth's face tightened, not in anger but resignation. "You don't know what it's like, this end of things. Any more trouble attached to him, at his age? He'd never be able to live on his own again, have his own place.

Probably be stuck in a facility somewhere. You know what that would do to him?"

The object of their discussion was playing with his fork, humming under his breath as though to tune them out. Tonica looked at Ginny, who shook her head. "We need to prove that he wasn't in breach of his lease to stop the eviction."

"Right. And we're assuming that this Cooper's going to be willing to listen to anything we find?"

"Legally . . ." Ginny let her sentence trail off. The law might, technically, be on their side, if there was no actual proof of wrongdoing, but that didn't always mean much. From the look on Seth's face, he was well aware of that. If Deke couldn't handle going to court, odds were the landlord knew that, and was using it to get rid of his tenant. But why? That was the question her instincts were telling her to follow.

"It's almost one," Deke said, looking up at the clock, suddenly tense again. "I have to go. I can't be late for work."

"Yeah," Seth said. "C'mon, I'll give you a ride there, old man."

"Who you calling old man, old man?" Deke teased Seth, getting up from the booth. Having told strangers his problems, he seemed to have shed them entirely: if Seth said these people could help, then there was no more reason to worry.

Ginny could work with that. She was used to people dropping their problems in her lap.

"Nice meeting you, Deke," Tonica said. "Seth, we'll talk to you later, okay?"

"Yeah, sure." Unlike his friend, Seth was still worried, but he seemed resigned to that, as well.

"Why did we agree to this, again?" Teddy asked, watching the two men leave.

"Because Seth asked us. Because"—and she made an unhappy face—"we're both pretty sure now that he's right, that Deke wouldn't do well in a drawn-out legal process."

"Right. Christ." Teddy shook his head, running his hand over his hair again, letting it slide down to rest against the bunched muscles in his neck, as though the pressure would ease out the inevitable headache he could feel coming on.

"He seems like a nice guy," Ginny said. "Sweet. Not altogether there, or even sure where there *is,* but nice."

"But?" He waited, wondering if her take was going to the same place as his own.

"But I'm not sure we can take his version of reality as gospel."

"Ya think?" The sarcasm came out a little heavier than he had planned. Teddy shook his head, not even trying to hold back his reaction now. "Ginny, that guy's taken more than a few hits, and I'm pretty sure the package wasn't well wrapped to begin with. Even assuming the dogfighting thing was a feint, did you listen to what Deke was saying, and how he said it? He's told himself there were no dogs in the house, because he knows he would be in trouble if there were. That's a vastly different thing than there being no dogs in the house."

Ginny frowned at him, but didn't challenge his evaluation. "I'd thought there was something weird about the phrasing, but if he's as messed up as you say, how do you know he's *not* telling the truth?"

The headache arrived, right on schedule. "You're doing that 'give the world a third chance' thing again, Mallard. People are going to suspect you're actually a bleeding-heart idealist. And we don't know a damned thing except what we've been told, first by Seth, who's invested in his old buddy not being guilty, either for friendship or guilt, or maybe both, I don't know." He'd known Seth too long to be able to read him well. "And then by a guy who not only has reason to lie, if he is guilty, but might not be able to differentiate between reality and lie."

"Okay, even if he was housing a couple of dogs and nothing else, could we use that inability to keep him from being evicted? I mean, say that he didn't realize, or understand . . . ?"

"Doubt it. That could leave him open to claims he's not fit to sign a contract, which would mean he couldn't rent another place. That's what we're supposed to be *preventing*, remember?"

They both fell silent, and Ginny drummed her fingers against the table, her eyes unfocused in a way that told Teddy that she was thinking, hard. He waited. She might bow to his people-reading skills, and depend on him to schmooze witnesses into giving up their secrets, but she was the one who put together the puzzle pieces, and saw the patterns. They needed a plan of action, and she was—hopefully—coming up with one.

"First things first. We really need to talk to a lawyer, someone with some experience in this, no matter what Deke thinks."

"I know a handful of lawyers." And he waited for Ginny to say "of course you do."

"Of course you do."

They'd gone beyond keeping score, but he made a mental hash mark on his side of the board, anyway. "But none of them deal with this sort of thing," he went on. "Real estate, I mean. Still, they know people who might, and friend-of-a-friend webs occasionally catch something." He'd owe them a favor in exchange but he was starting to get used to that. Teddy didn't like asking favors for himself, but favors on behalf of other people, that he could do. "So yeah, I'll see who I can scare up."

"Second," Ginny went on, "or maybe even before the lawyer because they'll want to know, we need to find some proof that nothing illegal was going on in the house. Specifically, we need to be able to say that there weren't any dogs living in the house. Which means getting inside. Preferably without Deke around to muddy the waters. But we didn't get a key."

Teddy thought of the little house they'd looked at briefly, and rolled his eyes. "I'll lay you decent odds they locked the front door, and the back's open," he said. "Or a ground-floor window's been left open. As friend of a friend, I'd be perfectly justified in going in to make sure nothing's been disturbed until Deke can come by to pick his things up." Truthfully, he suspected the cops wouldn't be impressed by that argument, but he didn't expect it to be tested. That wasn't the sort of neighborhood where the cops made regular patrols. "I've got to get to work, but I'll go over there tomorrow morning." Two days in a row, awake at an ungodly hour. But there was no time to do it today, not the way traffic got on Friday afternoons, and he sure as hell wasn't going to do it after shift. Breaking and entering was bad enough; doing it at three in the morning was a good way to get shot. "Unless you want to go over there?"

"I can't. I've got a new client meeting this afternoon, in town. And I'm not going to rely on mass transit to get me out to that neighborhood and home again."

She had a good point. Depending on the buses to get there would take forever. Better to leave that to the guy with the car.

"But I should be able to do some digging," she went on. "I mean, even if Deke did something stupid, there's no way he's the ringleader or mastermind of anything; Seth was right about that. So if something was going on, I mean, more than Deke maybe having a couple of mutts in the backyard, something on the level of a dogfighting ring, there's got to be more involved—someone else pulling the strings. Right?"

Teddy nodded, following her logic. Deke was more

victim material than criminal, anyone could see that. If someone else was involved . . . They might not be able to use that fact directly, but maybe something would come out in the digging that they *could* use.

Teddy had no problem using a little careful pressure—blackmail was such an ugly word—to solve this, and from Ginny's expression, she felt the same. Deke might not be an innocent, but he was definitely being victimized.

"Be careful," he said. "This guy Cooper sounds like a sleaze, and if there is any truth in the accusation, dogfighting isn't the kind of hobby nice people take up. Don't poke too hard, okay?"

Gin gave him a classic are-you-kidding-me face. "I know how to hide my tracks," she said. "Go, before you're late for shift again, and have to fire yourself."

Traffic was actually not bad, heading north along the highway. He checked his watch and decided that he had time to swing by his apartment and change to more work-appropriate clothing before shift started, rather than having to rely on the emergency clothes he kept in the storeroom.

Teddy lived a half-hour drive from Mary's, in an older apartment building that made up in creakiness what it lacked in charm. But the space suited him: it came with a parking space, and his neighbors were quiet during the morning hours when he was asleep. When he was *supposed* to be asleep, anyway. He didn't really need much more than that.

The first thing he noted when he closed the door was that the message light on his phone was blinking. Teddy groaned. Someone had left him a message on his landline in the time between when he left the apartment to pick Ginny up and now. "Three guesses as to who it is, and it doesn't count if they're not related to me."

He shook his head, deliberately turning his back on the phone, and went over to the area of the studio that doubled as his bedroom. He pulled a black T-shirt out of the dresser even as he was unbuttoning the shirt he'd worn to the meeting, and toed out of his dress shoes. Tossing the shirt and his slacks onto the bed, he dressed quickly in jeans and the T-shirt, then replaced his shoes with work boots. A sturdy toe box and nonslip soles were a hell of a lot more important behind the bar than looking good, and it wasn't as though his feet wouldn't hurt at the end of shift no matter what he wore.

A quick check of the time told him he was doing fine—and if he was a few minutes late, well, despite Gin's parting crack, that was the bonus of being the manager. God knew there had to be *some* bonus to it.

He was about to head out the door when guilt tagged him, and he paused by the phone. "Damn it . . ."

Hating himself, he hit the play button on the phone and waited.

"Theo. It's Maggie." He could see her, glaring at something across the room, maybe putting the fear of God into a peon, as she spoke. "Please call me, okay? No more bullshit. I know why you're ducking our calls and I don't blame you a bit but you need to stick an oar into this, too."

No, he thought, he really didn't. He had a bar to run and an investigation to make, and a life to lead, and all of that was on this coast, not back on the East Coast, where he'd—he'd thought—left all of his headaches. And his heartaches.

Maggie sighed. "Okay, it's Friday, and barely noon your time, so you're probably sleeping—or pretending to be asleep and ignoring me"—and despite himself he laughed, because she was right, that's exactly what he would have been doing—"but please, call me? You're an idiot, I love you, bye."

"I love you, too," he told her, when the message ended. Teddy deleted the message, picked up his jacket, keys, and wallet, and headed out. His cousin knew he wasn't going to call.

3

Penny spent most of Friday evening tucked on a high shelf along the far wall of the Busy Place. It was dark enough there that she couldn't be seen—and was therefore left alone—but she could see the humans perfectly well. Not that she cared about most of them: only a few. Two. Her whiskers twitched. Maybe three.

Ginny wasn't there, which meant Georgie wasn't, either. Theo was behind the bar, working with the other male who came in sometimes. Not the blustering old one, the younger one who was always trying to bribe her with treats, as though she were a dog.

She could tell even at this distance that Theodore was thinking things he wasn't happy about. Her human's ears didn't move and he didn't have whiskers, but his shoulders and hands moved differently when he was unhappy. But she didn't know what he was unhappy about. Was it the way the younger male was behaving? Or was it something else? Was it about the new sniffing they'd started? How was she supposed to help him if he didn't talk about it where she could hear?

Georgie was able to go with them, hear what was happening, see what they were up to. But Georgie wasn't here. Neither was Ginny. Was Ginny off doing things? Had she taken the dog with *her? Penny felt her tail twitch in frustration. She didn't want to get in the car, didn't want to go strange places, not unless she decided where she was going. But she needed information!*

So when the lights came up and the Busy Place emptied, and then Theo turned the lights out again, Penny slipped out through her own exit and approached the car, giving her best "where are we going?" meow. There was no way Theo could resist that.

When the alarm went off Saturday morning, Teddy rolled over and groaned, slapping a hand over the clock to shut it off. It had been a hellish shift: Jon had nearly quit over yet another imagined slight, then two college kids decided to get into a dustup on the street outside. And when he'd finally been able to call it a night and close the place down, Penny started acting up, as though she didn't want him to leave—or she wanted to come home with him.

"Sorry, sweetheart," he'd told her, lifting her body and firmly placing her, again, outside the coupe. "I may be your human, but you're the bar's cat. You stay here."

Penny had actually hissed at him, frustration in every quiver of her whiskers, and he'd had enough: he'd left her by the side of the road, come home, and fallen into bed, the new blinking light on his landline a match to the message light on his cell.

"No," he told the ceiling now. "I am not awake. I am very much not awake."

But there were things to be done, so he rolled out of bed and into the shower.

He'd ignored the message indicators until the morning, and then—out of some faint hint of guilt or masochism—let the messages play out while he brushed his teeth, listening to Maggie's voice fill his studio apartment. Apparently, she'd been the designated nagger.

"Theo? I know you don't want to get involved, but you should be. You're part owner, too. Call, okay?"

He deleted the messages again before he left the apartment. What could he say if he called? "Do whatever you want and tell me when it's done?" They knew his feelings on the subject. It wasn't a matter of life or death, just selling an old summerhouse nobody had time or energy to keep up anymore, and yeah, it had been in the family for two generations, but it was just a house. Sell it already.

But his cousins and sisters all wanted to *talk it out* and *make a group decision*. Better just not to call and let them sort it out, avoid all the yelling and guilt.

Of course, if he really wanted to avoid the guilt, Teddy thought, walking to his car, he should stop listening to the messages altogether. But he couldn't bring himself to do that. He didn't *want* the responsibility, but he couldn't make the final, full break, either.

"And if that's not the story of my life, I don't know what is," he told himself.

The sky was blue, the air dry, and Teddy found himself humming under his breath as he drove, despite his earlier bad mood, as though he were taking a pleasure drive instead of planning to break, enter, and snoop.

He contemplated parking around the corner, just in case

anyone called the cops, but decided that trying to explain why he hadn't parked in front of a house he claimed to have every right to enter . . . yeah, no reason to borrow trouble. He parked at the curb in the same spot he'd taken on their first visit, got out, and walked back up to the house.

Oddly for a nice Saturday morning, there didn't seem to be anyone taking a walk, working outside, or just hanging out on their front porches. Maybe they were all sleeping in. Teddy felt a moment's bitter jealousy, and promised himself another cup of coffee as soon as this was done.

This time, he skirted the front porch, knowing that the door would be locked, and walked around to the back. There was a wooden gate at the side of the house, but the door was a simple lift latch and the hinges didn't creak when he pushed it open.

The backyard was surprisingly large, an expanse of dirt and sparse grass. Like the house itself, it looked like a space that with a little money and effort could be nice, but right now was barely on the plus side of run-down. There was a cellar hatch snug against the side of the house. The aluminum door was dented, but the padlock and chain across the handles were sturdy enough to resist anything short of a lowland gorilla yanking on it. Teddy scanned the yard, but didn't see anything that might have suggested dogs had ever been out here: no animal-sized shelters, no chain wrapped around a tree where a dog might have been tied, no remains of dog poo in the grass. Of course, everything might have been cleared out already, or he might be missing something that would be obvious to a dog owner—Ginny really should have come here, not him.

The cellar might have been barred, but the back door, as he'd expected, was unlocked. Teddy shook his head: he knew that there probably wasn't anything in the house worth stealing, and anyone who snuck up on Deke deserved the knuckle sandwich they'd probably get, but it was still stupid.

The back door opened into the kitchen, which looked like it hadn't been updated since the house was built in the 1950s. White linoleum and battered, peeling countertops were topped by wooden cabinets. He checked a few of them, and found basic pots and pans, some cereal, and packets of instant coffee, but not much more. There was a pizza delivery flyer taped to the refrigerator door, and inside a carton of eggs, soy milk, and more small packets of condiments than Teddy had seen since his college roommate's collection. Clearly, Deke wasn't a happy homemaker, kitchen edition.

The rest of the small house was similarly barren. They'd seen the main room through the front door earlier: two battered sofas and an old television and VCR, plus piles of old paperbacks. Teddy picked one up and looked at the cover, curious. *The Parsifal Mosaic,* by Robert Ludlum.

"Classic," he said, and replaced the book where it had been. There was a room off the back that was clearly the bedroom, if only because there was a narrow single bed against the far wall, and a closet full of clothing that looked remarkably similar to what Deke had been wearing the day before. The only other room was the bathroom, which was exactly as depressing as Teddy had expected it to be: threadbare towels, denture polish, and medications. He glanced at the bottles, but didn't recognize any of the names. He took a picture of each one with his cell phone, so Ginny could check them later. He didn't think it would be relevant, but it might be.

"If this is getting older, man, I opt out." The old-man bathroom gave him the creeps.

He went back out into the main room and looked around. Ginny had a cleaning service come in every week, and she was moderately compulsive about keeping things neat, but every time he'd been over there, Georgie had toys under the coffee table and left abandoned by her food dish, not to mention the quilted dog beds, one in the office, the other by the sofa. There was none of that here. If there ever had been dogs in this house, that had been cleared up, as well.

There was a narrow staircase at the other end of the main room. The stairs creaked badly, leading to an open space about half again the length of the house. The ceiling was low, barely a crawl space, and it was filled with cardboard boxes, all taped and marked in black, some with a woman's name on them. A lifetime, packed away but clearly not forgotten. Teddy felt another twinge of guilt, and decided not to pry. He might be wrong, but he was pretty sure nothing here had anything to do with the case. And if he was wrong . . . well, these boxes weren't going anywhere.

"If there's anything, it's going to be in that basement," he said, going back downstairs. "Damned unlikely that there wouldn't be an internal entrance, as well as the outside door . . ."

A quick search found another door in the kitchen, bolt-locked, that opened to a steep flight of stairs going down. The wall switch cast a bright light onto the steps, and after making sure that the door was wedged open, just in case, Teddy went down into the basement.

The smell hit him before he was halfway down. His nose wrinkled, and his eyes watered a little. Urine, he realized. Like a pipe had burst in the bathroom upstairs. No, not burst, leaked. A slow leak over years.

"Man, did nobody ever come down here?" He almost went back upstairs, but instead breathed through his mouth and kept going. Another light switch at the bottom revealed a space running the entire length and width of the house, doubling the square footage. On one wall was the door that must lead to the backyard; on the other side there were two windows, high up and blocked by the hedge outside. The floor was cement, and looked cracked and stained. There were tables along the far wall and what looked like a laundry basket. He went closer, and nodded. An old plastic laundry basket, filled with more of the threadbare towels he'd seen upstairs. Was there a washing machine down here?

Something made a noise, and Teddy froze. If anyone ever asked, he would totally deny being scared of rats, but he wasn't exactly *fond* of them, either.

He waited a moment, trying to place the sound. Was it upstairs? Outside? He thought he saw something move on the other side of the windows, a sway of greenery, but then the noise came again, closer. Inside.

"Here, kitty kitty," he said, hoping for a best-case scenario.

There was a low whine, and Teddy turned, tracking the noise. Behind the table, in the shadows. Moving cautiously, in case he was wrong and it really was a rat waiting to leap out and eat his face, Teddy bent down and reached out a hand. "Hey there. Hey, boy. C'mere, boy."

His hand reached a small, warm bundle of fur, and a warm, wet tongue scraped across his fingers, making Teddy laugh in relief before he sobered again. Not a rat, no. But proof there had been at least one dog here, despite Deke's claim.

Normally, Ginny was able to make a plan of attack, and then attack it without hesitation. That was her stock-in-trade, her MO. Friday afternoon, despite a good meeting and plenty of time afterward to work, she was deeply unsatisfied with the research she'd been able to do on the case. Oh, the legal stuff about tenancy and leases had been simple enough. But the rest of it . . .

"Damn Seth for mentioning dogfighting, anyway."

She hadn't wanted to click on any links, as she'd admitted to Tonica, because she'd been afraid of what she would see. Considering that even before Georgie came into her life she'd teared up at those manipulatively evil ASPCA ads . . . no. So she'd put a tight filter on and stuck to the text sites, the newspaper articles and dry legal findings about the mechanics of dogfighting. That was what she needed, to discover what might be involved in this, why they might need Deke, and his little house. Just one link that might give them a hold on *how* Deke might be tied into this . . . or if it was impossible that he could be.

Even avoiding the more graphic sites, by midmorning Ginny knew more about dogfighting, both the historical basis and the modern iteration, than she had ever not-wanted to know. "Gambling and drugs," she muttered, drawing a triangle on a sheet of paper. "Dogfighting, gambling, and drugs. That says mob, right?" Apparently the government agreed, since there was a push to use RICO charges to nail dogfight organizers after the Vick case in 2007.

"You'd think someone who got violent profession-ally would have gotten his aggressions out, and not have to watch dogs get hurt for his jollies," Ginny muttered. "People suck."

She found a site that offered to set people up with—oh God—a dogfighting starter kit. They were blunt about the money that could be made. Even allowing for marketing BS, it was still in excess of a thousand dollars pure profit for each fight, and that didn't take into account any sideline betting that was probably changing hands. House share would be gravy on top of that. And none of it reported to the IRS.

Ginny really needed to scrub her brain after this. But one of the things that seemed pretty clear was that there needed to be space for a dogfight. A "fight ring" was twelve feet or more. A little suburban house, even with minimal furnishings, didn't seem large enough. Although it might have been used as a training area; the articles she'd read said that fighting dogs were sometimes kept caged up, beaten, and starved until they were desperate enough to fight, just to get fed.

She took a sip of her coffee, and grimaced at the now-cooled bitterness, although the taste could have been less the temperature, and more the fact that her stomach hurt to begin with. She drew a box above the triangle and wrote "Deke" inside it. Then "Deke's house" in smaller letters. "Tonica will find anything there is to find, if there's anything to find."

Her left foot stretched out under the table, searching for the shar-pei sprawled under it, wuffling in her sleep. The desire to have the dog nearby, to get down on her knees and hug the dog, apologizing for her entire species, was intense.

"If you hadn't ended up at the shelter, baby, if I hadn't adopted you . . ." She didn't know where Georgie had come from, only that she'd been found as a puppy, abandoned. The shar-pei was a marshmallow, but you wouldn't know it to look at her, square-chested and solidly built under that loose skin. Shar-peis had been bred as fighting dogs once. And she'd bitten people, to protect Ginny. . . .

"I need to teach you not to go with strangers," she said.

"We'll work on that, next training session." Georgie was too much of a sweetie, generally willing to let anyone pet her. That had never seemed like a bad thing before.

And that reminded her—a quick check of the time and yeah, Tonica should be back soon. He'd agreed to give her and Georgie a ride to the vet today, rather than having to haul out on mass transit. It would save her at least an hour of travel time, and they could discuss the case along the way.

"You ready to go to the V-E-T, Georgie?"

The dog had no opinion one way or the other, although she perked up immediately when Ginny came back into the office holding her leash. "C'mon, kid. Walkies, then we're going for a drive."

When they came around the corner back onto her street, Georgie having done her business, Tonica was waiting for them, jeans and leather jacket like a postadolescent hood, leaning against the side of the car and taking in the midday sunshine. But he had something in his arms, was holding it like he wasn't quite sure what to do. . . .

Ginny came closer, and then stopped, Georgie bumping at her heel.

"That's a dog."

"I can see why you like investigating things," Tonica said, his voice drier than it had any right to be, considering there was a dog in his arms. No, not a dog, a puppy. Ginny reacted automatically, stepping forward and reaching out.

"Don't hold him like that, he's not a beer, he's a puppy, you have to support his body."

Somehow, she ended up with a double handful of warm, wiggly dog, and Tonica was stepping back with a look of relief on his face. "Oh hi there," she said, taking a closer look. "Aren't you adorable?"

"It's not adorable," Tonica said. "It's a sad, rat-shaped excuse of a dog."

"Terrier of some kind, I think." The ears were upright and sharply pointed, and the muzzle was adorned with long silvery whiskers, while large brown eyes looked at her like she was the bestest thing since kibble. Georgie pressed up against her leg, face upturned as though to ask "whatcha got there, Mom?"

"Don't even start with me," she warned the puppy. "I'm a one-dog woman and that job's already taken." She reached down with one hand to pet Georgie, just in case the older dog was feeling threatened, then looked at Tonica. "Where did you find it?"

"Where do you think?" Tonica made a face. "In the basement of Deke's house, where he swore there were no dogs, ever."

"Hell." Ginny felt the dog shiver in her arms, as though it knew they were talking about it. "Anything else?"

"No." Tonica went down on one knee and patted his thigh, calling Georgie over to him. She went without any reluctance, accepting his petting. "No sign of kennels, cages, or any indication that anything illegal or bloody had ever happened there. But Parsifal there is a pretty big neon clue."

"Parsifal?" Ginny looked down at the terrier puppy. "Tonica, that name's bigger than he is."

"Get in the car, Mallard."

She laughed, still cuddling the puppy, and watched while Tonica opened the door and coaxed Georgie inside. "It's a good thing we're going to the vet, then, anyway. We can get him checked out, make sure he's healthy, and see if he's got a chip to tell us who he belongs to."

The look that Tonica threw her, as he got behind the wheel and started the car, was telling, and chilling. He didn't think the puppy was chipped, didn't think that any owners were going to show up with relief and claim him.

Neither did she.

"Georgie, settle down. Georgie!" She held the puppy in one arm and shoved the other dog's nose gently, until she sat back down. "Stay," Ginny said sternly. "You know better than to try and get up in the car. Shut up, Teddy," she said, not even looking at the driver, but knowing he was grinning. "If your puppy ruins Georgie's up until now perfect car manners . . ."

"Not my dog," he said, but kept any other comment to himself.

"Hello."

The puppy flopped on his side, and craned his short neck around Ginny's arm to better see who was talking to him. "Hello."

"*I'm Georgie.*" *The shar-pei came a little closer, shoving her nose into the space between the front seats, but still keeping close to the floor, so Ginny didn't get upset again.* "What's your name?"

The puppy looked at her quizzically. It had whiskers like Penny's, long and silvery, and twitchy.

"C'mon, Parsifal," Ginny said. "Stop squirming, will you?"

"Parsifal," Georgie said. "That's your name."

"All right," the puppy said. "What's a Parsifal?"

"I don't know," Georgie admitted. "Penny will know."

"What's a Penny?"

"She's a cat," Georgie started to say, and the puppy scrambled under the warm hands holding him, trying to get up. "Cat? Where?"

"Seriously, dog, stop wiggling!"

"Not here. Later." Georgie shushed the puppy, telling it to stay still. When Ginny used that voice, it was time to put your nose on your paws and pretend to be asleep.

They spent the rest of the ride staring at each other, Georgie curious, the puppy fading in and out of sleep.

As they slid back into traffic, Teddy's attention was split between dealing with the road and Ginny's talking to the two dogs, trying to get them to settle down. He noticed the sedan that moved into place behind them, a late-model Chevy in dark blue, the kind that made airport runs for half the price of a cab, but he didn't think much of it.

He certainly didn't recognize it as the car that had been parked across the street from Deke's house when he arrived that morning.

The driver, an Asian man in his late thirties, kept exactly one car length behind, slowing and speeding as they did, never getting too close, but not letting them out of sight until they reached their destination. While they parked in the open lot attached to the building, the sedan idled along the curb around the corner, waiting until they went inside.

The driver then picked up his cell phone from the seat next to him and entered a number.

"He picked up a woman and a dog, and went to a veterinary office in Washington Park. No, the dog was a big one, full-grown. No, no sign of the old man. Hell, I don't—no, sir. Yes, sir."

He grimaced, then nodded. "I'll make sure of it, sir." He ended the call, then pulled away from the curb and drove away.

4

Scott Williams wasn't the closest vet to where Ginny lived, by a considerable distance, and Teddy was quite sure that he wasn't the cheapest in town. But they'd met him when he was volunteering at the shelter they were investigating, and Georgie had liked him. After a less-than-stellar experience with her first vet, Ginny had decided that she was willing to spend a little more money and time for a vet Georgie had rapport with.

Especially since Teddy was sucker enough to drive them there when he had the time.

"Hi, Ms. Mallard, hey, Georgie," the receptionist called out when they came in. "We're running a little behind, but we'll be ready for you in a few minutes. Oh, and who's the cutie?"

"I'll assume you're talking about the four-legged one," Ginny said drily. "This is Parsifal, and no, he's not mine. Neither's the two-legged one." Ginny tilted her head in his direction, and Teddy was suddenly under the intense scrutiny of five-foot-nothing of receptionist, and an only-slightly-taller male vet tech who showed up as though drawn by the scent of New Puppy.

"I found him," Teddy said awkwardly, feeling himself shift from foot to foot, even as the technician lifted the dog from Ginny's arms and was expertly checking it over. "He'd been abandoned, I guess?"

"You guess?" the receptionist asked.

"I found him in an abandoned house. We were . . . it's complicated." They weren't cops, or even licensed investigators; despite his earlier bravado, technically he'd been trespassing, since Deke hadn't actually given his okay, and since he was in the process of getting evicted Teddy didn't even know if his permission would be valid.

"Well, you did a good thing, taking him in," the receptionist said. She was short, and round, and dark-skinned, with gray hair that curled around her head like a halo. "No collar? He's a little thing, but we'll see if he's chipped, and check him for all the usual, yes?"

"Um, yeah." Teddy had the feeling that he'd just somehow been maneuvered into taking responsibility for the puppy. But it was for the case, right? The dog was evidence.

He heard a door open and close, and then there was a scrabble of claws on the linoleum as Georgie abandoned Ginny and raced forward, reaching up to put her paws on the newcomer's knees, putting her head within easy scratching range.

Dr. Williams laughed, rubbing her flopped-over ears with affection. "Hi there, Georgie. You're so good for my ego."

"She knows you have chew treats," Ginny said drily. "Not to knock down your canine charm, or anything."

"That *is* my canine charm," Williams said, even as he

took a treat out of his coat pocket and gave it to Georgie. "And I see you've brought us a new patient?"

They must have had other animals in the back, other things to be doing, but Williams took the puppy from the tech and studied its eyes and ears, stretching out each leg briefly. The puppy stared back at the silver-haired human, whiskers trembling, and then lunged forward and licked his nose.

"Oh, yeah, you're a real terror," Williams said with a laugh. "C'mon in back, I'll check him out quick while Alan does up Georgie, and get you on your way."

Teddy declined to go in the back with the puppy, feeling the need to distance himself from the entire situation. Not his dog. Ginny and Georgie disappeared into another room, and reappeared about fifteen minutes later. Georgie seemed as unflappably happy as ever, her stubby tail wagging when she saw Teddy, perfectly content to flop down at his feet while Ginny went up to the counter to pay.

The vet came out with Parsifal a few minutes after that, waiting until Ginny had finished at the counter before addressing them both.

"Well, the good news is that the young fellow appears to be a healthy four- or five-month-old pup. I'm putting down mostly border terrier as a breed—there's probably something else tossed in there, but not enough to worry about. He's a cheerful thing, good-tempered. A little scrawny, and definitely underfed right now, but proper care and feeding should take care of that. He'll probably max out at ten pounds—not quite a pocket pup, but most apartment buildings won't have an issue with him. He's going to need a lot of exercise, though: they're active breeds, terriers."

Teddy nodded, not sure what he was supposed to say at this point. Next to him, Ginny echoed his nod.

"But . . ." Williams's voice dropped in the way that never brought good news. "I saw a few things that worried me. I assume that you were not planning to breed him?"

"What?" Teddy looked at Ginny, and then back at the vet, who seemed to be expecting him to answer. "Um, no. No, I wasn't."

"Good. I would suggest that you have him neutered sooner rather than later, just in case. I suspect his line's already been inbred to the point of . . . well, not damage, but you may run into trouble when he's older, and these are not genes you'll want to pass on to another litter."

"Yeah, okay. I'll, um, I'll make an appointment." Teddy wasn't going to keep the dog, but it was the least they could do, to make sure the little guy was adoptable. He'd charge it back to Seth, part of the unexpected expenses of the job. Maybe, if Deke could find a place, the two of them could stick together, two misfits, through no fault of their own. Teddy was pleased with that idea, even though he had no idea if the older man liked dogs, or could afford to keep one.

"How can you tell?" Ginny asked. "About the problems, I mean."

"It's not definite, not without lab testing, but there are small things you can guess from," Williams said, answering her question without hesitation. "The way his ears fall, the shape of his muzzle, the way his hindquarters aren't quite squared . . . there are certain things we see, especially when you have too small a breeding population, or a breeder is focusing too hard on one particular aspect and forgets to monitor others." His mouth tightened, like he wanted to say something more, but didn't. "But I don't see anything that should cause serious medical issues right now. He'll make a fine companion for someone."

"And he wasn't chipped?" Thank God Ginny remembered to ask. Teddy was having trouble focusing on everything the vet was telling him, much less coming up with questions.

"No. And we ran the missing pets database and nobody's reported anyone with his description missing. I take it you're about as unsurprised by that as I am."

Ginny just shrugged, an entire conversation in that move.

"I see." Suddenly he was talking to Teddy again. "He's got his starter shots, but he'll need boosters later on. We'll set you up with some puppy chow to start, and remember to make sure he gets more time on the sidewalk than Georgie-girl. He's not used to holding it as long, right now."

"I still have some wee pads," Ginny said, possibly a sympathy offering, as though she could tell Teddy felt like someone had just rammed him with an invisible truck. A small, cute, furry truck.

"I'm not keeping him," Teddy said, pretty sure that nobody was listening to him.

Williams didn't miss a beat. "Well, if you decide against it, and Ginny doesn't want to be a two-dog mom"—he paused, but she declined to pick up the bait—"let us know. We might be able to find a foster for him, so he doesn't have to go to the shelter."

Teddy didn't want to drop the dog off at the shelter, either, any shelter. Most especially not the one they'd met Williams at, which had been hit with the double whammy of one of the owners embezzling funds, and an employee using it as a front for exotic animal smuggling: they were still in business, but struggling to maintain funding. Teddy felt bad about that, but they'd brought it on themselves.

"We'll see," he said, and could swear everyone in the room snickered.

Deke. He was definitely going to try and pass the dog on to Deke.

Although Georgie got to ride on her own in the backseat, due to Parsifal's size and lack of training, he was introduced to a plain cardboard carrier with "I'm New!" printed on the side. He was dubious, but eventually stayed in long enough for them to close the top and load both dogs back into the coupe.

"So, what are you going to do with Parsi?" Ginny asked. "I mean, you can't just leave him in your apartment while you're working, not while he's a puppy, anyway. And I'm *not* taking him home, so forget about it." She would, if he pushed. But she wasn't going to give in just yet.

"Mary's," he said, putting the car into gear and pulling out of the parking lot. "We already have a house cat; we can put up with a house dog for a few days. Maybe someone there will be dumb enough to want to rescue him. You want to be dropped off at home, or . . . ?"

"We'll go with you," Ginny said. "Parsi could use some familiar company, and we still have to go over everything for the job." They'd been too distracted by the dogs to talk about anything on the way over.

"Yeah, okay." He didn't sound enthused about it, but she figured he was *still* distracted by the puppy.

She looked back, checking to make sure that both dogs were okay, and then looked at him. "So, did you learn anything, poking around the house?"

Tonica chewed on the inside of his cheek, fingers tightening and relaxing on the wheel. She waited. Unlike some guys she knew, Tonica never hesitated to say what he was thinking, even if it sounded dumb. He liked talking it out; that was one of the reasons why they worked well together.

"I don't know. There wasn't anything I could put a finger on, but something about that basement, the way it had smelled . . . I don't know," he said again. "But there was something hinky going on there, Gin. The smell in the basement was . . . pretty bad. Multiple dogs, bad. Like the shelter's kennels smelled, only multiplied a hundred times, and minus all the bleach they used to clean the place up."

"Dogfighting bad?"

"Blood, you mean? Maybe. I'm glad to say that I'm really not all that familiar with the smell of stale blood. And no, I'm not going to get my nose trained in case we need it later, Ginny," he warned, hopefully heading that idea off at the pass. "I don't think anything happened there, though. You were right, there wasn't enough room."

"I've seen bullfighting," Ginny said, seemingly out of nowhere. "Once, when I was in Spain. It was . . . beautiful, and horrible, and dangerous. But the humans took a risk, too. This . . ."

"It's all violence, Gin. And the animals don't get a say in it."

She nodded, and stared out the car window, worrying at a fingernail with her teeth. He glanced over at her, listening to the sounds of the dogs behind them, restless.

"I know Deke said he didn't do anything, and I'm inclined to believe him, but my gut—and my nose—tells me that there were dogs there—one at least, and I doubt he showed up on his own. If whoever's got those dogs is involved in dogfighting, the way the landlord claims, that's a federal crime. Do you think we should call Agent Asuri?"

The federal agent had cleaned up the aftermath of their first case, and had warned them against taking another. But they had gotten the feeling that she was a straight shooter. They could probably trust her to not freak out at them if they called her now, before they got in too deep.

"Not until we can clear Deke," Ginny said. "We promised no cops unless we knew for sure he was guilty, and feds are as bad as cops. Worse, maybe. And we're not assuming he's guilty yet. Are we?"

Teddy hesitated, then shook his head. "No. Not yet."

★ ★ ★

The driver of the dark blue sedan parked his car by the curb, away from a tree that might drop sap or something on the finish. He hated having to go back to a scene; he was supposed to be certain places at certain times, and that routine kept him safe, unnoticed. But he'd been interrupted earlier, by the other man's arrival, and the boss didn't accept jobs unfinished.

There were three young girls playing some game on the front lawn of the house next to the old man's place. The driver glared at them, waiting until they got bored and drifted to the side of the house before he got out of the car. If anyone had seen him once, it could be shrugged off. But if someone saw him there again, hours later, questions might be raised. Even with redirected plates on the car, he couldn't afford anyone asking questions that might be traced back to him, and through him the boss.

He ignored the front porch, going around back to the cellar door, pulling a key from his pocket, and opening the lock. The door slid open easily, and despite the darkness, he went down the steps with the ease of a man who had done it a hundred times before.

His nose wrinkled. The air was rancid, the smell of ammonia enough to make him gag before his nose and lungs adapted by the bottom step.

His hand touched the switch at the bottom of the stairs, and the basement flooded with light. He walked the perimeter of the room, checking the corners and under the wooden tables with the air of a man who had misplaced his car keys. After a single circuit around the room, he dropped to his knees with a grimace, looking under the tables. Nothing caught his eye, and his shoulders relaxed slightly.

A noise in the house above him—a heavy creak and bang—made him freeze, half under the table.

"Shit." The hand not resting on the concrete floor reached for the holster at the small of his back, fingers closing around the pistol butt and pulling it slightly out of the leather.

Footsteps moved across the floor, and he counted steps, visualizing where the walker was heading. Across the living room, toward the bedroom, not the kitchen.

Damn it, the old man was supposed to be gone.

He got to his feet, pistol now in his hand, and waited for five long breaths, letting each one settle before taking the next. "Go to bed, old man. Or jerk off or do something, but don't go into the kitchen."

He had his orders, and he'd do them, but he didn't want to kill some dumb old man if he didn't have to. Sloppy work.

There was the creaking of furniture, and then the distant sound of water running, hard and long enough to be a shower, not a sink. The intruder put his gun away, and, with a last glance around the basement to make sure he hadn't missed anything, left the way he had come, closing the door softly behind him and locking it back up again.

The boss could rest easy. Nothing had been left behind that might say what had happened there.

5

Two Bastards and a chaser, check." Stacy smiled at the customer, her hand already reaching for the glasses under the counter.

Teddy had to force himself not to offer help or advice. He was just there on a Saturday afternoon as unofficial official backup; he'd promoted her because she could handle it. And if Jon went through on his lame-ass bravado from last night and quit, she was going to *have* to handle it, plus more, until he could hire someone new. But it was hard to stop himself from making a suggestion occasionally.

As though she knew what he was thinking, Stacy looked up and made a face at him. He rolled his eyes and continued pacing back and forth, his cell phone pressed to his ear.

Ginny was ignoring them both, her research spread over the table they'd claimed as their own, handwritten notes with yellow and green highlighter marks on all of it. A lager, half drunk, and a glass of ginger ale, untouched, sat nearby, condensation beading along the sides.

Georgie was under the table, gnawing on a rawhide bone, with the smaller puppy occasionally giving it a pat with tiny paws, as though considering taking a bite, as well.

Teddy eyed his beer longingly. He had been listening with varying levels of patience, but this conversation had been going on long enough. "Look, I'm just saying, we need to get the kitchen fixed up. We're not going to pass inspection this year unless we do."

There was another pause on his part, while the other person spoke at length. Teddy pressed fingers against the bridge of his nose, feeling another headache inch into the back of his skull. He really wanted to get back to work, not be having this idiotic conversation.

"No, we can't just slap some paint on it. We need a new fridge, and a new floor. Come on, man, just spend the money now and there's less trouble later."

A renovation was going to be a massive pain in the ass, but less of one down the road than having to deal with the health department. But Patrick was so wound up planning his new bar, he kept putting off anything to do with his existing one. If Teddy heard "expanding my brand" one more time, he might be tempted to take a brand to the speaker.

Another customer pushed through the door, looking around as though half embarrassed to be coming in so early in the afternoon. Mary's didn't do a rousing business before 5 p.m., since they didn't have a TV to show the games, but Teddy was in no position to judge anyone who needed that 2 p.m. soother.

"Yeah. Yeah, fine, all right." He cut off Patrick's latest rant about contractors without caring how it sounded. "I'll do some research, get you the numbers. Yeah, fine."

He ended the call, and sighed, dropping the phone on the bar and putting his head down into his hands.

"That's why they pay you the big bucks," Stacy said from where she was rearranging glassware at the other end of the bar. The new customer—he looked familiar, vaguely, so not a newbie—let out enough of a laugh to prove he'd heard their banter before, so Teddy just lifted his head enough to glare at her. "Don't get sassy just because you're on weekend shift," he warned her. "I do the scheduling, and I can put you back on weekdays and floor duty in a snap."

"Yeah, but then you'd have to work with Jon all weekend, *plus* wrangle the paperwork."

Just the thought of it made his head ache even worse. "If I ever try to promote you?" he told her. "Quit."

"I hear ya there, boss."

He shook his head at her and went back to their table. Ginny was still intent on her tablet, so he reached down to the small bundle of fur, rubbing the pointed ears until Parsifal craned his entire body around to lick his hand. Overhead, there was an unhappy hiss. Teddy looked up and waggled a finger. "Penny, hush. He's just a guest. Be nice."

To say that she hadn't reacted well to the puppy's arrival would be an understatement: she had taken one look and made for the top of the bar's shelves and stayed there, no matter how much Ginny had tried to coax her down to meet the newcomer. Apparently, Mistress Penny-Drops was a one-dog cat. Although she hadn't seemed happy with Georgie, either, for the first time ever.

"You sure you don't want a puppy?" he asked Stacy now.

"You going to pay me enough to move to a larger place that takes dogs?"

"Go fill orders, and leave me to my headaches."

She saluted him. "Quiet right now," she said, casting an eye over the drinkers settled around tables in the back. "I'm going to bring up more vodka, 'kay?"

"Bring up another bottle of Dalmore, too!" he called after her.

The puppy scrambled to his feet at the shout, and looked up at Teddy with eyes that could probably have taken Attila the Hun down at the knees.

"What?" he asked it. "You gotta pee, there's your pad on the floor. And you've been fed already. Damned expensive food, too."

Behind them, Penny gave another hiss, but it sounded halfhearted.

"Hey, little guy." Ginny pulled herself away from whatever she was doing and pulled something out of her bag, holding it low in front of the puppy's nose. "Here's a chew toy more your size, so you can leave Georgie's bone alone."

Parsifal took the toy—what looked like a small rubber mouse—and crunched it experimentally between his jaws. It squeaked, and Teddy sighed.

"Hey," Ginny said, looking around as though the sigh had reminded her. "Did Seth show up yet? I want to ask him something about Deke's run-in with the law."

"No, he's not scheduled to come in until later. How

many toys do you carry around in that bag of yours, any-way?"

"Oh, yeah, 'cause you never bought Mistress Penny up there any catnip mice. So what was all that about?" She meant the phone call.

"Oh good Lord, don't ask." Being manager of Mary's while Patrick went off and opened a new bar across town had never been in his career plan, but here he was. Then again, he'd never thought about private investigations, either. He supposed that was what happened when you refused to make plans: life made 'em for you.

He sat down and picked up his beer, taking a hard slug. "I swear, between my family and Patrick, I'm changing my phone numbers. Anyway, that ate the time I planned to go over your notes, so just give me the Inigo Montoya sum-mation."

"Right." She took a sip of her ginger ale, then wiped the sides of the glass with her napkin. "First off, there's no way that Deke didn't know that there were dogs in his base-ment," she said. "Right?"

Teddy sighed again. "Yeah." He liked the guy, from what he'd seen, but he'd been the one to find Parsifal, and there was no way the little guy had just wandered in from outside and gotten stuck in that basement. And Deke was still living in the house, at least for a few more days, so squatters couldn't have set up, even assuming the landlord wasn't keeping an eye on things, so they couldn't blame anyone else.

Plus, there had been that smell in the basement. The

shelter case had been enough for him to recognize the smell of a kennel, even underneath the faded stink of industrial-strength cleansers. Animals had been kept in that basement. More than one small puppy, for more than one or two days.

"Damn it." Clearing someone of a false accusation was one thing. This . . . He had told Seth that if it looked like Deke was guilty, they were dropping the case. But the evidence of one puppy wasn't enough to convict of illegal behavior, just dumbass lying to the people trying to help him.

"But we've already established that he's in denial," Ginny was saying. "I'd love to spring Parsifal here on him and see what happens, but odds are he'd go into exactly the kind of meltdown Seth was afraid of. The only thing worse than a client who lies is a client who might not even be aware he's lying."

Teddy would almost rather be dealing with his family than a depressed and disheartened Ginny. "So what do we have?"

"While you were arguing with Patrick, I did some digging on the landlord. Public records, gotta love 'em, and then I did some real estate hunting." She sorted the papers, and pulled one out. "The guy owns five different houses in greater Seattle: two in Lynnwood, another in Rainier Beach, one in West Seattle, and Deke's. All of the houses are just on the edge of slumlordhood, but staying on the right side so there aren't any formal complaints filed."

"Nice. So?"

Ginny looked at him like he'd missed a clue somewhere.

"He's a slumlord. It's not exactly whiffly, but it's kind of whiffly."

"Whiffly? What the hell is whiffly?"

"You know." She made a vague gesture with her hand. "Off. Weird. Suspicious."

Teddy shook his head. "Hardly whiffly, Gin. Lots of people own property. And yeah, okay, borderline slumlord, maybe, or at least Bad Landlord of the Year. But that doesn't mean he was involved in anything that was allegedly going down in Deke's place. Hell, a couple–five years ago, real estate values were way down. Now they're going up again, all over the city. He might be looking to flip them; that's why he's kicking Deke out."

Ginny had that expression on her face, the one that said she was going to be bullheaded stubborn. "You're right. But do you have any other place to start? Some magical dog-hoarding connection I missed?"

He sighed, and looked over to where the two dogs had collapsed in a joint nap. "No." He finished his beer, and nodded. "All right. Fire up your spreadsheets and let's see what we've got."

Penny curled herself comfortably on her perch, tail over nose, and watched the humans with one eye while keeping her ear cocked on the interloper. Georgie had tried to get her to come down and join them, but the cat had merely twitched her whiskers at the smaller dog in disdain, and stayed put.

"C'mon, Penny." Georgie tried again, hoping the cat would

have changed her mind now that she'd seen the puppy wasn't a threat. "Don't be like that."

The tabby flicked her tail, and half slitted her eyes, still watching. She was going to be exactly like that. The newcomer was curled up against Georgie's side, its ears twitching occasionally as it dreamed. Bad dreams, not good play-hunt dreaming.

If that fact bothered the cat, she refused to let it show.

"Penny." Georgie was trying to be reasonable, but the whine at the end showed her uncertainty. Penny was never like this, she didn't throw sulks. "Listen! They're on a job. We can't help them if we're not talking to each other." Her curled tail gave a single wag, and she looked hopefully up at the cat, while the puppy started and woke up, eyes blinking at Georgie, then turning to look up at Penny. "Pennnnnny," Georgie coaxed.

The cat's ears twitched irritably. "Don't do that. Makes my whiskers hurt."

"Then come down here."

Penny sighed, then uncurled herself and leaped gracefully from shelf to counter, and then down to the floor, pausing only long enough to allow Stacy to give her an absent pat.

She came around the edge of the bar, and was greeted by a skitter of claws and a too-inquisitive nose. "Hi? Hi!"

Penny lifted her paw and swatted the interloper. The puppy went down in a sprawl of limbs, and then bounced back up again, one ear flipped inside out, and its eyes bright with uncertainty. "Hi?"

Penny sighed, and Georgie shoved her much larger paw out between the two of them. "Parsi, stop. Penny. Parsifal's important. He's evidence! Ginny said so!"

Penny turned her gaze onto the puppy, coolly thoughtful. He whined a little, deep in his throat, but lowered his gaze and bowed his head in submission. He might be young and dumb, but he wasn't stupid.

All right, maybe she could work with that.

Teddy barely spared a glance at the antics of the animals, watching Ginny instead as she tapped her fingers against the table, her eyes focused somewhere other than the screen of her tablet. They needed to get a large-screen monitor, so he could look at whatever she was working on, without standing over her shoulder.

"What do we have that's cold solid fact?"

While he waited for her to answer, he took a quick survey of the bar. There were a half dozen or so people at the tables now, and another five bellied up to the bar itself. Stacy was taking orders while obviously, casually, eavesdropping on them. Penny, having deigned to come down, was now curled in her usual spot across Georgie's front paws, the puppy sprawled on its tummy next to them, occasionally turning his head to look from one to the other. Nothing out of place, nothing he needed to worry about.

"All of the houses are about the same size, zoned for residential," Ginny said. "They all have fenced yards, no garages, street parking, and a single tenant: male, between the ages of fifty and eighty, most of them retired from a blue-collar field, or long-term unemployed. And not a single one of them could actually afford to rent out an entire house, even one that was a little run-down. Not based on their stated incomes, anyway. Not unless they're picking up more than Social Security or unemployment."

"That's not exactly building a case for the home team, Mallard. Huh." He didn't want to ask, but . . . "You got their names, and their income, off the Internet?"

She gave him a look, like he should know better by now. Really, he thought, he should. "And a few phone calls, yeah. It's not quite as easy as finding who lives where, but it can be done."

"Cold calls and favor-trading? Man, I hate the research part of this."

"Good thing I'm good at it, isn't it?" Ginny finished her ginger ale and pushed the glass forward for a refill. "Now focus, please."

"Have you always been this bossy?"

"Yes." The answer came from both Ginny and Stacy, in unison, and Teddy laughed, getting up to refill their glasses. Stacy made a face at him when he leaned over the bar to hit the tap, but didn't try to stop him.

"So," he said, lingering by the bar, "the next logical question is—was their landlord a generous angel who liked to make sure the faded end of society didn't end up homeless, and Deke just got caught on a bad day, or was something else going on?"

"Something else being, what?"

Fair enough question. "The landlord freaking out because there's dogfighting going on?" The accusation had to come from somewhere, and while Parsifal didn't seem like a dogfighting kind of dog, he was still a stone on the "guilty" side of the weights.

"I really doubt the guy didn't know. I mean, Deke's lived there how long, ten years? And the landlord never had a clue? So why now?"

"You think the landlord's involved somehow? I don't know, Gin, it still feels reachy. I mean, why would the landlord be the one to accuse him, and kick him out? Wouldn't he want to keep it quiet?"

"Yeah. I don't know." Ginny made another face. "Although there are a lot more dumb people than there are criminal masterminds."

He raised an eyebrow and nodded, conceding the point. "Maybe he did just catch wind of there being dogs there. Maybe he's looking to get a higher-paying tenant in. Unless we can prove that there are dogs in the other houses, and that the guy knows, we're stuck on that front. We're good, but I really don't think we can bullshit our way in and ask strangers if they're hiding vicious dogs in their closets. So we need to find another lead."

Ginny flipped through several pages of notes, and sighed. "Deke doesn't seem to have anything else I can dig into. I mean, he doesn't own a car, isn't a member of any shopping clubs or delivery services, he doesn't seem to have any memberships in anything except the Association of American Boxers, and a few magazines—*Ring News, Sports World Weekly,* and *Playboy.* Well, he's got focused interests, anyway. No Pet Fancier or PETA subscriptions."

"But no *Dogfighting Monthly*?" Teddy shook his head,

aware that he wasn't going to beat Ginny's PETA crack. "Maybe we should be focusing on the boxing angle? I mean, I like Seth, and Deke seems like an okay guy, if a little soft on the corners, but boxing's a violent sport. It's not inconceivable that someone there might get tangled up in watching dogs fight, too."

"Already on it," Ginny said, her fingers flying on the tablet, comfortable as though she were working on a full-sized keyboard. Teddy, who could barely manage to text on his phone, just shook his head and watched. "Nothing's coming up connecting boxers with dogfighting. Football players, yeah. Baseball players, even, and a couple of race car drivers and"—her eyebrows rose—"some actors. But no boxers. Or hockey players, for that matter. So much for the stereotype of violent people playing violent sports. But I've put out a few more feelers, see if anything comes up from the depths of the Internet. And one of us should probably hit the news archives, just to cover our asses."

"Newspapers? Really?"

"Don't start, Tonica," she said. "Just because I prefer the 'Net doesn't mean that I ignore other alternatives. There's still a lot of the world that hasn't been digitized."

"And you consider that a personal affront," he guessed.

"Damn right I do. Meanwhile, you need to poke at Seth and Deke, see if they let anything more slip. I'm pretty sure, knowing Seth, there're details he's not sharing."

Teddy wanted to protest—it felt wrong, to poke at a friend, a coworker—but she was only dividing things up according to their strengths: she researched, and he, well, poked. "If either of them takes a swing at me, you're paying for my ER visit. My insurance sucks."

"Hello, self-employed here," Ginny said. "Mine's not much better. They swing, you better duck."

Stacy had wandered to the other end of the bar to fill orders while they were talking, but came back then, pausing until they both looked up at her. "Hey, boss, I'm going to take a break before things start to pick up, okay?"

He glanced at his watch. She was right, the rush would hit in about half an hour. "Yeah, I'll keep an eye on things."

She nodded thanks, and then turned to Ginny. "You want me to take the pups for a constitutional?"

Ginny checked her watch, too, while Teddy took over behind the bar, and then looked over at Georgie, who had raised her head as though she knew she was being discussed. "Yeah, that would be great, thanks."

Teddy didn't think Georgie needed another walk already, but he wasn't her owner. And maybe Stacy would bond with Parsifal, and solve that problem.

The younger woman picked up the leashes, one worn and pink, the other brand-new and black, from where they were coiled on the table. "Hey, Georgie, you want to go for walkies? C'mon, pup, let's introduce you to the wonders of hydrants, huh?"

"Parsifal isn't really up for a long walk," Teddy warned her. "You're going to end up carrying him most of the way."

"Yeah, well, my pocketbook weighs more than he does. I think we'll be okay. C'mon, guys, walkies!"

"She should try that at six a.m., see if she's so cheerful about it," Ginny said, watching the younger woman clip leashes to both dogs and usher them out the door, Parsifal barely managing to keep up.

"I don't think Stace has even *seen* six a.m., unless it was from the other side." It was a side effect of their job: you worked late nights, not early mornings. And her other job was working as an artist's model, and he didn't think artists were much for 6 a.m., either.

"Hey, Seth," he heard her say as she went out the door-way, which gave Teddy just enough time to put on his work face before the older man came inside. He had Deke in tow, both men looking exhausted.

"Good morning, ladies," Teddy called to them. He reached over and pulled two bottles from the chiller and popped the tops, sliding them across the bar. "You guys look like you could use this."

"Thanks." Seth took it, drained half the bottle. Deke merely held his, his thumb rubbing back and forth across the label.

"You guys look like a few miles of bad road," Ginny said with an utter lack of tact, frowning at them. She wasn't wrong, although it wasn't as though either man was a commercial for clean living and bright eyes, even at his best.

"They fired me," Deke said, his voice carrying exhausted outrage, as though he'd been saying it over and over and it still didn't make sense to him. "Why did they fire me?"

"We talked about this, Deke," Seth said, and Teddy was pretty sure he hadn't ever heard the older man sound so much like a worn-down patient. "You knew the job was short-term. And they gave you two weeks' notice."

"But everyone there liked me. They said so."

Seth rubbed his face with his hands, pinching the bridge of his nose between his index fingers. "Nonprofit center, Deke. Budget ran out, and you were low man on the salary pole. It's not about . . . anything else. Just bad timing. C'mon. Take your beer and help me get the kitchen set up, okay? Leave these people to their work."

Teddy and Ginny watched the two older men head into the back, and then Ginny shook her head. "That is a man who wouldn't have any luck if it wasn't for bad luck."

"I'm almost afraid to stand next to him, yeah. Considering the news, I think I'm going to take a rain check on talking to them about . . . anything right now, okay?"

"It's not going to get any easier to ask them," Ginny said, and then held up her hands in surrender when he gave her a look. "Hey, you're the schmoozer; you pick your moment. Just don't wait too long."

Ginny could have argued for going in after Deke right away—hit him when he was down, which was an asshole thing to do but probably effective—but part of their deal was that she gave way to Tonica in things like this. Anyway, Parsifal was getting walked, so they couldn't drop him into the older man's lap just then, anyway.

She had a sudden spurt of guilt—intentionally surprising a guy they already knew wasn't tight-wrapped, on what sounded like a particularly bad day, wasn't cool. But it was for his own good, and what else were they going to do?

She turned back to her work, entering the names of the renters into a grouped search, hoping that something might jump out and trigger a revelation.

As usual, working put her into a slight fugue state. She was aware of Tonica dealing with someone who wanted a refill, of the murmur of conversation, but none of it really reached her. When there was a change in light when the front door opened, though, she looked up, expecting to see Stacy and the dogs returning. Instead, a figure lurked just in the frame, leaning forward as though uncertain of his welcome. "Excuse me?"

"Hey," Tonica called, a professional smile on his face. "Come on in, we're open. Quiet right now, but open."

The man stepped inside, looking around the place. He seemed to like what he saw, giving it a small smile and a nod. "I'm looking for, um, Seth Wilbernosky?"

"Wilbernosky? Huh." Ginny looked up at that, tilting her head as she took in the newcomer. Short, blond, pale even by "we never see the sun" Pacific Northwest standards, and that was saying something. He wasn't wearing a suit, just a jacket over slacks, and a button-down shirt, no tie. Hair was a little shaggy for a G-man or cop, too, although that wasn't a deal killer. "What did Seth do this time?" she asked, anyway.

"What? Oh, no." The guy came all the way into the bar and reached in his pocket, handing Ginny a business card.

"Larry Zimmerman. I'm with the county social services.

Mr. Wilbernosky was down as the contact person for one of my clients, and I wanted to speak with him, but he wasn't answering his phone, so . . ." Zimmerman gave a half-apologetic shrug, like he did that a lot.

"Yeah, he doesn't have a cell phone, so you were reaching his landline. Seth!" Tonica half turned, and called toward the back. "Get your scrawny backside out here. Please."

"So why did you need to talk to Deke?" Ginny asked, making a wild guess.

Zimmerman gave her a long look. "Are you a family member?"

"No," she admitted. "A concerned friend."

"Well, as a concerned friend, I'm sure you understand that such things are private."

As shutdowns went, it was pretty polite, but definite. Ginny nodded, acknowledging that she'd stepped over a line, and things might have gotten awkward, except Penny took that moment to appear, stalking toward Zimmerman with her tail erect and her whiskers quivering, in full investigative mode.

"Oh hey, honey." Zimmerman leaned down to pet Penny as she wound herself around his legs. "And who are you?"

"That's Penny," Tonica said. "Hope you're not allergic."

Before Zimmerman could answer, Seth came out, and Stacy came back in with the dogs, the puppy, as predicted, cradled in her arms. "Everyone did all their things," the younger woman announced, handing Georgie's leash to

Ginny and depositing Parsifal on a stool, interrupting any-thing Seth or Zimmerman might have said to each other.

"And who are these pretties?" Zimmerman asked, as the shar-pei sniffed happily at the stranger's outstretched hand.

"This is Georgie," Stacy said, "and that bundle of cute is Parsifal."

Ginny started to say something about Parsi looking for a forever home, if Zimmerman was dog-inclined, when Deke came out, an apron wrapped around his waist and the bottle of beer still in his hand. "Hey, Seth—oh. Hi, Larry."

"Hi, Deke," Zimmerman said, masking any surprise he might have had at finding the other man there. "You missed our meeting last month."

"'S'not mandatory."

"No, but it does help keep you focused. How are things?"

"Crap. I lost my job, and I don't have anywhere to stay." Deke's voice managed to be both placid and bitter, as though he'd accepted that life wasn't ever going to give him anything nice.

Zimmerman went into alert mode, the same way Geor-gie did when she heard an unfamiliar sound. Ginny could feel her stomach tense, even though she didn't know what he was reacting to.

"What happened to the place you were renting?"

"Landlord kicked me out." Deke's face screwed up, like he was about to go into the entire story, and you could hear the thud of the other shoe dropping. Ginny didn't know why Deke rated a social worker checking up on him, but she was pretty sure Larry was going to want to know *why* Deke was about to become homeless, and that meant talking about the accusations, and odds were that would create exactly the mess they were trying to avoid. She lifted her gaze to Tonica, hoping he'd have an escape route, but before either of them could say anything, Seth jumped into the conversation.

"They're having a disagreement about the specific terms of the lease. Nothing serious. We expect it to blow over in a few days." Seth lied like a champ. Either that, or he really had that much faith in what she and Tonica could do.

"You're still there, then?" Zimmerman asked. "Do you need an advocate to help you? I can arrange someone to come in—"

"No, we got it handled," Seth said. "Really."

Zimmerman had flipped open his notepad and was writing something down. "He's staying with you, in the meanwhile?"

Seth scowled, then looked at Deke and nodded once.

"All right, I'll need your address, then, since someone who shall remain Deke failed to inform me of this."

"It's not my fault," Deke said, protesting, but with the resigned voice of someone who isn't surprised he's in trouble again. "It's because of the dogs. I didn't do nothing wrong!"

Tonica opened his mouth like he was about to say something, and Ginny shot him a glare—she would have kicked him if she'd been able to reach, and if it wouldn't have been so obvious.

"The dogs? These dogs? Deke, you know what your lease says." Zimmerman frowned at him. "I didn't know you even liked animals."

Georgie took that moment to shove up against Deke's leg, and Penny advanced across the counter, knocking her head against his shoulder, as though they were flanking him, showing that yes he was, in fact, an animal person. Deke absently reached out to knuckle the top of Penny's head, between her ears. Normally, the tabby didn't allow liberties like that from anyone except Tonica, but she almost seemed to welcome it this time, and Parsifal let out a sharp yip and raced to sit on Deke's feet, chewing on the laces of his shoes as though upset at being left out.

"He's . . . Seth's," Ginny said. "The puppy, I mean. Georgie's mine."

Seth blinked, then nodded. "Yeah. Don't blame me for the name, he had it when I got him." The older man scowled at Ginny, as though asking why the hell she'd saddled him with supposed ownership of a dog he'd never seen before. She gave a helpless shrug, not sure why she'd done it, either. They'd planned on shoving the puppy in Deke's face, yes, but this wasn't the time. They needed Deke focused right now, not flustered. Seth was Deke's friend, and that would cover them in case anyone had seen the puppy in Deke's house, since she didn't think that admitting that the dog was an illegal tenant and possibly an escapee from a dogfighting outfit would be in anyone's interests. . . .

They hadn't even been on this case for forty-eight

hours, and already it was all muddled and confused. Usually it took them at least four days to hit this point.

"Well, it's good you have somewhere to stay, until this is worked out." Zimmerman cocked an eye at Deke, who was surrounded by the three animals like some sort of furry honor guard. "The puppy's yours, isn't it, Deke, not your friend's? It's okay. I think you should have gotten a pet years ago, personally. And this pretty tabby girl here, is she yours, too?"

Ginny couldn't stop herself from smiling in relief. "Penny . . . belongs to herself."

There was something in Zimmerman's voice that told Ginny that this guy was on their side. Or Deke's, anyway, which was even better. He wasn't going to intentionally cause problems. But she still didn't like the fact that he'd come to check on Deke just then. From the look on Tonica's face, neither did he.

"So why the urgent visit?" her partner asked, then raised his hands in the universal sign for "not that it's any of my business."

Zimmerman flipped back to professional mode, although he didn't shut Tonica down the way he had Ginny: they'd passed some sort of test, she guessed. "His employer let us know that he'd been let go, since we'd gotten him the job in the first place. I wanted to do a check-in, make sure that everything was okay. Especially since he missed his last check-in . . ." The glare that accompanied that was worthy of Ginny's mother at her worst.

"Ain't obligated," Deke said again, still petting Penny, not looking up.

"No, you're not," Zimmerman agreed. "But I can't help you if I don't know there're problems. We've talked about this before, Deke. You need to keep your nose clean."

Right, Seth had said something about Deke being a guest of the county for a while. Ginny hadn't been aware that they did follow-up on things like that—with the budget cuts, she'd think everyone would be too overworked to give a damn about one harmless ex-boxer. Just Deke's luck he got assigned to someone who still gave a damn, exactly when he needed people to *not* notice him.

"So, he's not in trouble or anything." Tonica made it sound like a statement, not a question.

"He's going to need to get another job," Zimmerman said. "We'll work on that. But so long as he has a place to stay, everything should be all right. I'm sorry about the job, Deke, but you handled it well. That's good."

Ginny assumed that meant he hadn't hit anyone.

"I still haveta go downtown?"

"We can consider this to be this month's meeting," Zimmerman said. "But I want to see you next month, yeah. No excuses this time!"

There was a tense stretch after Zimmerman left, having gotten Seth's promise to get Deke to his appointment next month and refused Teddy's offer of a beer. Then Seth let out a deep sigh, looked at the puppy still gnawing on

Deke's bootlace, and turned and looked at Ginny as though this was all her fault.

"More damned animals? And you shove it onto me?"

"Well, it didn't seem like the right time to mention that oh, we found it in Deke's house, abandoned and half starved, did it?" Ginny pitched her voice low so that it wouldn't, hopefully, carry over to the customers who had so far pointedly ignored what was happening at the bar, but she was still obviously pissed.

Teddy winced. Ginny had a long fuse but a sharp temper, and Seth managed to ignite it more than anyone else. This was just one of the few times he hadn't done it intentionally.

"What?" Seth's voice was satisfyingly shocked at her bombshell, and he glanced at Teddy as though looking for verification. He nodded once. That was enough to turn Seth's attention back to Deke. Teddy felt sympathy for the older man, facing that glare, which could have melted steel.

"Damn it, Deke. You lied to me!"

"Did not!"

"Then you gonna tell me that you don't know how a dog got into your house? Didn't know it was there, all this time you were swearing you were innocent?"

"I never went down there!" And Deke clamped his mouth shut like he'd just gotten an electric shock or something, his eyes wide and a little more scared than Teddy liked seeing in an adult. Or a kid, for that matter. In anything. He'd had a cousin who had that look once, after a stint in rehab. Like he knew he was half a step away from screwing up his last chance.

"Deke." He shot a sideways look at Seth, a "shut up and back down" look he used just before a fight broke out, when he thought he could still talk things down. Seth knew the look and sat down on one of the bar stools, muttering under his breath. Ginny had taken Parsifal onto her lap, Georgie at her feet. Penny sat on an empty stool, washing her paw without any interest in what was going on around her.

"Deke," Seth said again. "Come on, man. We're trying to help you. But you need to be straight with us."

"I am," Deke said, his voice sulky.

"C'mon, Deke." He waited.

"I never went down there," Deke said again. "There was a separate entrance, the root cellar door. They used that. I didn't look, didn't ask. Lease said no dogs in the house. They weren't in the house."

"Logical to a fault, if not exactly legally accurate," Ginny said. "Who used the door, Deke?"

Deke shrugged, still sulky and sullen. "They left money in the mailbox, every month. Five hundred, cash. I didn't ask."

That would explain how he could afford the rent. Teddy kept his gaze on Deke, not letting him look away. "And you never heard anything? Really?"

Deke looked even more guilty.

"Deke, tell us."

"Sometimes. There were . . . noises. Things moving

downstairs, sometimes a whimper or . . . howling, some-times." Deke shuddered, a whole-body shake. "Like huge rats, or . . . demons."

"Demons?" Ginny's eyebrow almost broke her hairline, Seth rolled his eyes with an expression of long-suffering patience, and Teddy tried to keep things on track. "Focus, Deke."

"I didn't do anything wrong. I didn't look, I didn't listen. He had no right to kick me out of my house."

Seth slapped his hand down on the bar, causing Parsifal to jump and Penny to stop washing her ears and look at him. "Your lease said no pets, man. You told me—"

"They weren't pets!"

"Deke!" Teddy let his voice rise, just enough to cut through both of them. "Stop splitting hairs, and help us. Who were the guys who were keeping the dogs down there? Anything you can remember, at all. What did they look like, what cars did they drive, how many of them were there?"

Hopefully, the specific questions would focus the old man enough that he could answer, and not melt down. There was a pause, and everyone could practically hear the gears spinning in Deke's head. Teddy kept still, watching, trying to convey with his gaze that he wasn't going to let Deke skate on this, not until he came clean.

"I only ever saw two," he said finally. "One of them came every day. A kid, maybe fifteen, sixteen. Scrawny but tall, like a tap would take him out. Every morning, around seven."

"Before school," Ginny said quietly. "Probably to feed the animals."

"How long was he there, Deke?"

"Dunno. Half an hour, maybe."

Enough time to feed animals, but not much else. Depending on how many dogs were down there. Teddy tried to remember the layout of the room: even if they'd all been little things, you couldn't fit more than five or six cages down there.

"And the other?"

"Older than the kid, but not old. Asian, maybe Korean. I never saw his face well enough to tell." Teddy was impressed Deke could tell the difference at all; most people didn't pay that much attention. "He'd come by once a month, mostly when I was at work, but I saw him a few times. He'd go downstairs, then leave me the money."

"And that was it?"

"There was one other guy," Deke said slowly. "I only ever saw him once; he came with the second guy. White. Light hair. Maybe in his fifties? Not anyone you wanted to cross. He had that look, you know? Not a fighter, he wouldn't hit you clean, he'd take you out from behind. Like Jasper, you remember him?"

Seth nodded, then shook his head. "Fixer, used to hang around the fights back when I first started. Not someone you wanted to cross, ever. Never got his hands dirty but had guys who'd do the deed for him. Deke, you *idiot*."

"I didn't . . ." Deke shrank in on himself even more, and his hands twisted in his lap. "Okay, okay. But how else am

I gonna get rent, Seth? Money don't go so far anymore. I don't, I can't . . ." He reached down to pet Penny, who had leaped down from the stool and was now twining around his ankles. The motion seemed to calm him a little. "I don't have a job, I don't have a place to stay. I know Seth said I could stay there but he don't got room. Am I gonna get locked up again?"

The meltdown they'd been afraid of was starting to bubble to the surface.

"No," Ginny said, even as Teddy hesitated. "You're not. Calm down, all right? Here," she said, and handed him the puppy. "I think you both need some quiet time. You come over here, and let him get to know you, okay? And I'll have Seth make up a sandwich for you while Parsifal has his dinner. That good?"

For someone who claimed to have no maternal instincts whatsoever, Mallard wasn't doing half-bad. Teddy watched as Deke let her guide him to the nearest empty booth, waiting while he slid onto the bench, the puppy held carefully in his arms. Parsifal, as though knowing what was expected of him—and still worn-out from his walk—gave Deke's hand a long, slurpy lick, then curled up in his lap and fell asleep.

Showing a rare sensitivity—or knowing that she was in no mood for his shit today—Seth waited until Ginny came back to pick up the conversation again.

"That's all he knows. Deke ain't smart enough to lie. Not that much, that long." Seth shook his head. "You still think you can clear this mess up? He's an idiot, but . . ."

"But you're right, he'd never do anything to hurt an animal," Ginny said. "That much is obvious. We'll do the best we can."

"But not tonight," Teddy said, with a look around the bar. More of the tables were filled now, and the sound level had risen to the point where conversation was getting difficult. Nothing they couldn't handle, but he was on shift soon, and he needed to focus. And no matter that he seemed calm for the moment, they needed to get Deke out of there before the poor bastard had his—admittedly deserved—meltdown and said something else he shouldn't, in front of someone who might not be sympathetic.

"Seth, take the rest of the night off. I think we're gonna shut the kitchen down tonight. Start training people for when we're doing renovations."

"Renovations?" That was enough to break through Seth's concern. "What? Damn it, what the hell is Patrick on about this time?"

Teddy shook his head. "Trust me, don't ask. That's my headache for now. Just take Deke home, keep him out of trouble, okay?"

"Yeah, all right." Seth scowled again for good measure, as though to reassure everyone that he wasn't getting soft, and went over to the booth where Deke and Parsifal were sitting.

"So what next?" Ginny asked. "Because I'm going to admit I'm out of ideas."

"For now? I've got a shift to work. You can chase leads, and we'll start again tomorrow, hopefully with more sleep."

"I um, kind of have plans tonight . . ." She raised an eyebrow and dared Teddy to make a crack.

The temptation to say something was trumped by the urge not to get smacked. "At least someone around here's got a social life. Go, have fun. Only," he paused, as though he'd just thought of an objection. "I'm not sure I can in good conscience send Seth home with both Deke and a puppy. You okay taking junior home for the night?"

"You mean I had a choice? I'm not sure Georgie would let us go home without him." She sighed, and gave him a look that let him know he wasn't fooling anyone. "How is it that you're allegedly fostering him, but I'm doing the actual work?"

He held up his hands, palms out, in a protestation of innocence. "Hey, cat person here. And I paid for his shots, but you're already set up for four-footed roommates."

Ginny had to acknowledge the truth of that. Teddy wasn't a pet person. He'd fought against admitting that Penny had claimed him, resisted any suggestion that he get her a collar and tags: only the thought that the tabby might end up in a shelter if animal control caught her got him to agree to having her chipped. And even that had felt like a betrayal. Although, he had to admit, Penny hadn't seemed particularly bothered by either the trip to the vet or the implant.

Ginny went over to talk to Seth and Deke, holding out her arms to take Parsifal, smiling a little as the puppy made a contented wuffle and snuggled down in her arms. Georgie groaned and got to her feet, her square-chested body and wrinkled skin making her seem even larger compared to the much smaller terrier. "A couple of days, kid," he heard Ginny say, "that's all you get. My building's a one-pet-per-apartment deal, and as small as you are you don't get to stay."

Teddy smirked a little, hearing that, and watched the odd threesome leave, then looked up to the shelves where Mistress Penny usually resided, watching over her domain. "What do you think the odds are that she adopts the little fuzzbutt anyway?" Then he frowned, not seeing the usual drape of tail curling over the edge. "Huh." He backed up a little, and looked again. No Penny. He looked at the door, as though he'd spot her there, then did a scan of the area behind the bar. Nothing furred-and-tailed.

Not that her disappearing was anything new or novel. She was her own cat. She'd come home whenever she finished whatever she was chasing. He didn't feel at all abandoned, damn it.

"Hey, barkeep!" one of the newcomers yelled as he settled in at the bar with several of his friends. "Service around here sucks!"

"Yeah, bite me, Taylor," he replied, flinging the bar towel over his shoulder with a flourish, and moving down the bar to where Taylor waited, grinning obnoxiously. "It's not like you ever buy the good beer, anyway."

He tucked the case into the back of his brain, put it away until the morning, and focused on the things he could do something about. His real job.

But even while he was pulling beers and telling Taylor

that no, the kitchen was closed tonight, get over it, part of him kept thinking about Deke's fear, and Parsifal's sad eyes and malnourished body, and the kind of person who could get off on hurting animals, and he couldn't let it go.

He wasn't an animal person. And he knew you couldn't save everyone, not even folks who got as far down on the scale as Deke. But he didn't like bullies, or abusers. The landlord might or might not have known what was going on, but there was no way that Parsifal had been the only animal down there, not with a kid showing up every day, not for five hundred dollars a month, not the way the space had smelled, days after it had probably been cleared out.

Those animals had been there for a reason, had disappeared to *somewhere*, for some reason. And he was pretty damned sure the reason didn't bode well for the dogs.

There had to be a trail, something that would lead to the actual culprits, clear Deke, and stop whatever was going on. They just had to *find* it.

Penny hesitated once she left the Busy Place, sheltered by the shadow of the building. She watched Georgie padfoot away, her human and the puppy with her. The urge to follow them, to make sure they got home safe, was a sharp tug in Penny's whiskers. But Georgie was there: she wasn't always the quickest, but she was strong, and brave, and she had smelled the hurt-fear in the smaller dog, too, for all that the puppy was easily distracted by comfort and new sensations. Georgie knew to be on guard, protect the puppy. Penny had things to do, other things, important things.

Except . . . she didn't know how to do them. Uncertainty dragged at her fur, itched her paws: she was a hunter, listen and smell and quick-move-pounce. But the prey was too quiet for her to hear, too well hidden for her to see. She could smell *it, hurt-fear and mean-sour, but that wasn't enough.*

She leaped onto a fire escape ladder and made her way to the rooftop. A hunt like this needed quiet and moonlight for proper thinking.

Settled on a narrow ledge, her tail swished back and forth slowly while Penny thought. The humans had talked about other dogs, and bad men. About fighting. Dogs fighting.

Dogs fought for the right to make a den, or because they were afraid.

The puppy was afraid.

The answer was where the puppy had been.

But the place where the puppy came from was too far away, Georgie said they'd gone in the car for too long; she couldn't nose a trail, couldn't find it on her own. And the puppy was too young— too dumb—to tell them anything useful.

Humans were good at finding things, and stopping other humans from doing bad things. The older human smelled of fear, too. Fear, and the sadness like old dirt. Maybe he knew something? But then, why hadn't he told Theo and Ginny?

Her tail lashed again, and her eyes narrowed, ears alert. When a bird hid in the branches, when a mouse went under a leaf, you waited. Eventually, they moved. Penny just had to be patient.

6

I t's cold." The puppy was shivering, brown eyes wide and doleful. Georgie tried to cuddle it closer, but she was awkward with the much smaller body, afraid she might crush it or something. Penny was smaller, but she was shaped differently, and draped over Georgie's paws rather than huddling. And she was Penny, who always knew what to do. Parsifal didn't know anything, and Georgie had been left alone, and she didn't know anything, either.

But the puppy was cold. "Come here," she told him, curving her body so that the smaller dog fit against her chest. "It's all right." They could get under the blanket, but Herself didn't like it when Georgie did that. Herself yelled and Georgie was a bad dog, and wasn't allowed to sleep on the bed that night. And Georgie didn't think that the floor would be warmer than the bed.

"Where are the others?"

"Ginny just went out for a while," Georgie said. "It feels like forever but she comes back, she always comes back. And Penny is at the Busy Place, or out hunting, and Teddy . . ." Georgie paused. She wasn't actually sure where Teddy was. He had a den of his own, she'd been there once, and they were always taking her in the *den-that-moved, but she didn't know* where *he was right now, and she didn't like to say things she wasn't sure of.*

"Others," *the puppy insisted, his tail flipping with frustration. He was too little to really be clear, and couldn't explain what he meant. Georgie, driven by instinct, licked the top of his head the way Penny did for her when she was upset, and the puppy flopped down again, his voice muffled by the blanket they were lying on. "Where are my others?"*

Georgie knew she wasn't as smart as Penny, or even Ginny, but she wasn't dumb, either. "Oh, others! Littermates, you mean? There were other dogs with you, where you were?" The satisfaction of figuring out what Parsifal was talking about made her happy, but then she dropped her muzzle down in frustration. "I don't know, Parsi. I don't know where they are. But Ginny and Teddy will find them." Georgie had faith in her humans. They could do anything. With a little help.

She needed to talk to Penny.

"Hey," Max said, halfway through their appetizers. "What's the deal, Ms. Fabulous? This is supposed to be our night out, away from jobs and significant others and all that, and you're . . . quiet. That's not the woman I know."

"Sorry." Ginny played with her fork, and then tried to smile at her friend. "I didn't quite leave the job in the office, I guess."

"Same old Virginia Mallard, Overachiever." That was funny, considering Max was just as much an overachiever, running his small catering company, if not more so. "So what's up? Clients getting to you?" Max leaned back and gestured imperiously, clearly prepared to hear yet another hopefully entertaining rant about impossible demands and wildly improbable expectations. "C'mon, tell me, what're besties for? You were working on a cruise, right?"

Mrs. Mastello and her family of thirty-two, off on an Alaskan cruise, yeah. "Nah, they're sorted. At least until one cousin decides that she doesn't want to room with the other, or a grandkid's college exams require a different flight out, or . . ." She waved her own hand, her fingernails—blunt-filed and unpolished—flittering as though to say that was same-old-same-old. Ginny was in demand as a private concierge, sorting other people's plans and problems, not just because she was good at it, but because very little flustered her anymore. She just assumed that her clients would be unreasonable, and charged them accordingly. "No, it's not that. We, um, we took another case. Tonica and I, I mean."

Max just looked at her, waiting for the rest of the story. She compared that—against her will—with the expression Rob had worn when she told him the same thing. Her boyfriend's face had gone from expectation, maybe amusement, to something else. Worry, maybe. Disappointment, certainly. He wasn't dumb enough to think that he could issue ultimatums—they wouldn't have lasted this long if he were—but he didn't shy away from voicing his opinions, either. And she respected that . . . most of the time.

"You know I don't talk about jobs when I'm still working them," she said now.

"Yeah well, I thought you said you weren't sure if you even wanted to continue with all that?"

"A friend needed help." Although she wasn't sure Seth actually qualified as a friend; not really. Not hers, certainly, and maybe not Tonica's. But he'd asked, and neither of them had been able to say no.

Max had known her for years: they'd been in the same cubicle farm, before the company was bought and they were scattered to the wind. He knew better than to push—for now. "Too much to hope that you're not going to get shot at, or attacked by a giant cat, or arrested this time?"

Ginny thought about Parsifal, curled up on her pillow when she left the apartment this evening, Georgie asleep at the foot of the bed, and smiled. "No giant cats, I promise."

Thinking about Deke's very real fear, and Seth's worries, she wasn't comfortable promising anything else. No guns would be ideal, and not getting arrested . . . well, they'd never actually gotten arrested, just scolded by people carrying badges. That wasn't the same thing at all.

But Max was right about one thing: she wasn't working tonight. Even overachievers needed down time. So she forced herself to pay attention, listening to Max's story about a client of his own, while hoping that the puppy hadn't torn her bedroom up too badly, or had an unfortunate accident. And she absolutely did not think about dogfights, or gangsters, or a man left confused and homeless because other people were jerking him around. . . .

Deke was on a string, she thought. Like a marionette, on someone else's stage. Was the landlord the player, or was he being played, too? And if so, who was pulling the strings, and why?

"Gin." She looked up, and Max was looking at her, his dark brown eyes kind, and a little amused. "You sure that's all that's bothering you? Nothing's wrong with you and wossisname, is it?"

"What? No." She smiled, and let him catch her right hand, the one currently without a fork in it. His fingers were warm, and she thought again that she was fortunate in her friends. Just like Deke. "No, nothing's wrong there, except maybe me missing him. I promise."

That was mostly true. Rob would either get over his reservations about her taking the job while he was away, or . . . or he wouldn't. They'd agreed to take on this job because Deke needed help. And the reality was that neither of them, not her or Tonica, was going to stop, or say no to someone in need. No matter how much they knew they probably should.

Teddy fully intended to sleep in Sunday morning. When you didn't hit bed until nearly 2 a.m., feet and knees aching from standing all night, six hours of shut-eye was the bare minimum, and eight was better. Barely getting four, two nights in a row . . . sucked.

But the universe hadn't gotten the sleep-in memo, clearly, because his cell phone chimed well before it should have, the morning light still dawn-pale. He reached for the noise with his eyes still gummed with sleep, and his heart filled with thoughts of murder. Who the hell was calling him? Maggie wouldn't dare call him now, not about the damned house, and Mallard texted. If it was a wrong number he was going to murder someone, God's own truth.

When his eyes could focus, he saw the time—6:40—and groaned, but accepted the call.

"Nothing's on fire, nobody's dead," Seth said, his voice even more of a smoker's cough than usual.

"Then why are you calling me?" he growled, already feeling his brain waking up, because if Seth was calling him it had to be an emergency of some sort.

"Deke's disappeared. I woke up this morning, and he was gone."

Teddy sighed, letting his head fall back on the pillow with a hard thump. "Goddamn it."

"Teddy, we need to find him. He's going to do something stupid."

"Yeah, I got that. All right, look, I'll call Jon in early, and between the three of you, you can cover today's shifts. You're dog in charge, all right? If Patrick calls, tell him *nothing*."

"But I—"

"I need you to be at the bar. Don't worry, Seth. We're on it."

He ended the call and stared at the ceiling, then texted Ginny, giving her the bare essentials and telling her he'd be there in an hour. Hopefully, she'd be awake, and not too badly hungover.

Or maybe he hoped she was. If he had to suffer, everyone should.

He gave himself time for a shorter-than-normal run, just enough to get his blood moving and his skin sweaty, and then threw himself into the shower while the coffee brewed. The drive to her place was quick—for once there were no construction delays—and he slid the Saab into a barely legal parking space, double-timing it to her apartment.

It was only as he was coming out of the elevator on her floor that he remembered that she'd had plans last night. He wanted to meet the guy she was dating, but he kind of hoped he'd gone home already, assuming he'd stayed the night, because this was an awkward as hell way to introduce yourself.

Ginny met him at the door, fully dressed, awake, alert, and not too obviously hungover. "Seriously? Seriously? This was not supposed to be a missing persons case, Tonica."

"It still isn't," he said, following her inside. There was no sign of another person in the apartment.

She was staring at him, her arms crossed over her chest, her expression one of cool disbelief. That had been one of the things he'd liked about her, back when they first met: that cool, like she could play with the boys even wearing high heels and lipstick. It was the attitude, the "I can deal with this, don't try to bullshit me" vibe.

And never mind that he knew her tells now, too; knew that she wasn't anywhere near as cool as she wanted to be.

"He's not missing," he went on. "He's running away from home. Or not-home."

"Oh, because that's so much better." Her hazel eyes were filled with scorn, but he could see the worry underneath—the same worry he was feeling. "What the hell was Seth thinking, to let him walk out like that?"

She'd dropped down onto the sofa while she was talking, legs pulled up under her, and was tapping her fingers against her leg. He looked down and saw Georgie and Parsifal sprawled together under the table, the remains of toasted bagels and cream cheese scattered on the table's surface. Only one mug, so no mystery boyfriend today.

"He was thinking Deke was a grown man who can't be kept under house arrest?" He was trying to keep his tone mild, for his own sake as well as hers.

That got a snort, and a look. "Seth should have known him better. Hell, I barely know the guy and I know better."

"All right, yeah." He admitted defeat on that one. "I don't know what he was thinking except he can't stay awake twenty-four-seven and guard the guy, Gin."

And now, even though Seth had sworn he'd cover for him at Mary's, Teddy was pretty damned sure that Seth was out there looking, taking his old Honda CB750 around town to all the haunts he thought Deke might run to, the places he might hide.

"We're not going to find him," he said to Ginny, taking a seat in the armchair opposite the sofa. He was pissed, almost as pissed as Ginny, but he'd had time to cool down and think it through on the drive over. "And there's no point in us worrying about what he might or might not be doing, because we can't know. We need to stay on the case. Find out what's going on, ideally before that idiot makes it worse."

Parsifal came out from under the table and tried to chew on the end of his bootlace. Teddy lifted him away with one hand, but when the puppy came right back, he let him. "We don't know his hideouts, his bolt-holes. We'll let Seth look; he'll call us if he hears anything." He hoped. "Does he have your number?"

She gave him another look; he was collecting the entire set today. "Why would Seth have my number?"

"Right." And Seth didn't have a cell phone, so there was no point in texting it to him. "So I'm contact person. Once the bar's open, I'll call Stacy and bring her up to speed." And warn her about not talking to Patrick, too.

"I feel bad, dragging her into this," Ginny said.

"Don't. She's enjoying it, trust me."

Ginny seemed to accept the truth of that. "Do you think we should call that guy, Zimmerman, see if he knows where Deke might go?"

"No." Teddy's reaction to that was immediate. "And you got his number? I thought you were in a relationship?"

"I always get people's business cards," she said primly. "It's just basic networking. You never know who might need my services . . . or vice versa. But yeah, you're right. He seemed like a good guy, but not high on Deke's confessional list. Odds are he wouldn't have any more idea where to look than we do—and he obviously didn't know what was going on in the house." She sighed. "So we stick with what we were doing, chasing down who was actually behind the dogs being there—and who took them?"

"And why, yeah. I think so. But carefully," Teddy said. "Everything Deke said, it sounds like the people involved are unpleasant, to say the least. And now that we've started poking the nest . . ."

They investigated crimes, yeah, but mostly the jobs had been reasonably benign: looking for a missing person, or missing money. They'd gotten surprised by the violence before, and somehow, weirdly, that made it okay. Going in *knowing* that there was violence lurking underneath, that was different. It was stupidity aforethought.

"And that brings up the next question," Teddy said. "Is it time to be calling the cops?"

"And tell them what? We don't know anything they don't, except that there was a dog in the house, which isn't actually a crime except for making the landlord's case for him, and oh, wait, that isn't going to *help* Deke, is it?" Her voice was sharp, but it sounded different from her usually being angry. He studied her, the way her fingers weren't drumming on the table in thought, but now clenched into a loose fist, at how she kept reaching her leg out to rest a bare foot on Georgie's back and then pulling away, as though afraid she'd communicate her mood to the dog.

He knew the signs by now. She wasn't angry, or scared. She was *mad*. Mad at Deke, or him, or the entire known world, Teddy didn't know, but it wasn't a good sign. Ginny angry was bad enough, but once she got mad, she tended to speak her mind, which meant she should not be allowed anywhere near other people, especially people who might be useful. He enjoyed having the sharp edge of her humor whetted against him, but other people didn't.

"We need more info on the other players," he said. "The mysterious stranger who was paying Deke, to start. The guy with the money is usually the one with the power."

"Yeah." She was thinking again, ire overtaken by logic. "Yeah, I'll start with the teenager, though. We have a better description, and he's got to be local if he's coming on foot, so that helps. Also, teenagers are easier to find than adults; they see no point in staying off the grid. I should be able to ID him, and then we can find out who hired him. I can run Deke's description of the other guys, too, for whatever it's worth, but I'm betting that turns up empty. We don't have enough to go on; the fact that he's Asian is, well, not going to cut the list down much here in Seattle. And the older white guy with cold eyes? Yeah, good luck with that. Even if we had a decent description . . ."

Teddy nodded. Her computer-Fu was good, but professionals knew how to not leave tracks. Especially professional criminals. "Just don't do anything too obviously illegal online," he said. "The cops were already giving us side-eyes in November. I doubt they're the forget-and-forgive sort."

"We probably should get licensed," she said absently, already reaching for her laptop, which had been sitting, closed, at the edge of the table. "One of us, anyway."

"Yeah, right. No." He'd read enough of the *Moron's*

Guide to Private Investigations to know how much paperwork and brain sweat that involved. Plus, there were rules you had to follow, to *keep* your license. Things you had to say, or couldn't ask. "While you're doing that, can I borrow Georgie for the afternoon?" It was an impulse, but it felt right.

"What?" She looked down at the dogs, slanting her gaze under the table as though to make sure that they were both there, and then looked back up at Teddy. "Why?"

"I want to borrow her for the afternoon," he repeated. "Look, Parsi's too little to actually be useful. But Georgie's got good instincts. So I want to take her back to the house, maybe sniff around a little. Let her sniff around. If you think she'd be okay with that?"

He'd never taken the dog on his own; it was always the three of them when Georgie came for a ride. But the dog seemed to like him, as far as he could tell, so maybe it would be okay. If Ginny agreed.

She tilted her head at him now. "What do you think she's going to find?"

"I don't know." He shrugged. "But we're not exactly overflowing with ideas or leads, so maybe using a dog to find dogs isn't so far-fetched?"

"So you want to use her to 'fetch' a lead for you?" But Ginny was considering it, rolling the idea around in her head, so he let the pun go, and waited.

"Yeah. All right. And walk her around the neighborhood, too. People like her, they come up to her all the time, ask questions, just randomly strike up conversations.

See if you can talk to the locals, if they saw anything hinky happening at the house, or better yet, can tell you it was an absolutely calm, no-hinky household."

He nodded. "See if I can pick up gossip, check."

"And watch them. How they react to Georgie." Ginny was sitting forward now, the simple act of having a plan, even if it wasn't hers, reigniting her brain and giving her focus. "She's a sweetie, yeah, but shar-peis were fighting dogs once. And she's still exotic enough, if anyone's looking for fighting dogs, or used to being around them, they might say something. . . ."

"You do your thing, I'll do mine," he said with a mock scowl. She rolled her eyes but didn't argue the point. They were getting better about not arguing, when it mattered.

"Hey, Georgie," she said softly. "You wanna go for a ride with Uncle Teddy?"

A soft thump of a tail responded, and then the larger dog emerged from under the table, looking first at Ginny and then up at Teddy, as though she'd understood what was being asked. Parsifal abandoned Teddy's bootlaces and pounced on Georgie's front paws, thinking this was the start of some great new game. Teddy scooped the puppy up and held him, while Ginny went to get Georgie's leash.

"Sorry, guy," he told the puppy. "You don't get to come with us."

Ginny came back with the leash, and handed it to him, taking Parsifal in exchange. He held the leash where Georgie could see it, getting her attention away from Ginny and the puppy. "Gonna help me with an investigation, oh hound?"

Georgie was a quiet dog, rarely barking and never growling without cause, but she let out a quiet yip that Teddy decided to take for a yes. "All right, then," he said, snapping the leash to her collar. "But you gotta look butch, kid. I need a rough guy, not a sweetie, today. Can you do that?"

"The command you're looking for is 'watch,'" Ginny said. "Like this." And her voice went deeper, her words bitten off more crisply than her usual soft tone. "Georgie, *watch*."

The dog had been sitting while Teddy hooked on the leash, but now she went up on all fours, her chest squared, her head up, looking around the room not so much alertly as warily. Teddy blinked, realizing that it looked familiar because it was the expression he'd see on the local cops' faces some weekend nights when they stopped by, when the crowd got louder than usual and they were trying to see where trouble might be coming from. Not expecting trouble, but aware of the possibility.

"Perfect," he said. "Um, how do I get her to stop?"

"Georgie, okay, it's okay." They watched as Georgie seemed to sigh and shake herself out, then looked up at Ginny as though waiting for a treat. "Pretty much 'it's okay' after a command sets her back to normal. She's not too picky about who says it, though, so be careful."

"Why does that not surprise me a bit," he muttered, shaking his head. Georgie might be able to muddle her way through being a guard dog when needed, but she was still the sweetest marshmallow on four legs he'd ever seen.

Deke felt guilty. Not because he'd lied to Seth, because he hadn't, really, just fudged the truth. And maybe danced a little around what he shouldn't have said, the way he used to dance around a punch, so he didn't get laid out cold. He felt guilty because Seth had gotten other people involved. Because Seth was trying to take care of him again.

Nine years ago he'd been dumb and gotten mixed up in things he shouldn't have. Seth had saved his bacon then, talked to the judge, made it all go away so long as Deke kept his nose clean, and Deke *had*. And then they'd offered him the money, and he'd thought that because he didn't know anything, he couldn't get in trouble, and then when he got in trouble he thought that if he just didn't say anything it would all go away, but he hadn't, and it didn't. Now his mess was someone else's mess and it shouldn't be.

He hated being a problem.

The bus jolted to a stop again, and he put a hand on the window, the cool surface of the glass making him aware of the faint tremble in his fingers. He pressed harder against the glass, fighting the urge to curve his fingers into a fist.

Deke knew he took too many punches, and he hadn't been smart to start. He'd thought he was doing the right thing, being like the three monkeys—see nothing, hear nothing, and don't say nothing. Instead he screwed it all up. So he was going to try to fix things now. He was going to find the guy who paid him, and . . .

And he hadn't thought that far out. Finding the guy was the first step, though. He'd figure the rest out once he did that. And he knew how to find him. Or he thought he did, anyway. Sammy's. It had all started at Sammy's.

Letting his hand drop to his leg, he dragged his palm nervously across the denim as he watched the city go by. About a year ago now. He'd been still working out then. Not much, just a few rounds with the bag, some rope work. Mostly it was to be around people he understood, who understood him. The guy had been scoping him out, watching him, making Deke uneasy before he finally approached him with an offer.

Deke wasn't smart, but he knew he wasn't the only dummy out there. Someone else said yes, too. Someone there would know how to find the dog-man. And Deke would get him to call off the landlord, and then it wouldn't be a problem anymore.

Deke nodded at the landscape, and reached up to pull the cord to get off at the next stop. His mess, he'd take care of this.

He wasn't gonna let Seth down again.

Teddy had never taken Georgie anywhere on his own, but she padded along obediently when they left the apartment, not at all distressed to be leaving Ginny and the puppy behind. She balked slightly at the car, but Ginny had shoved a handful of treats into his hand before they left, and two were enough to remind Georgie that the backseat hadn't eaten her before so it was probably safe. He kept an eye on her, checking in the rearview mirror to make sure that she didn't get any stupid ideas in her doggy head, but once they pulled into traffic she lay down with her head on her paws, and beyond the occasional full-bodied sigh, didn't move until they reached their destination.

"Come on, girl, out. C'mon, Georgie, out!"

Once the shar-pei realized that there was grass for her to sniff at and pee on, she was much more energetic. Teddy urged her along the sidewalk, heading for Deke's house but keeping an eye out for anyone who might be a source of gossip. The only person visible, though, was an older guy walking toward them, a plastic bag with a store name blazoned on it in one hand, his cell phone in the other. He saw them and put the phone away, his body language clearly telling Teddy that he was going to approach them. Ginny had been right. Score one for the dog.

"Nice-looking dog you got there. What is it?"

"Shar-pei," Teddy said, easy as though he'd said it a million times. "Mostly purebred, not entirely." The older man grunted and studied Georgie. "What, thirty-five, forty pounds? Looks like it's mostly muscle." Teddy tensed up slightly, really not comfortable with someone eyeing Georgie like that, even though that had been the vague plan. Then the stranger bent down and offered Georgie his hand, palm down, for her to sniff. "You're a sweetie, aren't you? I can tell from the eyes. You're a lover, not a fighter, aren't you, girl?"

Georgie licked his hands and wagged her stub of a tail.

"Yeah, you got her number all right," Teddy said, amused. "Her name's Georgie." He remembered how Ginny knew the names of all the dogs whose owners came to Mary's, but only about half of their owners'. Maybe the best disguise was to be Georgie's Owner rather than giving a fake name, or worrying they'd somehow leave a trail, or . . .

"Hello, Georgie. Hey, Kevin," and the stranger half turned, looking over his shoulder at another man who had been sitting on his porch, a few houses down. "C'mere and meet Georgie."

Kevin brought his daughter Lucy, who was, she announced proudly, seven, and another man, who didn't give a name. They were all in their late forties or early fifties, Teddy guessed, with the look of men who'd held blue-collar jobs all their lives, settled and comfortable with it.

"You guys are all dog people, huh?"

"I had a dog," Lucy said. "But it died."

"A mutt," Kevin said. "Good dog. Dumber'n butter, but a good dog. We keep thinking about getting another one, but . . ." He shrugged, and Teddy got the feeling that the idea of adding another mouth to feed wasn't a thing they could do right then. Too bad, since they had a puppy looking for a home.

"Looks like a good neighborhood for a dog," Teddy said casually. "I was driving around and Georgie decided she needed Out, Now, so I've been looking around . . . Any houses up for rent?"

"A couple, yeah." The unnamed man frowned, then jerked his head toward the house Deke had been living in. "I know that one was rented out but the guy living there, I haven't seen him around, and things got all kinds of quiet, so I'm guessing he's gone."

"Quiet? Was it noisy before?" Deke hadn't struck him as the kind of guy to hold wild parties or blast music, but the one thing he'd learned over the past year was that people did all sorts of shit you'd never expect.

"Not noisy, exactly," Kevin said, and the first man laughed. "Quiet but busy. I don't know what old Deke was doing in there but he had pretty regular visitors. Not the kind of people you'd invite in for a beer, either, if you know what I mean."

Not the teenager, then. Cold Eyes? Kevin looked like he wasn't going to say any more—they were the kind of people he didn't want to talk about in front of a small child? Maybe. But trying to get rid of the kid would shut them all up, so that wasn't an option. So instead Teddy raised an eyebrow, and looked a little worried—which wasn't hard to fake. "The kind of thing that might lower property values?"

That made all three of the resident adults shift uncomfortably, looking at each other, and *not* looking at the house in question. Interesting.

"No," the first man said, and his face—weathered, his eyes watery around the edges—was open enough to be honest. Probably. "Nothing like that. We'd have called the cops if they were that kind." A glance at the girl, then away. "Just every now and then there were people showing up, carrying boxes away, or bringing some in."

"Not boxes," Kevin said. "Crates. About yay big." He showed with his hands, about three feet apart. "Most of 'em light enough for one guy to carry. They left some, took some. Every couple–three months.

"They loaded 'em into a van," Kevin added. "Sweetie, don't let Georgie lick your face. I know it feels funny, but remember what we told you about germs?" He returned to the conversation at hand. "And Deke was never around when they showed up, far as I could tell. That was the weird thing. You got people taking stuff in and out of your house, you'd think you'd, I dunno, watch once or twice?"

Not if you were convincing yourself it didn't happen, that if you didn't see it you weren't involved. But Teddy just nodded thoughtfully. "People are weird," he said. "Okay, you ready to go now, Georgie?" He had wanted to take her into the house proper, see if she reacted to the smell in the basement, but he couldn't do that now, not while he was being watched.

The locals made their farewells to Georgie, and he loaded her back into the car, only having to resort to the bribe of one treat to get her settled into the back this time. Maybe they'd come back after dark, use the "looking at the neighborhood" excuse if anyone caught them. Or even visit with a Realtor, if the house was up for rent already. That might be the better move, yeah. Come in officially, and nobody would raise an eyebrow.

He got behind the wheel and pulled out his cell phone. "Ginny, hey," he said to her voice mail. "I don't know if this will be useful or not, but the locals saw crates being brought in and hauled out every couple of months. You're the one doing research, but that doesn't sound like any dogfighting scenario I ever heard of, does it?" Unless they were getting rid of bodies. Jesus. He felt a full-body shudder hit him. "Call me."

He dropped the phone onto the passenger-side seat and stared out at the street. His body was humming, like he'd touched a live wire, and there was an itch between his shoulder blades. That meant there was something he'd seen or heard that was important, that was triggering something in the back of his brain. But he knew from experience that if he tried to chase it down now, he'd lose it. The best thing he could do was ignore it, until it was ready to be an actual thought.

Normally he'd go for a run, let his brain chew on the problem while he focused on the physical, but traipsing back across the city to return Georgie, then go home to get his running shoes would take too much time.

"You up for the beach, Georgie?" he asked the lump in the backseat. "I could really use some salt air and sand right now." It wasn't the grand old lady Atlantic he'd grown up with, but the bay was pretty good for thinking, too.

7

Georgie didn't like getting sand in her toes, but chasing the waves was good, even though the water was cold. And it made Teddy laugh when he threw a stick for her and she caught it, and she liked it when humans laughed, they smelled better and petted more.

But she wished Penny were here. She was sure he had taken her to that street to sniff out something, to find something for him, but she hadn't been able to. The strange men had smelled like sweat and meat and a little like the Busy Place, late at night, and the little girl had smelled like water and soap, but none of those smells meant anything to Georgie, nothing out of the usual, and without Penny she didn't know if she'd missed something.

They were supposed to be sniffing out something to help the sad man. Georgie hated not being able to help.

An hour walking on the beach hadn't given Teddy any clarity on the case, but his mood was definitely lighter, watching Georgie run in and out of the waves, a short bit of driftwood in her mouth, the loose folds of her skin more obvious when she shook water out of her coat.

Fortunately, other people were having more luck than he was.

"What?" Teddy had to shift his phone to his other ear, because Georgie was up against his right side, trying to lick his fingers. She was too well trained to actually go after his burger, but cleaning grease and meat smell off fingers was apparently acceptable. He probably should have gotten something less messy from the food truck, but he had a weakness for greasy hamburgers. "He did what? No, Seth, shut up, I'm already out, I'll go get him. Yeah. Gimme the address."

He'd always carried a notebook and pencil in the glove compartment; since he'd started hanging out with Mallard, he'd had to replace the notebook once and the pencil twice. He scribbled the address, and read it back to confirm, then ended the call and dropped the phone onto the passenger seat, next to the food wrapper.

"Damn it. All right, Georgie, get back. Sit down. Sit, Georgie." She had sand all over her paws from walking up and down the narrow strip of beach, and he wasn't going to let her get back into the car until they'd been brushed off.

The dog whined a little, but finally settled back down and obediently lifted her paws for brushing, one at a time. He knew they probably should have a carrier or something for her, the amount of time she spent in his car, but Georgie was mostly good about lying down. He'd seen dogs with their heads hanging out of car windows and always thought that looked like a disaster waiting to happen, no matter how much fun the dogs seemed to be having.

"Change of plans," he told the dog, pulling the car out into traffic and pointing her south on Alaskan, heading downtown. "Because apparently, Deke is exactly as much of an idiot as I thought."

Georgie just settled her head on her paws, and wagged her tail once, as though she thought there might still be burger taste at the end of the ride.

He thought about leaving her in the car when they got to their destination, then thought about what Ginny would say about that, and brought her along. He suspected nobody was going to give him much grief about a serious-looking dog in tow, not down here. Not even with a pink leash.

From the street, the place didn't look impressive: a blank gray wall with a small window covered in old newspaper cuttings, and a single solid metal door. If it weren't for the sign on the wall, he'd think it was the back of a warehouse or something.

Inside, the air was thick with sweat, and filled with noise. It was a warehouse, if one that had been converted to another use years ago. Where there might have been pallets and machinery and workers, there now were punching bags and roped-off rings, and men—and a few women—jumping rope or doing impressive-looking pull-ups, and generally making Teddy feel like a ninety-six-pound weakling, even though he was taller and broader than many of them. You didn't work with an ex-boxer without learning very quickly that judging by size could get you into trouble.

Speaking of which . . . He tugged at Georgie's leash to get her to quit sniffing one of the mats on the floor, and they walked across the gym to where an older man was sitting behind a battered metal desk, scowling at an open ledger book.

"Excuse me."

"What?" the man asked without looking up. As though drawn by his voice, Georgie put her front paws up on the edge of the desk and peered at him. He looked up then, when her claws clicked against metal, and his expression went from sour to surprised to almost-not-sour in fast succession. "You're an ugly mug, even around here," he said. "What do you want?"

Teddy was taken aback, then realized that the first comment had been addressed to Georgie, not him. "I'm here to pick up . . . a friend." Teddy made a face, hoping to convey his distaste for the chore without actually saying anything. "I'm told he was making a nuisance of himself earlier."

"Oh, you're Deke's babysitter. Yeah, he's in the office," and the man jerked his thumb toward the back, where a long glass window showed a series of desks behind the wall. "Just go on."

The air in the office was cleaner, although it still reminded Teddy of his old high school gym. Deke was slumped in a wooden chair in the hallway, and the high school resemblance carried over to detention.

Georgie let out a single low woof, and Deke looked up, his face crumpled in exhaustion. "Oh. Hi."

"What the hell," Teddy started to say, when the other man in the hallway with Deke interrupted. "It's okay, no harm, no foul. Well, a little harm, but no foul." He was at least thirty years Deke's junior, black, with a shiner starting on one eye, and a split lip. "Deke got a little carried away, but nobody's pressing charges; we just figured someone should take him home, y'know?"

"Iffin you'd just told me what I wanted to know," Deke muttered, "none a' this woulda happened."

"Man, I told you I don't know, okay? You need to stay cool."

Their back-and-forth felt more like a comedy routine than an actual fight. Teddy could feel another headache coming on, but the feeling of relief—from Seth's phone call he'd thought he'd be dealing with cops and bail money, not two boxers sulking at each other—overwhelmed everything else.

"Thanks," he said now. "Deke. Take Georgie outside and wait for me, okay? And don't hit anyone else."

Deke and Georgie made their way back through the gym—watching them through the window, it was obvious to Teddy that the dog was shepherding the man, intent on her destination. Nobody stopped them, although a few people turned to watch.

"All right. Tell me, what happened?"

The other man sighed, and reached up to touch the side of his face, wincing a little. "For an old guy, he's still got a hell of an uppercut. But seriously, it was nothing, just him letting his temper slip. Around here, that's got more repercussions than, y'know, in your average office."

"Yeah, I get that. But what did he lose his temper about? He said you wouldn't tell him something?" If Deke had gone off on his own, and come here, and been asking questions, there was probably a reason for it. Maybe not a good reason, but it was all they had right now. He looked at the other man more carefully: too old to be the high school kid Deke had mentioned, and not old enough to be the other guys, even if he'd been the right race.

Bruised guy looked shifty. "He um, he wanted to know if I knew how to get in touch with someone. I didn't."

Teddy shifted his weight, not wanting to leave Deke and Georgie on their own for too long, but not wanting to leave without an answer, either. "Uh-huh. Who?"

The guy actually fidgeted, looking down the hallway as though hoping for reinforcements to save him. "Look, it doesn't matter, okay?"

"Yeah, actually, I think it does. Who was Deke trying to get in touch with?" Teddy wasn't about to try what Ginny called his Intimidating Bouncer routine here, and he didn't think Understanding Bartender mode would work, either. But he shoved just enough of both into his voice, hoping that something would click. "Look, man, I get that you don't want to get involved. Just give me a name." Deke wasn't going to, or *couldn't,* that much was clear. "I don't care about contact info, or how you're involved in all this. I just need a name."

The other man sighed. "Hollins. Lew Hollins. And you never heard it from me."

When Teddy got outside, Deke and Georgie were waiting for him. Georgie had curled up on the sidewalk, in her usual "I'm waiting on humans" pose, while Deke was leaning against the wall, hands shoved into his jacket pockets, staring squint-eyed up at the overcast sky.

Teddy stared at him, and then shook his head. "Come on. Let's go."

"Go where?" Deke was already walking when he asked, so it was obvious that he didn't really care. Or maybe Georgie was that good a herder, heading instinctively for the car parked along the curb and dragging him along. Either way, Teddy didn't care.

"I'm taking you back to Mary's. The bar," he clarified, when Deke looked confused. It was early yet, but at least there they'd be able to keep an eye on him, keep him from haring off on another idiotic adventure that might get him . . . well, maybe not killed but sure as hell deeper in shit. He supposed he should call Seth and tell him the prodigal child is en route. . . .

As though on cue, his phone vibrated in his pocket. He looked at the caller ID and accepted the call. "Hey. I've got Deke. No, Seth found him, I just did the pickup. What's up?" He hesitated before opening the car, listening, then nodded. "All right, yeah, we'll meet you there." He put the phone away and glared across the roof at Deke. "Come on, get in. Ginny says she's got something."

Ginny had to wonder when her life had come down to this, ranting about the man—men—in her life, not to sympathetic friends, but sharply pointed ears and a long, twitching tail. But any ears were better than none, at least until human ears arrived. And she could have gone somewhere else, she supposed, but that felt disloyal, like cheating.

Besides, she'd have ended up at Mary's anyway, eventually.

Her companion made an inquisitive noise, which she took as a cue to continue. "Anyway, I swear, sometimes Rob reminds me way too much of my dad. Because you know they always have to be right, always have to be . . . right. And when you try to tell them that they're wrong, they just give you this *look,* like you don't understand what's really going on. Am I right?"

Penny raised a paw and batted at Ginny's hand, gentle claws pulling her fingers closer, until she could take the bit of cheese away from the human.

"I'm pretty sure you're not supposed to have that," Ginny said, picking up another piece of cheese from the sandwich wrapper. "But I'll tell you what, you've got better table manners than most."

In her lap, Parsifal whined, and looked at her with over-sized, overly soulful puppy eyes.

"All right, one for you, too, then. But only one. Your puppy tummy is too delicate. There are already too many doggy effusions in my life, without you adding more."

"Girl, you need to get out more," a voice said next to her, and then added, "Oh my God, you have another one?"

"Not mine," Ginny said, lifting Parsifal up with one hand. "You want?"

"Oh hell no, get that rat away from me," her friend said,

tossing her long coat into the booth and sliding onto the bench opposite her. "Is that why you called me down here? Because oh hell no."

"No, but I do have a favor to ask, kinda related."

"Of course you do." Shana signaled to the bartender. "And I'm getting at least one drink out of it; otherwise you would have asked me over the phone, which means it's something I'm not going to want to do."

"'Not want' is a bit of an overstatement . . . ," Ginny hedged. After Tonica had left her apartment earlier, after she'd hit a wall on her research, she'd done some thinking. About the situation, about the possible solutions. But all she could think about was Deke, the look in his eyes when Seth had yelled at him, the way he'd held his body tight when Zimmerman questioned him, the resignation in Seth's voice when he talked about trying to keep the older man out of trouble.

The way she hadn't been able to stop thinking about how many ways there were for one fragile old man, without hope, to decide to end it all. Never mind that they'd found him, there were too many ways this could go wrong.

She remembered their first client who hadn't kept a low enough profile, despite their warning him, and paid the cost. Not again. Not if she could stop it.

They needed to buy some time, keep Deke from falling into *more* trouble. So the first thing, clearly, was finding Deke a place to stay, somewhere he couldn't *find* trouble—since Seth wasn't able to stop him.

Shana lived out on Bainbridge, with room for an extra

houseguest, and the island was difficult enough to get to that Deke would have no choice but to stay put. She just had to find the right way to ask. . . .

"Scotch-and-soda for her, make it a double," she called to Jon, who nodded. He might be a diva, according to both Tonica and Stacy, but he didn't give any of that 'tude to the customers.

"All right," Shana said, putting her bag on the seat next to her, and turning her attention to Ginny. "Spill."

"Okay, so. This puppy. He's got a story. . . ."

By the time Tonica came in, Deke and Georgie trailing behind him, Ginny had finished selling her plan to Shana, who looked about as unhappy as expected, but had agreed, anyway. The fact that Parsifal was being well-behaved and adorable helped, as did the scotch-and-soda.

"I'll make it up to you, I promise."

"Yeah, you will," Shana said. "Now go say hello to your dog before she expires on the spot."

Georgie was, in fact, dancing in place a little, looking at Ginny with anticipation.

Not too long ago, the shar-pei would have charged across the floor to greet Ginny after any time apart. Months of expensive training and a little maturity had checked that urge, and now she only tugged once on the leash to indicate where she wanted to go, and then waited for permission. In the middle of all the worry, Ginny felt a flash of pride.

She lifted her hand and called, "Georgie, come!"

Thankfully, Tonica let go of the leash in time.

"So what happened?" she asked Tonica, when the two humans joined them. Georgie was pushing against Ginny's knee, while Parsifal reached down from her lap to pat the larger dog's nose. "Where was he?"

"He is right here," Deke muttered, looking around the bar, obviously trying to spot Seth.

"Downtown, trying to beat information out of a guy half his age." Tonica had an odd expression on his face that she couldn't quite decipher, until he shot a look at Shana like he wasn't entirely comfortable talking in front of her. The other woman took the hint and got up with a smile at the newcomers. "If you'll excuse me, I need to use the ladies'."

Tonica watched her go, then shook his head. "Deke's lucky the guy's mother taught him not to hit crazy people."

"Hey." But this time Deke's protest was halfhearted at best.

"No cops involved?"

"No. Nobody wanted to make a fuss. I get the feeling it's the kind of place where if the cops show up, half the regulars would fade out the back door."

She raised her eyebrows, and he laughed a little. "Okay, no, it's not that bad, but it probably was before gentrification kicked in hard enough to shove them up a few rungs."

"It used to be lots worse," Deke agreed, as though that were a thing that he missed. Ginny thought he probably did, and almost understood it: things could be simpler when they were bad.

Tonica started to say something, and then made a face, smoothing it out only to show professional charm as Shana came back. "And we haven't met? I'm Teddy, manager of this fine establishment."

"I'm Shana Markonis, and Ginny warned me about you."

"I did no such thing," Ginny said, "so stop trying to get me in trouble. Deke, sit down, your hovering is making me nervous, and if you try to bolt again I'll sic Georgie on you." She waited while Deke slid into the booth next to Shana, who moved her coat to make room.

Tonica scanned the bar, his gaze lingering on Jon briefly. "I should go make sure that Jon has everything under control."

"He doesn't," Shana said. "But he's very cute."

Tonica just sighed, and went under the bar to speak to the other man.

"What?" Shana widened her eyes at Ginny. "He is cute!"

Ginny couldn't disagree, and watching the two of them standing next to each other, Tonica with his buzz cut and no-nonsense stance, in one of those boring gray sweaters he favored, versus Jon's long blond ponytail and bright red button-down, was like looking at a spectrum of Male Appeal. Not that she'd ever tell either of them that.

"The tip jar is going to be overflowing tonight," she predicted, then turned her attention to Deke. "So what the hell was that all about?"

"What was what all about?" He slid a glance sideways at Shana, similar to Tonica's, as though asking why they were talking in front of her.

"Don't give me that crap. You ditched us, ran off, and

Teddy had to haul you back from what sounds like massive stupidity . . . so what the hell were you trying to do?"

"Wait, this is the guy you want me to babysit?" Shana asked. "Girl, he doesn't look like he could be that much trouble."

"He is," Ginny said grimly.

"I'm sorry," Deke said, and Ginny shook her head.

"That might work on Tonica," she told the older man. "I'm the tough one in this partnership, and I don't melt that easy." A partial lie, but a plausible one. "What was so important that you had to flit off on your own?"

"The only guy who can clear me is the guy who hired me," Deke said, like it was the most reasonable thing in the world. And, Ginny had to admit, it was. How he'd thought he was going to convince the guy to do that . . .

Her eyes narrowed. "I thought you said you didn't talk to him, didn't know who he was?"

Deke's gaze shifted, and Ginny sighed. "Deke, I swear . . ." She bit her lip to keep anything else from getting out. He might have been a tough guy once, but she'd watched enough noir movies to know how to handle him, she thought. Not threats, the way Seth would, or man-to-man pep talks. He was old school, and an old-school boxer, and that probably meant that he would be uncomfortable saying no to a woman, if she played it right. She might be an only child, but she knew how to work the kid sister thing when she needed to. And she needed to get him on board with her plan.

"C'mon, Deke. I know you don't trust us, not the way

you do Seth, but Seth trusts us. Otherwise he wouldn't have asked for our help. But we need to work together, okay? Keeping secrets is what got you *into* this mess."

She waited, aware of Shana sitting very still, like she was front row at a play, and Parsifal snoring a little in Deke's lap, tiny puppy snorts.

"I knew how to find someone who would know," he admitted. "But they wouldn't never have talked to you. He wouldn't even talk to me, and I was convincing."

"You mean you hit him," Shana said.

He rubbed the back of his bald head and grimaced. "Yeah."

"Awesome."

Ginny was suddenly not so sure that her friend was going to be a good babysitter after all, the way the two of them suddenly grinned at each other.

At her feet, Georgie whined a little, a distressed sound, and shoved against Ginny's legs. "What is it, baby? Too much for you in here? Do you need to go outside and take care of business?"

"She went when we got out of the car," Deke said.

"Okay, then you just need some quiet time, huh?" She looked at the others. "You two, stay put. I'll be right back."

As she got up, she scooped Parsifal up off Deke's lap, noticing how the man's hands had instinctively curved to keep the puppy still. There might be hope for those two yet, she thought. "Just to give him a little down time," she said, trying to be soothing. "Overtired puppies have a tendency to forget their bathroom training."

That got Deke to let go, fast.

Usually, when Georgie was restless, she'd bring her out front where a "doggie relief station" had evolved next to the bike rack. But this case had her more on edge than normal, especially after Tonica was just parading the dog around in Deke's neighborhood, and she couldn't get the things she'd learned that morning about dogfighting out of her head, no matter how much she tried to distract herself. So instead, she took Georgie through the back door, past the tiny kitchen to the storeroom. There was a sheepskin pad there, and a bowl of water, for days when she and Georgie were here longer than usual. The Princess Pad, Tonica called it. Knowing the manager definitely had perks.

"That better, girl?" She knelt to place Parsifal on the ground and tugged at Georgie's ears, play-shaking the heavy, wrinkled head. "Better?"

Georgie licked her hand once, then settled on the pad with obvious relief, turning several times until everything was just right. Parsifal, meanwhile, was investigating the corners, sniffing at everything with obvious excitement. Ginny checked her phone for the time, and pulled a handful of treats out of her pocket, placing them on the floor next to the pad. "It's still a while until dinnertime, but you've been a good girl, you earned some treats."

Parsifal, hearing the magic word, came over as well to investigate.

A quiet thump in the shelves overhead told Ginny that Penny had arrived, and sure enough, the little tabby leaped down onto the floor and stalked over to where the dogs were resting.

"I'll just leave you three to it, then," Ginny said, standing up and smiling down at them.

Penny sat down in front of Georgie, tail curled around her hind-quarters, ears perked forward, ignoring the puppy. "All right. Tell me everything you were able to learn."

"What?" Georgie looked at her like she'd just asked if the dog could fly.

"When you were out with Theo! What did you learn?" The bits she had been able to catch from the humans' conversation had told her only that the little man was in trouble, that he was getting kicked out of his home, and that they didn't know who was caus-ing it. And that they were worried about something else. Penny had been a good hunter, patiently waiting, but things were moving again and it was time to pounce.

Georgie scratched herself thoughtfully. "We met some people, where the worried man lived. The neighborhood smells nice, like grass and dirt. A little girl scratched my ears. They seemed like nice people."

Penny kept her tail from thwapping the floor in frustration. "What did they talk about, Georgie?"

"Oh." The dog thought back. She didn't have the best memory in the world—time got messed up in her head, and she couldn't al-ways remember who said what, but she tried, because Penny needed to know.

"They talked about the house. About who went in or out. And what they were carrying. They brought boxes in and out. That was it."

"And you didn't hear anything else?"

"No. We went to the beach for a while, and he threw a stick for me"— and Georgie could obviously tell Penny wasn't interested in that, so she rushed over it—*"and then we went somewhere else, somewhere that smelled of sweat and rubber and blood, and then he made me wait outside with the worried man forever. And then they didn't talk much at all. And then we were back here."* It all came out in a rush, like she was afraid she'd forget something if she stopped.

Then Georgie shook her head, as though something might fall out of her ears if she only knocked them hard enough. *"No, wait. He said something, the same thing Herself was talking about while she worked. About bad people, and dogs. Bad dogs? Making them do bad things? And the worried man kept saying it wasn't his fault?"*

Penny's tail twitched once in agitation. Georgie wasn't a puppy anymore, but she'd been taken care of for most of her life. She hadn't seen some things that a cat on the street saw. The puppy had been afraid, before good food and petting calmed him down. The smaller older human was still afraid.

She thought about the worried older man, the one their humans were trying to help. He had large hands that had been gentle against her fur, and he smelled slightly of stale fish and newsprint, two smells that made her want to purr instinctively.

He wasn't one of those people, the cruel ones. She'd trust her whiskers on that.

He was losing his home, his den. His safety. She tried to imagine the Busy Place not being there, being blocked off to her, and her claws flexed nervously.

Her humans might not be getting anywhere, but they—she and Georgie—had an advantage the humans didn't. They had Parsifal.

Back at the bar, Tonica had finished whatever confab he was having with Jon, and joined Ginny, Shana, and Deke at their table. There was no sign of Seth, and Ginny admitted that she was relieved. This was going to be hard enough without the other man trying to butt in, either because Deke was his friend or because he didn't think she—a mere female—was competent, or whatever snit he had in his ear today.

"You kids look like you have things to talk about," Shana said. "Come on, Deke, let me buy you a beer."

"But . . ." Deke looked like he was going to dig his heels in. "This is my problem. I can help."

"I think you've done more than enough today already, Deke," Tonica said, and his voice wasn't one that encouraged back talk. Deke held his stare for about five seconds, then dropped it, and nodded. Ginny almost felt sorry for Deke. Almost.

She watched them go, Shana putting a hand on Deke's elbow that could have been comforting or house arrest, then shook her head and turned her attention to Tonica. "All right, what happened? Details, this time."

"Pretty much told you all of it already. Deke decided to go down to a fighter's gym and try to knock something out of one of his buddies. Who, thankfully, didn't want to press charges. Or return fire, since like I said, he was carrying the bruises, and our man Deke wasn't."

"Christ, he's an idiot," Ginny said with feeling. "Did you find anything in your neighborhood snoop? Was Georgie useful?"

"We didn't get to actually go in the house—too many people around. But yeah, maybe. Turns out Deke wasn't quite honest with us."

"Oh, there's a shock." Ginny shook her head hard enough that a curl fell out of the knot she'd pulled them into that morning. "What do I always tell you, Tonica? Clients *lie*. Even when they think they're being totally up front."

"Yeah well, like I said before, I'm not convinced he knows what's real and what isn't, entirely." He reached for a used coaster on the table, turning it in his hands. "To be fair, it's not like he was home all the time, but neighbors said that they saw people going in and out of the house on a semi regular basis. Carrying crates."

"Crates?"

He glared at her. "Did you even pick up your voice mail? Yeah, crates."

"Of course I did. But it didn't seem like an emergency situation, and I was kind of busy dealing with other things. Were they like packing crates, or . . ."

"Like carrying-live-animals crates, I think. Which would tie into . . . everything else. Mostly everything else." He dropped the coaster, frowning. "Something funky is going on, involving dogs stashed in Deke's basement. That much yeah we know. But it still raises the question of *what*? I mean, if you're going to have dogfights, you need people to watch 'em, right? That's where the money's to be made."

So where were they? And considering they didn't have enough room . . . was this just a way station?"

"Maybe, but I don't think it was for fighting dogs," Ginny said, waking up her tablet and pulling up a screen. "That's what I was busy looking into when you called. I did some more research after you and Georgie left, trying to get the pieces to fit, and then I remembered something the vet said, about Parsifal. Because there was no way even if he was full grown and healthy he'd be a fighting dog, okay? I mean, seriously. A ratter, yes, but if another dog went after him he'd just show his belly, or try to escape. Even if they made him mean, he'd be too little, unless they matched him against a Chihuahua."

"And?"

Ginny pushed the tablet over to him, not wanting to actually say the words.

"Jesus. Mallard." Tonica was reading the screen, his eyes flicking down over the text and then back again, as though he couldn't quite believe what he was reading.

"Yeah." Her stomach had been churning ever since she'd read the article, and the urge to gather up every small animal in sight and just hug them had pretty much swamped her.

"They . . . you think that they . . ." He stopped, running a hand over the top of his head as though he were smoothing the inch-long strands down. Not for the first time, she wondered if he used to have longer hair, and that was where the habit came from. "Jesus. Just when I think this entire thing can't get any sicker . . ."

She'd hoped Tonica would dismiss her fears, tell her that she was wrong. "It makes sense, though. Bait animals: cats, smaller dogs, rabbits . . . anything that won't fight back, I guess." Unwanted animals, from a shelter or the streets, anything they could get cheap or free. Bad enough to think of Georgie being trained to be vicious; when she thought of Parsifal being used that way, being hurt or killed, she had to swallow hard against the urge to either throw up or hit something. Or maybe both.

Tonica swore not quite under his breath words she was sure his mother would not approve of. "I want to take these bastards down so hard . . ."

Ginny appreciated the emotion, but they both knew that wasn't possible. "You know we can't, right? I mean, you've been saying it all along. Dogfighting, if that's what this is, it's a major operation. A lot of money involved. And where there's that much dirty money—we are way outclassed."

Outclassed as in, these were people worse than the guys Seth and Deke had been worried about, maybe. People who were used to violence—and didn't really care about sticking to—what had Seth said?—players the same size as them.

"So what, we throw Deke under the bus?"

"You know that's not what I meant," Ginny said sharply. "I just don't want us getting shot at or beat up again, okay?"

Tonica laughed, more of an exhausted huff than real humor. "Yeah, I'm on board with the not-getting-hurt part. So, we find a connection, someone who's actually responsible, and then we hand the entire mess over to someone with a little more firepower and have them clear Deke in exchange, agreed?"

She could do that. They could do that. Researchtigations. They weren't the goddamned Batman, they were goddamned Alfred. Or . . . something like that. "Yeah. I guess."

Tonica leaned back in the booth. "Well, we have a name, to start with."

"We do?" That was news to her. "Deke said the guy wouldn't tell him anything." She stared at Tonica, who was smiling now, just a little smug. She checked his knuckles for bruises, and then looked at his face more carefully again. No, Tonica wouldn't actually use his fists. Especially not if that's what the other guy was used to. "All right, yeah, fine, point to you. That's why we let you hang around. Stop gloating, and give."

"Lew Hollins. I don't have anything more than that; I didn't think it would be a good time to push. Whoever this guy is, he's tough enough to make a pretty tough twenty-something boxer hesitate to even give a name, much less spill his guts."

Ginny was already typing into her tablet, pulling up new screens and tapping out commands. "Lew Hollins . . . Lewis Hollins, age fifty-seven?"

"I have no idea, I just got the name." Tonica sounded cranky, and she gave him the finger out of habit, turning it to suggest that he sit-and-spin, she was *working* on it.

"There's a Lou—L-O-U—Hollins in Seattle, too. But he's seventy-nine. Probably not? Not if he's the guy who was paying Deke, based on his description, no. Okay, Lewis Hollins. Lives in Holmes Point, unmarried, a podiatrist? Seriously?"

"That might explain how he met so many boxers," Tonica said. "Seth said once that the feet gave out before the hands or knees."

"Huh. Yeah, I guess I could see that. Looking for a visual . . . there we go." She slid the tablet around and pushed it toward him again. Tonica took a quick look at the photo displayed: a lean, angular face, with silvery blond hair receding slightly at the top, and nodded. "Matches what Deke said about the third guy, don't you think?"

"I wouldn't want to cross him," Ginny said. "Hell, I wouldn't even want him working on my toes. Deke's right, the guy's got cold eyes."

She took the tablet back and skimmed the readout.

"And, sadly, a clean surface. He's not pinging anywhere on the usual menace-to-society boards."

"You expected him to? Really, Mallard?"

She shrugged. "It would have been nice. Right now, we've got nothing other than a low-rung boxer's word that he's connected to anything even remotely criminal, and it's not like the kid's ever going to testify, if what you said is true. We've got no thread to pull."

"So in other words, we're back where we started, even with a name?" Tonica sounded like he wanted to throw something—a glass, a punch, a temper tantrum. She could feel the tension coiled in his body, even though he still looked perfectly at-ease to a casual observer.

"Please, have I taught you nothing?" She forced a grin at him, feeling a little of her usual self-confidence come back. "When an avenue of research comes up blank? You just go down another avenue, and then another, until you find what you're looking for."

"You really shouldn't look so happy about that," Tonica said. "It's indecent." He shook his head. "All right, how do we drill down and find out if he's a bad guy or not?"

"First, we need to get Deke settled. If this guy's as bad news as we think, it's even more important that he be out of reach, somewhere safe. Especially if the kid he beat on tells anyone." The first rule of the job was to keep it impersonal, not care about the client. Every time things went wrong, in every detective movie she'd ever seen, it was because the detective was a sap for the client.

"Great. So what, we're going to stash him in a hotel somewhere? Buy him a ticket out of town and hope he can take care of himself? C'mon, Gin."

She looked across the bar to where Shana and Deke seemed to be trading stories of misspent youth, based on the way Shana was laughing. "Don't worry. I think that's in the bag."

The office was modern but still managed to look comfortable, the chairs ones you'd like to sit in, the surface of the oversized wooden table being used as a desk covered with a comfortable clutter of folders and files. There were three people in the room: a woman, sitting quietly in the corner;

the young boxer from Sammy's sitting in one of the comfortable chairs in front of the desk; and the man behind the desk, shirtsleeves rolled up, thinning hair mussed, and reading glasses sliding down his nose.

"No," he was saying, leaning across the table and looking directly into the younger man's eyes. "It's all right. You did the right thing. You're the working hinge in all this, and the last thing we want is someone looking at you. Better they should think you've given them everything you know, and leave you alone."

The kid exhaled, resting his elbows on the table like they were all that was holding him up now. "I'm sorry, boss. I just didn't know what to do. He was going to keep pushing and pushing, and I didn't want to hit an old guy."

"Yeah. First time you've had the spotlight on you, I get it. And those bruises look like they hurt."

The kid grinned, touching the greenish spot visible under his cheekbone. "Nah. I get worse than this during a fight. The old man's still got some moves on him. But I'm sorry, I—"

"Gerry. It's all right. I'm not angry. When I hired you to keep an eye on things, it was precisely because I knew something like this might happen. Go home, get some rest. We'll be in touch."

The kid slipped out the back door, and Hollins sighed, shaking his head. "Kids today, I swear. They think they're invincible. Dumb, but invincible."

The woman who had been sitting off to the side during their conversation looked up from her phone, her head cocked to the side. "Do we need to teach him differently?"

"What? Oh, no, no," he said, waving away her concern. "He's loyal, and useful. You don't screw with that, not without reason. I might have wished he kept his mouth shut, but at least he knew enough to come here and tell me, rather than hide like an idiot and hope I never found out."

She nodded, less because she was convinced and more because he didn't want to hear her doubts.

"Meanwhile, I'm more concerned about this new player. I want to know about *him*. Is he a competitor? A cop? Or just some poor schmuck trying to help out a friend?" Hollins let out another overly dramatic sigh. "I swear to you, I'd rather he was a cop. They're easier to deal with."

"I have already started looking into it. I should have that information to you within an hour." She paused. "And what about Mr. Hoban?"

"Who, Deke? Oh, don't worry about him, poor old bastard. His part in this has ended; he gets to exit off the stage like a good bit player." Hollins tilted his head, considering something only he could see. "It may be, in fact, that this entire play has run its course, and it's time to draw the curtain down. Take a memo, Jeanine."

She did no such thing, of course, but listened carefully as he spoke.

It had been a good run, but he was right: nothing lasted forever.

8

*P*enny hadn't been sure how she was going to question Parsifal. The puppy was so little, its thoughts focused on the moment, not remembering what had gone past or—well, it was much like most dogs, really. Only littler. And it was already scared of her.

But it had to be done.

Ginny came in to feed the dogs then, placing two bowls down on the floor, one with more kibble in it than the other. Penny's ears flicked forward, alert, as she stared past Georgie's shoulder at the puppy, who had put his entire face into his bowl and was chewing away happily. Food calmed. A puppy with food in its belly would be sleepy and not-scared.

Georgie nosed at her own food, then looked sideways at Penny. "He's only a puppy."

"I'm not going to bite him," Penny said. The tip of her tail twitched, but she kept it from lashing: Georgie was upset enough already, her protective instincts engaged.

It was . . . reasonably cute, she supposed. And it needed help. But it was noisy and messy and didn't belong here. The sooner she figured out what was going on, the sooner Theodore and Ginny could get rid of it. "I'm just going to ask it questions. That's all."

"You don't play nice," Georgie said, her muzzle lifted in what might almost be a snarl. Penny waited. Eventually, Georgie relented and let Penny walk past. Not that Georgie could have stopped her, not really, but . . .

"Hi." The puppy had stopped eating, and turned its head sideways to look at Penny. "Who're you?"

"This is Mistress Penny-Drops," Georgie said. "You met her before, remember? It's all right. She's pack."

"Oh." Parsifal studied the cat seriously, then reached forward to lick the side of Penny's face.

Penny sneezed, and backed away, her tail lashing furiously now. The urge to hiss rose in her throat, and she forced it back down. If she scared it, it would be useless.

"Penny . . ." Georgie's whine was anxious, a reminder. "Parsi, Penny doesn't like being groomed by us."

"Oh." The puppy looked crestfallen, its ears drooping and its tail tucked between its legs. Georgie gave Penny a long look, and then turned back to the puppy.

"If we ask you something," she said to it, "could you answer? Tell us everything you remember?"

"I can do that, sure!" The ears lifted slightly, but the tail remained cowed, his body flat against the blanket in submission. Georgie nodded to Penny, who kept her tail still, her ears forward.

"I need you to remember the place where you were," she said to it. "Before Theo—the big human—found you."

Those ears dropped again, and the little body shivered.

"Can you do that?" Penny asked, very, very still, like she would wait for a mouse.

"It's okay," Georgie said, moving around so that she was half on the blanket next to Parsifal, nudging into his side. "We're here, you're safe."

"Okay." The puppy was shivering, but its eyes were bright, and Penny felt a twinge of respect.

"Tell me what you remember, what you saw, heard, smelled. Everything, no matter how small." Penny didn't trust the puppy to know what might be important: they would figure that out later.

The puppy was obviously trying to think hard. "It was dark most of the time," Parsifal said. "Warm and dark. Except when the humans came to feed us. Sometimes then we were taken out of the den and ran around. The ground was cold, and the air smelled bad."

"We?"

"There were seven of us," Parsifal said solemnly. "I used to count us at night, when we slept, to make sure nobody had gone away."

Penny blinked once, and her tail slowly curled around her hind-quarters. That was important, she thought. "Some of them went away, before?"

"I think so. I don't remember so well. The warm one. And others? It was noisier, once. And then it was quieter."

"When the humans came. What changed?"

"It was brighter. They handled us, put us on cold things and talked. To each other, not to us. They didn't touch us much."

Parsifal sounded so sad at that. Penny looked up at Georgie, hoping she would know what to do.

"We'll find you a human who touches," the shar-pei said, nudging the much smaller dog with her nose. "All the touches and treats. Just tell Penny what she needs to know."

"I don't remember!" The puppy wailed, loud enough that

someone outside might hear. Georgie whined, deep in her chest, and Penny's ears went flat, then flicked back and forth as she tried to hear if anyone was coming to investigate the noise. They waited until it was pretty certain that no humans had heard. Only then did Penny let her muscles relax, and raised a paw, catching Parsifal's attention with the sharp glint of claws.

"Yes, you can," she said firmly, and touched the small dog on the tip of his black nose, not firmly enough for the claw to slice, but enough to remind the puppy of how easily she could. "You can remember the smells from the time you were born. The feel of the hands on you. The voices. Remember them all."

The puppy's eyes crossed, trying to keep watch on that claw on his nose.

"Tell me," Penny said, and the tip of her tail twitched, just once.

"Hard hands. Cold hands. Cold voices, like bones we've already chewed twice. They smell stale, old, and cold. Bones and . . ." The puppy whined, not having words to describe what little he did remember. "Like the high-voiced human."

Penny cocked her head, then looked at Georgie.

"I think he means the kitchen-man?"

Penny's whiskers twitched, and she tried to identify what Seth smelled like.

"Ash?" she said. "Burnt smoke, harsh in your nose?"

"Yes!" The puppy's tail thumped against the floor, he was so pleased to be understood.

"They smoked," Penny said to Georgie. "Enough that the smell lingered, like it does on Seth's hands." She always had to groom herself after he touched her, to get rid of the smell on her fur.

"And . . ." Parsifal seemed relieved when the claw lifted from his nose, but his eyes remained crossed until he shook his head and sneezed. "And blood."

"What?" Penny's ears flicked forward, and her whiskers trembled.

"Sometimes they smelled of blood."

Having settled the dogs down with an early dinner, Ginny went back to the table they'd commandeered for the evening. The kitchen was still closed, but Tonica had gone back and made them sandwiches, daring any of the customers to say anything. Nobody had. The food wasn't up to Seth's standards, but it was filling.

Not that she was all that hungry, after looking at the materials she'd dug up, yet again, and discussing it all with Tonica. She was pretty jaded about the world in general, she'd thought, but this . . .

"There's absolutely no connection between this guy and . . . anything," Tonica was saying in disgust. "And you're telling me that he's not even the kind of super-nice guy we could immediately be suspicious of on general principle?"

"If we were real detectives . . . ," Ginny started to say, yet again, and Tonica cut her off.

"Which we're not."

"If we were, the next step would be to put a tail on this Hollins guy." Ginny stopped, her mouth twisting. "Tail, right. Inappropriate puns aside, he's the only real lead we've got. We need to know who this guy is, what he's doing. He's the key."

"What, you think we should spend our time lurking after a podiatrist?" Tonica shook his head. "I'm already running on exhausted, Gin. And you are *not* going to do that alone. If this guy's actively involved, he's not a nice guy."

"Aw, your caveman tendencies are coming out again, Tonica," she said, drawing a quick, reluctant grin from him before getting back to the topic. "But no, I wasn't going to suggest actual physical stalking. You should know my methods by now, Watson."

"Cyberstalking?"

"I prefer to call it in-depth digital investigations," she said primly. "But yes. A full dossier, soup to nuts. We've already exhausted what I can do, though. At least, without getting into the dodgy areas that make you twitch."

He shrugged at that. She'd never actually broken the law, at least not noticeably, but Tonica had tighter reins on his moral propriety than she did.

"I have someone I can call on for help—but I'm going to need a suitable bribe." She looked sideways at her partner, trying to gauge his willingness to play along. It could go either way, now that he was the bar's manager in title as well as responsibility.

Tonica sighed, knowing what she had in mind. "Yes, all right. But only for a set time period, Gin. Two weeks, max. And I reserve the right to cut whoever it is off if they get drunk. *When* they get drunk."

"Don't worry, Greg's a lightweight. Two drinks and he'll be a happy little hacker."

"You guys know the most interesting people," Tonica said, then got up to snag another round—one ginger ale, and one lager, with a side of coffee—from the bar, and bring the drinks back to the table.

"Useful, anyway," Ginny said, already entering Greg's number. "He's not actually all that interesting, if you're not heavily into the hacktivist mentality. Hi, Greg," she said into the phone. "This is the real actual Gin Mallard. Call me when you pick up, I have a challenge for you."

She put the cell down on the bar, only to have it buzz and vibrate, indicating another call coming in. She picked it up, glanced at the display, and sighed. "I'll be right back."

She stepped outside, letting the door close gently behind her, and answered the phone. "Hi, Rob."

"Hey." His voice was thin through the speaker, familiar and affectionate. "You were going to call me this morning."

"Yeah, I'm sorry. I got wrapped up in a job, and—"

"A job or a job-job?"

"There's a difference?" There was to him, she knew. Rob loved his job, but he still thought like an office geek, where everything was split between "what I do for money" and "what I do that isn't about a paycheck."

"Ginny. We talked about this already. You agreed."

No, she hadn't. For once, she'd kept the peace and not argued with him. That wasn't the same as agreeing.

Her mother's voice whispered in the back of her head: "I like this one. He's got a sensible head on his shoulders."

So do I, Mom, she thought back at the voice. "Rob, don't. Don't lecture me on what I should be doing with my life, or where my energy is best spent. I'm not sixteen, and you're not—" She sighed. "You get a voice but you don't make my decisions for me. Okay?"

She waited.

"You're going to get into serious trouble with this hobby of yours, Ginny. I'm just worried about you, that's all."

"I know." If she'd thought it was anything else, she would have broken up with him already. "But I promise, there's nothing at all problematic about this; it's just helping out a friend of a friend who's getting harassed by his landlord."

That was the unvarnished truth. It wasn't the whole truth, but who really wanted the whole truth, anyway?

"All right, not fighting about this. Are we still on for tonight?"

She had to think a moment, trying to visualize her schedule, before she nodded. "Yeah, we're still good." If Greg got back to her, she could set him on the trail, hand off Deke to Shana and whatever schmoozing was to be done to Teddy, and be home well in time to Skype with her boyfriend. Let him think she'd spent the day in the office, not sitting on a bar stool at Mary's, arguing over tactics and poking into other people's business.

Best of all possible worlds, really.

She wondered, as she said good-bye, if Tonica should feel insulted that Rob was worried about the job, and not the fact that she spent so much time with the bartender, who was not, by any stretch of the imagination, unappealing.

She tilted her head, a smile tugging at the corner of her mouth. Her and Tonica? She tried to imagine that, and the smile turned into a laugh.

When she went back inside, still chuckling, she refused to tell him why.

That night's crowd was weirdly mellow. Teddy didn't know why it happened sometimes like that; nobody had started a study of barroom flow the way they studied traffic, but the signs were unmistakable. When he'd been hustling for tips, it had been the worst kind of night, people nursing one drink and not socializing much, but at Mary's that was less of an issue. He kind of liked it, which probably meant that he was getting old.

It also meant that Penny hung around more obviously. The tabby didn't like it when the bar filled up and got noisy, but on slow nights she'd come out and parade through the bar, pausing to let people admire her properly. Right now she had appropriated one of the regular's laps, and the woman—Molly, drank mostly bourbon—was petting her absently, raising her drink with her other hand, and occasionally pausing to turn the page of her e-reader.

There was a lot to be said for quiet nights. Especially when he had other things to do.

Tonica reached underneath the bar and pulled out a street map of Seattle proper, unfolding it so that he could get a clear bird's-eye view. No doubt Ginny had some app on her tablet that did the same, with quick zoom and book-marking, but he still liked the solid feel of paper under his fingers, especially for something like this.

Penny abandoned Molly and came to sit on the bar next to him, peering over his arm as though she, too, were fascinated by the map.

"This is where Deke lives," he told her, pointing at the map. "And this is where the other houses owned by the same landlord are." He picked them off, one by one, referring to his notes to make sure that he had the right street. "And this is the gym where I found Deke."

He studied the points, trying to find a pattern but not seeing anything other than the fact that they were all in lower-end or working-class neighborhoods. Which meant nothing, really: if you were going to buy a bunch of build-ings, and weren't wealthy—which the landlord wasn't—you'd have to go lower on the scale, that was all.

Then he looked back at the notes Ginny had compiled on the renters, shifting through the pages until he found what he was looking for, and he was never going to ask how she got access to this sort of thing. Every single renter had one thing in common with the others: at one time or another, in the past decade, they'd all had a guest membership at Sammy's Gym and Boxing Clinic. "And none of them for longer than six months, either." He double-checked, to make sure he wasn't hallucinating, then blew out a breath in what might have been a sigh. "And one kid who knew the name of the guy hiring dog-keepers. Might be coincidence, really probably not. Time to lay down some chips, see if we can shake out some actual dirt." He picked up his phone and chose a number.

"Louisa? Hey, it's Theo Tonica. Yeah, I know, I'm sorry, but I know for a fact that you don't even look at your pillow until one a.m., so . . . Listen, I need to ask you a favor that might run uncomfortably close to client privilege, or whatever you lawyer types say, so you need to think carefully before you say anything."

He waited while the other person spoke—heatedly—and then smiled a little, more sadness than relief. "Yeah, that's true enough. I'm not going to say all debts are cleared but we're a hell of a lot closer." Louisa was an old family friend, so the debts ran for years, in both directions. "Look, a friend of a friend is in trouble, and I need to know if he got into it himself, or if someone else did it to him. What can you find out about the owners—and the clientele—of a boxing gym called Sammy's?"

His eyebrows rose. "Oh really?" He reached with one hand underneath the bar, grabbing the pencil and pad of paper that was always stashed there, and dropped them down on top of the map, startling Penny, who paused in her study to blink at him.

"Uh-huh." He was writing awkwardly, one hand on the phone, the other trying to keep the pad in place while he wrote. "Really? And that's recent. . . . Yeah, okay. No, this is really . . . helpful. Thank you. Anything else you come up with, let me know soonest. Yeah, you, too. Come by anytime, first drink's on the house."

He put the phone down and looked at Penny. "Someone

at that boxing gym has been a bad, bad boy," he told her. "Tell me, how likely do you think it is that someone who was cited for running an illegal fight club a few years back might have branched out into dogfighting?"

Penny blinked at him, her golden-green eyes wise.

"Yeah," he said. "That's what I thought, too."

There was a surge in orders just then, swamping Jon, so Teddy put the map away, shooed Penny off the counter, and busied himself pulling drafts and mixing drinks. There wasn't anything they could do this late at night, anyway. They'd reconnoiter in the morning, see what Ginny had managed to put together on her side, and figure out what to do then.

Or, if they had what he thought they had, whom to call for backup. Because he, at least, tried to learn from his past mistakes, and not make the same ones again.

9

Deke picked at a fraying spot on the knee of his pants, and stared out the car window. The sun was going down, and none of the streets looked familiar yet. He wasn't used to being in this part of the city: it made him nervous.

The woman driving—Shana, her name was, he reminded himself, Shana something Greek—was humming under her breath. She didn't look happy, but she didn't look mad, either. And she'd said he was welcome to stay with her as long as needed, but he didn't know if she'd said that because Seth was standing there glaring at her, or if she really meant it.

He'd tried to argue, tried to insist that he could go back to his house if Seth didn't want him around anymore, that he hadn't been kicked out yet, that he was still able to take care of himself on his own. Seth had just looked at him like that was the dumbest thing Deke had ever said, and after a couple of minutes he'd given up. He'd never won an argument with Seth, not once in years, and Deke didn't expect that to change this time, either. But a man had his pride, he thought. He had to at least get in the ring.

Wasn't the first time he'd lose in the ring, either.

When he'd quieted down, Seth had pointed out that he'd just gone to Sammy's and tried to beat an answer out of a kid, and just because the kid wasn't pressing charges didn't mean Zimmerman wasn't going to hear about it, somehow, and when that happened Deke had better have the rest of his shit cleared up, which meant getting out of the way and letting Seth and the others do their job without worrying about him.

So now he was going to stay with this woman, this stranger. In her house. Just a few days, Seth had said. Maybe a week, tops. Then this would all be straightened out, and things could go back to normal.

Deke sniffed. He knew better. At least they were letting him go home long enough to get his things. He'd had to borrow socks from Seth this morning, and they felt all wrong on his feet.

"You okay over there?"

"Yeah," he said, after making sure she was talking to him and not the puppy sleeping in a cardboard box in the backseat.

That was the other thing. He was supposed to take care of the puppy. "You agreed to let them in your house; that's what got you into trouble in the first place," Seth had said. "You don't get to weasel out now."

Deke had never weaseled out of anything, and he resented the hell out of Seth for even saying that. He just didn't think it was fair, when all he'd agreed to do was not look, and not ask questions, and not talk about the dogs, not take care of them. He'd tried saying that to Seth, and lost that fight, too.

"Ginny's already got that mutt of hers to deal with, and ain't no way Teddy's got time to coddle it. Man up, Deke, it's just a puppy, for God's sake."

The woman had just laughed, especially when the thing had licked her hand, and said she wasn't going to walk it, or clean up after it.

One puppy probably wasn't so much trouble, for a couple of days. He liked cats better, though. Cats left you alone. Didn't pester you, or make you feel guilty.

The woman was a decent driver, he'd give her that, and the car was nice, purring along instead of rattling or squeaking. It wasn't brand-new, but newer than the bartender's old coupe. And it was worlds more comfortable than trying to ride on the back of Seth's idiot machine. Man was too old to be riding a damned motorcycle . . . He could feel his old bones starting to ease against the seat, and didn't even realize that he'd closed his eyes until they pulled up to his street and the car stopped.

Deke frowned, something setting his nerves off again. He glanced at the house, seeing nothing awry, then spotted three figures lurking along the trees that separated it from the neighbors. It was hard to tell at dusk, but he thought they looked like teenagers, the way they were skulking in the shadows, afraid someone would call the truant officer on them. Not that it was his house anymore to worry about, but he didn't like strangers around, especially not punk teenage strangers.

Not his problem, he reminded himself. He didn't have anything worth stealing, and it wasn't his house anymore, never mind what Seth said, and those other folks promised. He knew better than to get his hopes up. Losing his job, having Zimmerman come after him like that, and then the dustup at the gym—he was lucky they weren't already hauling him to some geezer home where they'd try to cut his meat for him, or not even let him *have* meat anymore.

He looked at the house again. It wasn't much: same peeling paint, same curtains that had come with the rental, same porch light that never gave off enough light no matter what wattage bulb he put in there. But it had been home, for a while.

"It don't look the same."

The woman glanced over at him. She was a looker, if you liked the dark-haired, sloe-eyed type, but about forty years too young for him, even if he'd been inclined to try. Besides, you didn't hit on someone who was giving you a place to flop.

"Yeah, I get that," the woman said. "Change sucks, especially when it's not one you want."

The blonde, Ginny, said they'd be safe with her, him and the little dog. Like they thought he was in danger. Deke scoffed. Like anyone would bother with him. Even punk-ass kids wouldn't take a swing at him.

All he'd had to do was ignore what was going on, take the money, and not ask questions, and he still somehow managed to do that wrong. And now he had to pack up his stuff and go live with some strange dame who, no matter she was a looker, was still a stranger and he didn't like strangers. He didn't like change and it was all change.

And now even the place he'd lived in for nearly ten years didn't look the same.

"Let's get this over with. All you need to do is grab enough clothing for a few days. I have a washer and dryer, so even if this drags out—which it won't," she added quickly, so he must have let panic show on his face, "you'll be okay. Come on."

Deke nodded once, then swallowed and got out of the car. He'd become a problem other people had to deal with, a mess they had to clean up. That was no fate for a grown man. Maybe it was time to just give in. Wasn't like there was anything worth fighting for anymore.

Left in the backseat, the puppy let out a woeful yip of abandonment.

"Hush, dog," he said. "We'll only be gone a few minutes, and the sun's down so you won't get overheated."

Deke didn't care about the dog, except he did, sort of. Thing was pitiful, and alone, and didn't seem like anyone wanted him, either, if they'd left him in the basement when all the other dogs got took. And if he'd been left, then Seth was right, that sort of made the dog his responsibility. His mess.

"We need to get food for it, too," he said.

"Yeah, I know. After we pack you up, okay?"

Inside, the house smelled musty, like he'd been gone for more than a few days. Or maybe it smelled like that all the time, and he'd never noticed. He left the woman standing in the living room and headed for the bedroom, trying to remember where he'd left his suitcase. He hadn't used it in years.

It was under his bed, where he'd thought. "Good to know the brain ain't entirely gone," he said as he put it on the bed, flipping it open and turning to look at the dresser. Socks, underwear, pants, a couple of shirts. Pajamas. Toothbrush and comb, and the pills the doctor made him take for his heart. He'd forgotten them when he stayed with Seth last night.

The suitcase looked half empty when he was done, so he added a sweater and a pair of slippers. He'd never been out to the island; it might get colder at night.

"Something to read," he said, and went back out to the living room. She was still standing there, hands behind her back as though afraid to touch anything. He grabbed a few books off the top of the pile, not even looking to see what they were, and went back into the bedroom, tossing them on top of the neatly folded clothing.

He closed up the suitcase and brought it back into the living room.

"That's it?"

"I ain't a girl, to need a steamer trunk for a coupla days," he said gruffly.

She smiled, like he'd said something funny. "We probably should check the kitchen, to make sure there's nothing in the fridge that might go bad." She said it like she'd wanted to do it herself but was afraid. Deke thought about the condition of his kitchen, and snorted. She might have the right of it, there.

"If it was gonna go bad it would have already," he said, but headed toward the kitchen, anyway.

"You're a man after my own housekeeping heart," she said, trailing along. "If there's anything worth taking, we should. I'm not sure what I've got in my kitchen other than a few takeout menus."

She almost ran into him when he stopped just past the kitchen arch.

"Deke?"

He could feel her peering over his shoulder, her height giving her a clear view of the door that led down to the cellar. It was open. Not much, but definitely open. He always kept it locked. Always. He never went down there.

Down there was where the big guy, Tonica, had found the dog. Maybe he left the door open?

Deke wasn't the smartest kid in the class, but he was no dummy, either. Tonica had seemed the cautious, conscientious type. The sort that closed doors behind him. And anyone else came poking around, poking around *down there,* odds were they weren't leaving him an early birthday present.

He thought about the gangly forms he'd seen outside the house when they pulled up, and the look of the man who paid him every month.

"Get out," he said. "Now."

Part of him wanted to look, to see what was going on down there, in the basement he never went into. But even if it was empty—and why *wouldn't* it be empty? why would anyone leave something there, after they cleared everything out like Tonica said?—something was screaming under his skin that he shouldn't go closer, that he should get the hell out, too.

So he did.

They'd made it as far as the living room, the woman reaching down to grab the handle of his suitcase, when he heard a sound he'd never wanted to hear again, the muffled pop-and-hiss of something exploding. Fifty years fell off him in an instant, as he grabbed the woman by the back of her shirt and hauled her toward the door. Precious seconds spent opening it, the sweat on the back of his neck running cold, his skin prickling in anticipation of the next blow, the one that would break windows and knock them through a wall.

They were halfway across the lawn when the house blew.

There was shouting, and something snapping, crackling, and the smell of something familiar, unpleasant. He licked his lips, and tasted blood. Had he gotten knocked out again?

"Deke. Deke, can you hear me?"

"Woman, I hear you fine, stop your yelping."

No, the yelping was the dog. He was lying on his back, and the dog was yelping, and why was he lying on his back? That was a damned fool thing to do because his body felt like hell. He must have taken a KO, but wait, he wasn't in the ring anymore; he'd quit years ago.

The smell was smoke, he recognized it now. The combination of that and the taste of blood in the back of his throat made him feel queasy. He groaned, and tried to sit up, to see what the hell was going on.

"Sir, no, please don't get up." Hands were on him, and unfamiliar voices were still shouting, and the wind was rushing around him, smoke and blood and the damned dog kept yipping. Deke just said the hell with it, and passed out again.

Ginny had gotten the call from Shana, as close to hysteria as she'd ever heard her. "Fire" and "hospital" had managed to get through, and Ginny had met her at the emergency room where Deke had been taken.

"The doctors say he'll be all right; he got knocked out and they said he was dehydrated. But he'll be okay. Oh God, Gin, the entire house went up. It was horrible."

Ginny let her babble a little longer, until the words started to dry up, and the shaking stopped. Shana was a mess, Parsifal cuddled on her lap despite the dirty looks the nurses kept throwing her, but when Ginny suggested that she go home, Shana refused. "I told you I'd give him a place to stay, and he needs it even more now, right? He saved my life, Ginny, getting me out of there."

Ginny decided not to point out that Shana wouldn't have been in danger if she hadn't been talked into giving

Deke a place to stay. Instead, she patted her on the shoulder, made sure she had enough coffee, and went to talk to someone in charge, who directed her to where Deke was being examined.

By the time she found him, he'd been put in a corner of the ER, drapes pulled around him to give the illusion of privacy, and the doctor was long gone. She pulled the drape closed behind her and went to his bedside. "Hey."

"Hospital?" He didn't even open his eyes. She guessed that the sounds and smells were enough to clue him in.

"Yeah. What do you remember?"

"Fire. House." His voice was scratchy, like he'd been shouting. Smoke inhalation, she guessed. "How bad?"

"I don't know." She hadn't bothered asking. "But probably bad enough that even when we solve this, you're not going to be living there again any time soon." She paused. "I'm sorry." He might not have had a lot, but everything he'd had was probably now either burnt, or sodden from the firefighters' hoses. She should call Tonica, let him know everyone was okay, have him maybe check and see if anything could be salvaged. He had to have at least one friend in the fire department, right? She tried to remember if any of the regulars at Mary's had fire department patches on their jackets, but her brain—usually good with that sort of thing—drew a blank.

"Your friend, what's-'er-name, Shana?" Deke asked, bringing her attention back to the moment at hand.

"She's okay. She's in the waiting room. Won't leave without you. We're just waiting for them to release you."

Personally, she thought he should stay longer, but doubted he would agree. He probably didn't have the money for a hospital stay, anyway.

His eyes opened then, but he just stared at the ceiling. "And the dog?"

"Parsifal's okay, too. You guys are lucky the handyman was there; he called the fire department right away."

"Handyman?" He turned his head to look at her then. They must have washed his face when he was admitted. There was a bad bruise forming over one cheekbone, but otherwise he looked like he'd come straight from the shower, his sparse gray hair slicked back against his scalp, his eyes wide and the pupils overly large.

"Yeah, Shana said that's who dragged you away from the fire and called the fire department. The landlord had told him the place would be empty, so he went over to make sure everything was secure, and . . . well, he saw the fire start." Ginny hesitated. "How did the fire start, Deke?"

"I didn't do it."

Ginny had known that would be his first reaction: when something went wrong, he immediately assumed everyone would blame him.

"I know," she said. She didn't know any such thing, but Shana would have said something if she'd seen Deke light a match, right? And a house fire would need more than a match; it would need fuel, at least a can of accelerant, based on what she'd seen on television. "But you had to have seen something, heard something?"

"Stop badgering him, blondie." Seth's growl came from behind her, but he moved quickly to stand between her and the bed, as though he was protecting Deke from her. "You done enough. Or rather you ain't done enough."

"What?" Their usual antagonistic relationship, muted once Seth had asked for help, flared back at the hated nickname, much less the way he was talking to her. "How—"

"He near got killed!"

She could feel herself starting to splutter. "Are you blaming me for this? For the fact that his house blew up? Seriously?" She managed to keep her voice down, remembering where they were, but the urge to punch him in the nose was near irresistible.

"We just went back to get some things," Deke said, lifting a hand enough to grab at Seth's arm. "Wasn't her fault any more'n it was yours. It was my fault, for being dumb enough to say anything."

"Deke." Seth looked at Deke's hand on his arm, and then sighed, all the bluster sliding out of him. "Do you know what happened? Do you know who set the fire?"

Deke closed his eyes again, turning his head away. "No. Don't matter. House is gone, they done with me. I want to go now. Can we go?"

"Yeah." Ginny wanted to know what Deke knew, or thought he knew, but there was something so . . . defeated about the older man, she couldn't bring herself to push. And she wasn't sure Seth would let her, anyway. The sooner she got them somewhere safe, where they could figure this out without snarling at each other, the better. "Let me go find a nurse, and we can get you checked out."

The call had come in around seven, the not-a-cell-phone tone of the bar's landline unusual enough that everyone at the bar stopped and looked at it. Stacy had answered, and yelled for Seth. Seth had listened for a couple of minutes and then gone pale, muttering something about needing to go, an emergency. And then he'd said the words that made Teddy's blood cool with fear: "That damned idiot Deke."

He'd gotten a text from Ginny about half an hour later, and been utterly unsurprised to hear that whatever had happened had involved her friend, too. That was just how their luck went. Ginny was en route to the hospital, and would let him know what was going on once she knew.

And that had been the last he'd heard.

Not that he was stressing about it. They were all big kids and could handle themselves in an emergency and he'd stopped riding in to solve everyone's problems years ago.

And none of that had any bearing on why he took a break halfway through the night, went outside, and called his cousin.

He got her voice mail. Of course.

"It's Theo. My schedule's kind of crazy, but if we can schedule a group Skype one afternoon before five p.m., I'll do my best to make it."

He looked at the front of the bar, the warm lights spilling out through the front window, noise rushing out every time someone opened the door, and shook his head. He'd spent the past decade running away from responsibility. Looked like it had finally caught up to him.

Mary's closed at 2 a.m. on Sundays, officially. One of the bonuses of being manager, though, was deciding when you really closed. Teddy had made it an article of faith that anyone wandering into a bar after 1 a.m. was not the kind of patron you wanted to have, and if the bar happened to empty out before one, well, he had no guilt at all about turning off the lights and closing up shop. Tonight had been one of those nights: busy as hell until around midnight, and then dead, as everyone suddenly realized they had to go to work the next morning.

"And that's all she wrote, folks," he said, stretching his arms over his head and feeling things crack pleasantly along his spine. "We are done."

"You are the bestest boss ever," Stacy said. "No matter what I say."

Teddy was already closing out the registers. "Yeah, I'll remind you about that next time you're bitching about the work schedule."

It was their usual banter, undercut by the worry neither of them was talking about. They hadn't gotten any updates, and calling Ginny's cell phone had only gotten her voice mail.

He left Stacy to the cleanup, focusing his attention on balancing the till. Patrick went over the week's receipts every Monday, but the neater he left things, the fewer headaches everyone had.

They'd settled into a quiet routine, the clink of bottles and the swing and thud of the fire door as Stacy took the recycling to the bins out back mingling with the shuffle and thwack of bills being bound together. He did a final count, and then put the money into the safe.

And only then did he let the worry creep from the back of his brain to the front. He didn't want to call again, assuming that whatever was going on took all their attention, but the moment he got Stacy into her car and on her way home, he was going to.

When his cell phone rang at the stroke of 1 a.m., he grabbed it like it was a lifeline. "Mallard. Is everything okay?"

If it hadn't been she would have called. That was Mallard all the way through: if there's trouble you know about it. Her silence meant that everything was under control. He'd clung to that thought all night, but up until now he hadn't realized that he didn't believe a word of it.

"Yeah." Her voice came through, exhausted but clear. He could almost see her, leaning against the backseat of a cab, her eyes half closed and the look on her face she got when she was holding back a yawn because someone—probably her mother—had told her once that yawning was impolite, and she couldn't quite break herself of the habit. "Yeah. Shana is okay, a couple of scratches. Deke got treated for being banged up—the blast threw him back and he must have landed on a rock or something—plus they both had some smoke inhalation, but they're fine. So's Parsifal."

He hadn't even thought about the dog. "What the hell happened?"

"House fire. Started while they were in it, just managed to get out. And no, I don't know what or how. I didn't really think it was time to be interrogating the firefighters, okay?"

"A fire?" His mind flitted around half a dozen possibilities, and settled on one. "You think it was arson?"

"Maybe. Probably. It would . . . I don't know. Nobody knows. I'm exhausted and I just want to go home and sleep for about six hours, okay? I ended up taking Parsifal back with me. He was all sorts of traumatized by the noise and all the people, and Shana really wasn't up to dealing with them both."

He thought about teasing her about her one-dog-only stance, but decided it was too late, and they were both too tired. Tomorrow, though. Definitely tomorrow.

"Oh," she added, "and Seth fired us."

"Seth can't fire us," he said automatically. "He hasn't even paid us."

"Huh."

Proof that she was exhausted: that's the sort of thing Gin Mallard *always* thought of.

"Where's Deke? Does Seth—"

"Seth got sent home when he growled at a nurse. Shana's car is being held as part of the scene, don't ask me why, so Deke and Shana are on their way to the ferry terminal, courtesy of Seattle's finest and a squad car that probably smells of vomit. Everyone's accounted for, poppa bear."

He ignored the slam, and bit down the other questions he had: she didn't know; if she did she'd be telling him. Everyone was safe, that was the thing to focus on right now. "How are you getting home?" Please, God, don't let her be taking mass transit at this hour.

"Car service. Almost there."

"Good. Sleep, Mallard. This will make sense in the morning."

"It better," she said sleepily, her voice still managing to be tart. "Because right now it doesn't make any sense at all."

10

The alarm clock went off half an hour early. That had been intentional: Ginny had thought an extra thirty minutes might give her a leg up. What it gave her was the desire to pull her pillow and the covers over her head and sleep for another hour.

Georgie, obviously convinced that she had overslept and therefore failed her morning responsibilities, put her paws up on the side of the bed and burrowed her own wrinkled snout under the pillow, attacking Ginny's face with more than the usual enthusiasm, trying to power-wash her owner into wakefulness.

"Oh God, Georgie, stop." Ginny wiped her arm across her face, both to ward off Georgie's affection and to remove some of the inevitable slobber.

The shar-pei dropped back to the floor and sat on her haunches, a look of expectation clear on her face. "Time to get up, Mom!" she seemed to be saying. "The buzzing thing said so!"

Ginny groaned, letting everything that had happened yesterday drop back into her head, then sat up, turning off the alarm clock and reaching for the glass of water by her bedside. She blinked the sleep away from her eyes, and saw Parsifal on the doggy bed in the corner, staring at her with hopeful eyes and a quivering backside. Which, on a puppy that small, meant pretty much all of him was quivering.

No matter the crisis, a dog's bladder took priority. Well, almost-first.

"Let me start the coffee first," she told them. "Then walkies. Then . . . everything else."

The sun was about as awake as she was, the sky outside her windows still a dark blue as the light slowly reached the western side of the city. The dogs seemed content to wait at her feet, so she quickly checked her phone as the coffee-maker worked its magic. Other than a text from Shana saying that they'd made it to her house safely, there were no new messages. Ginny decided to take that as a good sign, not a bad one.

She checked the wee pad she'd put down the night before, knowing that Parsifal's bladder control might not be able to last that long, but it looked unmarked. She probably should check the doggy bed and make sure he hadn't done anything objectionable to it overnight.

That could wait, though. She poured herself a cup of coffee and felt her brain wake up a little with the first sip, then set the cup down, and told Georgie, "Leash, sweetie. Go get your leash."

She'd not gotten the new leash from Shana, in all the chaos of last night. Parsifal made do with one of Georgie's old leashes; despite being ragged, it would hold against the puppy's weight. He clearly didn't like it, but once he figured out that they were all going outside, he submitted without further wiggling.

Normally this would be a quick walk—in her neighborhood, the other dog owners were mostly office workers who didn't have time to chat in the morning, not the way they would in the evening—but Parsifal walked slowly, and wanted to smell *everything*.

Not that slow and early was all bad, since the earlier hour meant that she'd have the chance to see different dogs—and different owners—from the usual. Ginny wasn't, by her own admission, a networking monster; she was busy enough with the clients she had, and her reputation among satisfied clients was always her best PR, but in one of their discussions about work, Rob had reminded her that you couldn't ever rest on your laurels, not if you wanted to look more than a year down the road. So, if she happened to have a few of her business cards in her pocket, along with the dog treats and poo bags . . . well, nothing ventured, nothing gained, right? You never knew when your next client might show up.

At five thirty in the morning, though, the neighborhood was weirdly quiet. They'd made it around the corner before encountering another dog and owner. Parsifal cowered a little behind Georgie's legs, while the shar-pei immediately went nose-to-nose with the four-legged stranger.

"Okay, that is the silliest puppy I've seen in a while," the owner said, laughing at Parsifal. "But a handsome shar-pei, there."

"Isn't she, though?" Ginny said. "And Parsi's . . . well,

he's never going to win any beauty contests, no, any more than yours will."

The man laughed, not at all offended. "Yeah, Cassie's not what you'd call pretty. But I love her, anyway." The dog, an unholy mix of several somethings, with a rough black coat and bullet-shaped head over oversized legs, looked up at her owner as though she knew she was being discussed. "And she looks hard-core tough enough that I can leave her tied up outside the store or the library and not worry that someone's going to steal her away. The number of missing-dog signs I've seen lately, it's enough to make you want to buy one of those guaranteed bike locks for the leash, you know?"

"Yeah. I guess." Ginny studied Georgie, who was now sniffing at the other dog's hindquarters with great dignity. She'd seen the signs, but hadn't paid much attention to them. In light of what she'd learned, recently, that was a mistake. "I leave Georgie outside of Mary's, I never thought . . ."

"Downtown's probably safe enough, and shar-peis probably aren't on the shopping list—too large, and they can lay down a fierce bite, I bet. But be careful. You don't want her ending up in a lab somewhere, and someone could scoop that puppy up and walk away with him in their pocket."

He sounded serious enough to take seriously. Ginny bit her lip. "No. You're right." She paused, then knelt to offer her hand, palm down, for Cassie to sniff. "I had always thought that was urban legend, labs that don't ask questions about where their test animals come from. Like dogs being stolen for fights, that kind of thing."

"If there's a crappy thing humanity can do to animals, assume someone's doing it," Cassie's owner said.

Despite the topic, Ginny almost smiled. "That sounds like the voice of experience. You a cop?"

He laughed, gently roughhousing Cassie's ears. "That obvious, huh? Retired, Chicago. Came out here a few years ago, exchanging the cold for the damp. But the instincts die hard, if they die at all."

The dogs had finished their social exchanges and were clearly interested in moving on. Ginny raised a hand in farewell and let Georgie pull her on to the next interesting smell, Parsifal now looking back with longing, once the threat of a stranger was gone.

Her smile faded. "He's probably exaggerating," she said. "At least a little bit. Someone at the shelter would have mentioned something like that, if it was a serious problem, right? Or at the vet's office when we brought you in, right, Parsi?"

The dogs, intent on smelling the urine puddle another dog had left behind, didn't comment.

Still. She hadn't been down to the shelter in a while, and the vet's office was in a different neighborhood. Either way, the topic was too close to the case at hand for her to ignore, not when it fell into her lap like that. An uptick in stolen dogs, puppies abandoned in a basement—all right, one puppy, and other dogs presumably missing . . . Had Parsifal been stolen from someone? Was there a little girl or boy out there missing their puppy?

If there was, why hadn't he been chipped? Why hadn't anyone put up missing dog notices for him?

Ginny stared down at the two dogs. The reality was that nobody was missing Parsifal, not even the men who had abandoned him. And now that the house he'd been found in had burned, there was damn little chance they'd ever find out . . . anything.

But why had it burned? Her mind slipped from the question of missing pets generally and back to the specifics of the case. She would believe that Deke absentmindedly left the stove on or something, but from what Shana had said, they hadn't been home long enough, and the timing of it having been left on for days and only then. . . . No, the fire had to come from another cause.

But was it an accident, an empty house and a bad fuse? Or had someone set it on purpose, hoping to destroy evidence? If these people came and went when things got too hot for them—and she winced at the pun—then it made sense that they'd want to clear out any evidence. They'd moved the dogs . . . and a fire in the house of a guy who didn't have the best rep in the world, who had just gotten evicted?

"Enter Deke, practically a ready-made patsy. Damn it."

If the cops found proof of arson, there was no way they wouldn't be talking to Deke. Not even his being injured would protect him, not with everything else going on. The landlord had filed eviction papers, but he hadn't specified . . . but if he was questioned, too, and he would be, because it was his property . . .

She and Tonica needed to know what had happened there, and that meant talking to Shana—and Deke, if he was willing—and seeing if she could dig up any official reports yet, before the cops acted on anything.

Even for her, that was going to be a challenge and a half.

She flicked Georgie's leash. "C'mon, kids. Mom needs the rest of her coffee, and we all need breakfast."

And she had a lot of work to do, fast.

Teddy parked his car in Mary's lot and sat behind the wheel for a moment, enjoying the quiet. He might gripe about having to wake up earlier, now that Ginny had him chasing leads at ungodly hours, but there were some compensations. The morning hush was a marked contrast to the usual sounds coming from the bar, even before they officially opened. Too late for the cleaning crew, who came in around four in the morning, and too early for any of the delivery trucks to arrive. He half expected to hear the crash and clatter of Seth loading up the recycling bins, or the squeaky wheels of the dolly truck hauling supplies, voices raised in the store next door, where the owner was forever yelling at his teenage daughter, who worked afternoons at the counter, or the skateboarders who had decided their side street was a safe place to practice.

Instead, he heard birds in the trees, and the hum of traffic on the main road as people headed to offices, the occasional shudder of the downtown express bus as it pulled in and out of the stop, and that was about it.

It felt wrong somehow.

"It's quiet," he said softly, and then, "Yeah, too quiet."

He laughed at himself, then rolled up the window and got out of the car, feeling his leg muscles protest. He'd gone for a run this morning, but his body still felt like he was moving at half power. Spending a full shift on his feet was starting to take its toll. He could have tried for a parking space closer to Ginny's apartment, but he'd only have to move the car again later, unless he wanted to walk back after shift, and stretching his legs now would be a good thing.

"You're getting old, old man," he said. "Time to get a job that has actual medical benefits."

Mrrrp?

He looked down and saw Penny heading toward him, her tail upright and quivering slightly at the tip.

"Good morning, sweetheart," he said, bending down to let the tabby sniff at his hand. "I didn't expect to see you awake this early, either." He'd read up enough to learn that cats slept most of the day, but he supposed there was good hunting early in the morning, too. Penny always ate the food he put out for her, but never seemed particularly in need of it, more like a polite guest eating what her host offered.

The image that put in his mind made Teddy grin.

Remembering her insistence on trying to come with him the night before, he said, "I'm going to see Ginny. Want to come along?"

He hadn't expected an answer, obviously, but she put her paws up on his knee and indicated quite clearly that she wanted *up.*

Once she was settled on his shoulder, her claws carefully digging into his shirt, he took a few steps forward, making sure that she didn't suddenly object to leaving the parking lot. She didn't.

He felt somewhat self-conscious walking along the street with a tabby cat perching on his shoulder, but when other pedestrians barely seemed to notice, he eased up a little. He supposed, for Seattle, that one cat walking her human wasn't that big a deal. He paused once as they crossed the park to let Penny switch shoulders, and noticed that a few tourists taking pictures of the Witness Tree took a picture of him, instead. Patrick would probably tell him to pitch the bar, bring in some new money, but Teddy just smiled at them and went on. He didn't *want* tourists wandering into Mary's.

By the time they got to Ginny's apartment building, Penny had given up on his shoulder, and was riding cradled in his arm. He felt a little more self-conscious about that, but since she was purring quietly, and this was easier on his back, he just smiled again at anyone who gave him an odd look.

When he rang the buzzer to let Ginny know he was there, Penny finally leaped down from his arms and disappeared.

"Hey!" he said. "Way to dump your date!"

"What?" came through the speaker grid.

"Not you. Hi, it's Teddy. You decent?"

The door buzzing him in was answer enough.

Ginny met him at the door to her apartment with a coffee mug in hand, shoving it at him with a raised eyebrow. She was in what he thought of as her "off duty" clothes—jeans and an old university sweatshirt, her feet bare and her blond curls loose around her shoulders. He wrapped his fingers around the mug, took a sip, and went inside after her, fending off an inquisitive shar-pei at his knees, the puppy at his heels. Parsifal still looked like a reject from a Muppet factory.

"Have you heard from Seth since last night?" she asked.

"No. Although I didn't expect to. He's not exactly the reach-out-and-touch-someone kind of guy. You?"

"Seth calling me? Not likely. I heard from Shana, though. They made it home okay last night, and Deke's still sleeping in her guest room, not a wiffle of trouble out of him."

"Want to take bets on how long that'll last?"

"Not really."

There was a loud thump, and Georgie abandoned them both, trotting off into the kitchen. Parsifal let out a high-pitched yip, but stayed with the humans, leaning against Ginny's ankle and tripping over her bare feet.

"I see he's made himself right at home. Good to see you've made it clear that it's only temporary."

"Oh shut up," she muttered, reaching into her pocket and tossing a treat onto the floor for the puppy, who fell on it with the grace of a greased penguin. "What's gotten into you," she called to Georgie, heading into the kitchen after her. "You better not be into the garbage again!" Teddy followed, leaving Parsifal gnawing on his treat.

When he walked into the kitchen, he started to laugh.

Georgie had her nose pressed to the window, and on the other side, sitting on the fire escape, was Penny.

"Is that—" Ginny said, gesturing helplessly at the window.

"Yeah," Teddy said. "She came with me—and then abandoned me at the door. I guess fire escapes are more to her taste than elevators."

Ginny shoved Georgie aside and opened the window just enough to let the small cat slip inside. Georgie lowered her head and allowed the tabby to touch noses, then Penny twined around the dog's legs, tail erect and quivering slightly. "These two," Ginny said, "I swear . . ."

And then there was a scrabble of claws on the floor, and Parsifal skittered into the room, tail wagging and eyes bright. Penny took one look and hissed, and the puppy thumped his backside down on the floor as though he'd been slapped, looking mournfully at the other two animals.

"Penny, that's not polite," Ginny said, but Teddy laughed. "One cat to rule them all . . ."

"Do not get your geek on my dogs," Ginny said. "Dog."

"Uh-huh."

"I'm not keeping him. Sorry, Parsi."

"Your objections are getting weaker, and they weren't real strong to start, Mallard."

"They're not objections, they're facts. This is a one-dog apartment, and a scruffy terrier isn't the image I'm looking for." She glanced down. "Sorry, Parsi. I'm sure with a manicure and a wash-and-set you'll be fabulous."

Parsifal ignored them, his eyes still downcast, waiting for Penny to let him get up again.

"C'mon, my stuff's in the living room, might as well get comfortable."

They left the animals in the kitchen sorting out their pack hierarchy issues, and went back into the main room, settling on the sofa. Teddy was starting to feel more comfortable in her living room than his own apartment, which was a sad commentary.

Of course, she also had more comfortable furniture. He sank into the sofa with a groan of comfort. Definitely getting older.

"Before we even start talking about the fire, and what it might or might not mean," he started, "I called a friend of mine last night." He put his coffee mug down on the table after looking in vain for a coaster. "She works for the city attorney's office."

Ginny took her usual armchair, curling her legs up under her. "Useful friend to have."

"Not really." He made a face. "Friend of my sister's. I have a strong suspicion she was told to keep an eye on me."

He couldn't blame Ginny for snickering. It probably sounded ridiculous, a man his age being monitored. But explaining would require explaining his family. He'd managed to avoid doing that for years, and wasn't about to start now. Not even to Ginny.

"Anyway, I asked her, in a roundabout way, if she had any dirt, confirmed or otherwise, about the owners of the boxing gym, the place where Deke tried to beat the answers out of another guy. Because I couldn't shake the feeling that there was something seriously hinky about the place. I mean, yeah, the guy Deke tried to shake down's obviously connected somehow, since he gave me a name, but maybe there was a *reason* the guy who knew that name happened to be there? Especially since all the tenants of those rental properties also had a connection, however brief, to the gym?"

"What?" She sounded pissed that she'd missed that. He managed not to grin too smugly. "Oh, did I not mention that?"

"Connection how? And what did you find out?" She put her own coffee mug down, gesturing for him to stop with the suspense and get on with it.

"They all, within the past ten years, had a membership at the gym. Which really isn't that much of a coincidence, since if you're a serious boxer or ex-boxer who doesn't want to be working alongside some hipster, your choices are probably limited. But what made it *very* interesting is that, according to my source, the owner of said establishment, one Samuel Donner—presumably the Sammy for whom the gym is named—had a bad and very illegal habit of running fight clubs out of his back room. Or rather, it's not so much the fighting that's illegal as the sizable number of bets being placed on such fights. The state bans all amateur gambling, so I'm betting none of this was ever reported to the IRS. . . ."

Ginny blinked at him, and he could practically see the bits fall into place the same way they had for him. Probably better, with whatever she knew adding to the puzzle. That was why they worked so well together, why he kept coming back for more: because he could feel the energy building, even as her brain attacked the new information. He knew his strengths, but he also knew his weaknesses, and one of them was that he was, at heart, lazy. It took someone else lighting a fire under him to get him going. And Ginny, he'd discovered, was the best kind of match.

"Once you get your fingers dirty, it's easier to shove all the way up to your elbows," Ginny said. "I'd bet that it's a pretty quick jump from arranging fighters to beat the crap out of each other to getting dogs to do the same. Especially . . . if he's taking money in from the bets, you can be sure the fighters wanted a cut, too. But dogs . . ."

"Dogs are cheap," Teddy agreed.

"Especially if they're stolen," Ginny said thoughtfully.

"What?"

"This morning, when I took Thing One and Thing Two for their walk, I talked to a guy who was walking his dog, an ex-cop. The guy was, not the dog. Although . . . beside the point. He warned me about leaving them tied up unattended, that the number of dognappings around here has gone up recently. I don't know if he's right or just paranoid, but . . . he was talking about people stealing them for illegal lab testing, but what if someone's stealing them for dogfights, too? The research I did, that's a thing. People's pets end up in the ring, after they're treated badly enough to make them vicious." Parsifal ran into the room, clearly looking for people, and she scooped the puppy up onto her lap, cuddling him. "Who does that sort of thing, Tonica?"

He had no answer to give her.

"So you think maybe someone's got a dognapping ring for a dogfighting scheme, and was stashing them in Deke's basement?" He made a face, aware of how insane that sounded.

"It would explain the dogs being brought back and forth—in after they're stolen, then out to . . . you know." Labs, or dogfights, or some other fate that probably did not involve a loving home and chew toys.

"But why store them at all?" Teddy asked.

"Do I look like a dognapping mastermind?" Her hazel eyes widened in exasperation. "I don't know. But someone *was*."

Ginny with her teeth in the facts was a fearsome thing to behold.

She ticked off those facts on her fingers, tapping each blunt-filed nail with her thumb. "So now we have a potential cause, a potential suspect, and a potential connection linking all of these things to Deke."

"And, if this fire turns out to have been arson in fact, we have actual cops actually interested in the potential suspect—or suspects," he pointed out. Their gazes met, worry shared. "We need to be careful, or Deke's back in it again. Even if they don't like him for the bad guy, they'll still pull him in for questioning if he knew what was going on. And you know how that will end."

With Deke pulled back into the system, no matter how innocent he might be. Zimmerman might have his heart in the right place, but once wheels started turning, Deke could easily get crushed underneath.

"Which means keeping our connection to him out of any poking around we do." Ginny tapped her thumb and forefinger together, and then flicked them out, as though getting rid of a disliked thought. "Insurance claims. Those should be easy enough to lay hands on, at least, compared to anything else. That plus the crime report should give us an idea of the cause, if nothing else."

"I doubt we'll be able to get anything from the insurance company right away, no matter what contacts you pull," Teddy pointed out. He'd had to fill out a few dozen insurance claims over the years, and he knew that even a house fire didn't get done in any hurry, especially when not much of value was lost. And if there was a pending investigation . . . "So in the meanwhile, we follow up on the dogs?"

Ginny stroked Parsifal's fur, pursing her mouth in thought. "The first rule of research is start where you have an in, and see where it goes. Assuming we're not going to confront the guy your informant gave us . . . ?"

"Not until we know more, no." He was determined about that. "And we're waiting on your informant for that, right?"

"Right. Well, other than the potentially evil podiatrist, Williams was our best in, seeing if the vet community had any alerts, but we already tapped that and came up dry. So who else might know about missing dogs, or a potential dogfighting run on the area?"

Teddy rubbed his eyes, then ran his hand over the top of his head. "You think it's time to talk to our friends down at the shelter? See if they have a line on things?"

"Maybe." Ginny made another scrunched-up face. "Yeah. Flip a coin to see who has to talk to them?"

They'd solved the shelter case, but nobody there had been particularly happy with what they discovered—the petty theft they'd been hired to uncover had turned out to be the least of it. They probably wouldn't get thrown off the premises, but they weren't going to be welcomed with open arms, either.

"Sure." He reached into his pocket to get the coin he always carried with him.

"Yeah, forget about it, I know about that coin of yours," Ginny said. "I'll do it. I should rebuild fences, and I'm going to be taking Parsifal down there, anyway, eventually."

He raised his eyebrows at her. "Are you?"

"Don't start that again. Why don't you adopt him? Your hours aren't any crazier than most people's; he'd adapt. And you'd have a running companion."

"Yeah, with those legs?"

"So you could carry him. Like weights!"

He rolled his eyes, and she held up her hands, indicating that she would drop the topic if he did. He sighed, and nodded. It was rare he could hold something over her like this, but it really wasn't fair: she was obviously getting attached to the little furball and didn't feel she could keep him. Teasing was fair game, but not when it hurt.

Teddy put his coffee mug on the table. "You know what, this is stupid. We'll both go. This is business; we work better as a team—you distract them with annoying questions, and I charm them into telling us what we really wanted to know."

She rolled her eyes at his description of their working process, but didn't disagree.

Georgie hadn't wanted to go back into the Old Place. The last time she had gone in there, bad things had happened. She'd been left with other dogs, and her humans had been attacked, and Penny had almost gotten hurt, and now the sharp smells of the cages and the things they used to keep it all clean made her want to stiffen her back legs and not let them go in, not let them leave her sight.

"Georgie?"

Ginny's voice was questioning, not angry, not yet, but the rising voice that meant Georgie was doing something wrong.

Georgie let her leg muscles relax and followed at Ginny's heel, like a good dog. She let them leave her in the room with the carpet that smelled of too many other animals, where there were too many strangers. She put her head down on her paws and didn't whine when they left the room with another human, even though she knew she was supposed to be with them. She had to trust her humans. And she had to pay attention to what happened around her, be alert, see everything she could see, smell everything, and remember it. Penny said so. Anything could be important.

Georgie could do this. She could watch, and she could smell, and she could listen, and she'd remember, all of it, to tell Penny.

She wished they hadn't left Parsifal back home, though. She wasn't good at worrying about two things at once.

★ ★ ★

"Misappropriated dogs? I'm afraid it is a problem, yes. Medical labs willing to cut corners, unscrupulous backyard breeders, even the occasional pet hoarder . . . We try to screen everyone who adopts, as Ms. Mallard knows, but it happens."

Much to their surprise, Este Snyder, the director of the shelter, had agreed to speak with them. Ginny wasn't sure if the woman no longer held a grudge about what they had uncovered about the soap-opera-worthy goings-on there, or if she was professional enough to let it go for the moment and would go back to shoving pins in voodoo dolls after they left, but she welcomed the help.

They were seated in the back room office, still as paper-cluttered as it had been six months ago. Ginny noticed that the photos that had been there previously were now missing, and decided not to ask about anyone else they had met during the case. She would rather be thought rude than step into the middle of something messy. Again.

"If people know about this," her partner asked, "why—"

"Why isn't something done?" Este sighed. "You can make something illegal, Mr. Tonica, but you can't always stop it. Especially not when there is money to be made. And people . . . there are many people out there who don't see dogs and cats as having actual emotions, don't feel any obligation to the creatures we've domesticated."

He nodded, his hands folded in his lap, his expression fixed in polite inquisition. Ginny once again had a flash of envy at how casually comfortable he was, talking to people. Her stomach was in flutter mode, and she was trying to juggle too many thoughts at once. Even her tablet, ready at her lap, wasn't helping, because she really didn't have anything to write up.

"Truthfully, theft is more of an issue than gray-market adoption. We keep our prices low for families to adopt, but we also price it high enough to discourage idle or malicious adoptions. In addition, several states have databases of known animal abusers who are banned from adopting, and we ask for references, although we rarely have time to check them all."

"Someone warned me about dog thieves this morning, while I was walking Georgie," Ginny said. "I noticed that you have a lot of lost-dog posters in the lobby. Has there been an uptick recently?"

"Nothing that I'm aware of, although it's entirely possible. We track any reported missing animals, so that if they show up here we can alert the owner," Este said. "I have been told that gangs will hit a neighborhood over a period of a few weeks, and then move on. By the time the residents realize that there's been a pattern, and alert the police, they're gone." She shook her head. "It's a terrible thing." She glanced down at her laptop, obviously checking the time, and then stood up. "If I can be of any further help, please do call."

That was a more polite get-out-of-my-office than Ginny had been expecting. She stood and shook Este's hand, then waited for Tonica to do the same before they went back out into the lobby.

Georgie was waiting for them, lolling on the carpet while a little girl of about ten rubbed the dog's belly.

"You're disgraceful," Ginny told the shar-pei, reaching down to attach the leash without getting in the girl's way. "Come on, sweetie, let your playmate find her own puppy."

"We're getting a kitten," the girl said, and her grin was infectiously happy. "Maybe even two!"

"Lisa!" Her father called her over, and the girl got to her feet and, with a last pat on Georgie's head, ran to join him at the door to the large "socialization" room, where the cats were allowed to roam freely with prospective adopters.

"Good luck!" Ginny called, and the receptionist, a woman with a wild array of blond dreadlocks, gave them a dirty look, as though her wishes were enough to jinx the little girl. Clearly, not everyone had forgiven them.

"Pity they didn't want a tiny little puppy," Tonica said as they left. "I notice you didn't say anything to anyone about having an animal to surrender. . . ."

"Shut up," she said. They'd left Parsifal sleeping in the dog bed, with plans for Stacy to swing by later and puppy-sit, but Georgie had looked so pitiful, waiting at the door, as though she didn't want to be left out, Ginny had decided to take the larger dog along.

The little parking lot outside the shelter was half full. It was only just past noon, when the shelter officially opened for adoptions, and Ginny found herself eyeballing everyone she saw, wondering if they were legitimate, or the front for a vile dognapping scheme.

"Stop that," Tonica said.

"What?"

"That thing where you're assuming everyone's a villain. Stop it. Your hairy eyeball could scare off a saint."

"My what?"

"That. That look you give. It's a hairy eyeball, and it's terrifying. Even Georgie's scared."

"Go to hell," she said, but tried to rein in the side-eye looks. He was right, the odds that someone would be here, right now, with that in mind . . . Yeah. A little paranoia was healthy, but that was a bit much.

"You working this afternoon?" Tonica used to have Mondays off, but his promotion to manager had changed his schedule severely.

"Not until six. Carl's doing scut work and deliveries while Jon's at the bar."

"Carl and Jon?" She shook her head. "That's not going to end well."

He sighed. "Jon's a talented asshat," he admitted. "I wish he'd just quit already. He got up Stace's nose, that she's working weekends and he's not."

"And I bet she meekly backed down and agreed to give him Friday nights?"

"Oh, yeah." He chuckled, stepping over the parking lot curb to the sidewalk, and waited for Georgie and Ginny to join him. "Yeah, that's *exactly* what happened."

"So which is more tangled: bar politics, or this case?"

"This case," he said, but it took him a moment to decide. "At least with bar politics, I can see all the players, even if I don't know what they're up to. Here, not so much. We've got a cop, trained to be suspicious, who sees something and makes assumptions, but we also have the director of the local animal shelter who hasn't heard a specific peep."

"Yeah well, we already know that she's not good at seeing things she doesn't want to see."

"True."

They walked down the street, toward the busier downtown area. "So we're back to the name you got. Lewis Hollins. The podiatrist. Who, on the surface, is squeaky clean." Ginny smiled, a quiet, almost satisfied curl of her lip that he'd learned to recognize. "Squeaky clean always makes me curious."

"Yeah. We love that about you. I—" He stopped, and put a hand on her arm. "Gin."

She glanced at where he was looking. It seemed the normal urban streetscape: a handful of people walking on the sidewalk, someone crossing against the light, a small delivery truck too far from the curb. At first scan she didn't see what had caused him to react, then her sense of the scene recalibrated, and instead of a guy unhooking his dog from a signpost, she saw the way the dog *wasn't* reacting to him, the lack of enthusiastic greeting dogs gave even when you'd only left them for three minutes to run in and grab a cup of coffee. More, the nervous twitch of the guy's shoulders when he looked around, clearly uneasy, and she was heading down the street only a half step behind Tonica, Georgie loping along without question.

"Hey!" Tonica called. "You with the dog!"

The guy—a kid, really, for all that he had broad shoulders and a decent beard—half turned, then stood up, abandoning the dog and looking like he was about to make a run for it.

"Georgie!" Then Ginny hesitated, because did she really want to sic her dog on a guy who might just be an idiot, not a criminal? Before she could decide, Georgie still waiting for the next command, Tonica had taken the decision out of her hands. He'd already reached the guy, placing one large hand on his shoulder and using his I-used-to-be-a-bouncer voice to ask, "Where you going without your dog, son?"

"Not my dog," the kid mumbled, his eyes wide but not daring to shake Tonica's hand off. "Friend's. We're having a few beers, I said I'd walk the damned thing, if he picked up the tab. But it looked like it was going to bite me, so screw that, he can come get it himself."

Tonica kept his hand on the kid's arm. "Great. Let's go talk to your friend. Ginny, stay with the pup, okay?"

In case the real owner came by, she understood, which would be proof that the kid had been trying to steal it. Ginny would rather have gone along, because she trusted that kid about as far as she could throw him, but knew that Tonica wouldn't be dumb enough to go anywhere he could get jumped, or otherwise have the odds changed.

She watched them head off to the bar down the street and shook her head. She might leave Georgie tied up outside Mary's, but she could keep an eye on things through the front window. The poor dog was probably convinced he'd been abandoned. No wonder he was giving off unhappy vibes, especially if he didn't know his owner's friend.

"Georgie, sit," she said, making sure that her dog was a fair distance away from the other animal just in case the guy was right. Now that she was closer, she could tell that it was some kind of German shepherd mix, and either very young or terribly underfed.

"Poor thing," she said to it, keeping her voice low and not making eye contact, the way their trainer had advised dealing with possibly aggressive dogs. It whined a little but kept its head on the ground and its tail didn't wag, so she stayed put, out of potential lunging range. "You look like you need a bath. And a few weeks of good food. Your owner isn't treating you right, is he? I don't blame you for growling. But you shouldn't bite, not unless you're trained to do it on command. And even then you've got to be careful."

She knew she probably sounded like a nutcase; only the fact that she was wearing clean clothes and had taken a shower that morning was keeping passers-by from assuming she was a street person.

"What do you think, Georgie? Is this a good doggie or a bad doggie?"

Her dog gave a heavy sigh and inched forward a little toward Ginny—also, she noted, staying out of reach of the other dog, who had opened his eyes and was watching her, but otherwise made no move.

She decided not to offer her hand for sniffing, just in case, and settled in on her haunches to wait, falling into an almost pleasant fugue state as people skirted around the three of them.

"Kid's telling the truth," Tonica said, and she startled, almost falling over.

"That was fast."

"Yeah, well, the owner took one look at me and started babbling. Just got the dog last week, says he was cheated, that the dog's sick, and bad-tempered, no fun at all."

"Feeding the poor thing properly might have been a good start." With Tonica back, she felt confident enough to reach into her pocket and pull out a dog treat. Georgie perked up, but the way the shepherd's eyes fastened on her hand decided it for her. She put the treat on the ground and pushed it forward to where she thought the dog might be able to reach. It didn't growl, didn't lunge, but watched her hand carefully. When she pulled back, it shifted forward, and took the treat up so fast she wasn't sure she'd even seen him move.

"Sorry, guy," she said, after repeating it with a second treat. "That's all I got. So, we overreacted?"

"Maybe a little. Understandably. But what's interesting," Tonica went on, "is where he said he got the dog."

"Oh?" She looked up over her shoulder at him, having to shade her eyes against the sunlight to do so.

"From a guy he met down at Sammy's Gym."

11

The front of the gym didn't look any more impressive than it did the last time.

"I think I'm overdressed," Ginny said, looking down at her outfit, black pants matched with a button-down blue blouse, and her usual two-inch heels.

Teddy gave her a once-over, then shrugged. "I wouldn't worry about it. Pretend you're checking the place out for a client."

"Huh." She clearly hadn't thought of that, but he could see the immediate change in her. Shoulders back, head tilted slightly to the left, her mouth pursed just a bit, as though she'd eaten something and wasn't quite sure what it tasted like yet. He imagined that this was the perfect picture of a private concierge, set to do a job, and do it well. Then again, she was the only private concierge he knew, so . . .

Then the façade cracked, and she looked worried again. "Nobody's going to take a swing at us, are they?"

"Probably not?"

"I don't feel comforted, if that's what you were going for."

"I wasn't." Teddy grinned at her, and she huffed at him in response, turning to let Georgie out of the back of the car.

"A pity we didn't bring Parsifal with us," she said. "If someone recognized him, they might give something away."

"I doubt the people we're looking for are able to tell one puppy from another. Not unless it's proven itself in the ring. I'm pretty sure the only thing Parsifal could take on was a throw pillow, and even then I'm not sure he would win."

"Ouch. Poor Parsifal, he gets no respect at all."

"I respect his ability to take down people with the cute," Teddy said. "Speaking of respect, though, Georgie probably shouldn't come in with us." His gaze flickered over the dog, then back to the gym. "The clientele here probably won't remember me from my earlier visit, but they'll sure as hell remember her. She made quite the impression on people."

"I'm not going to leave her tied up outside in this neighborhood!" Ginny gave him a glare, daring him to argue. Considering the reason they were here, he really couldn't. It would be uncomfortably like staking a deer out in front of a lion pride, if what they suspected was true.

"All right, she can stay in the car." They were parked in the shade, and it was a cool enough morning that she should be all right for a little while. "Will that be okay, if we leave the windows down? Or will she get out and try to follow us?"

"Georgie, stay," Ginny commanded, and the shar-pei

whined a little, but went back into the car. Ginny pulled something out of her bag and unfolded it into a bowl, then filled it with water from her water bottle. "Here you go, baby," she said. "We won't be long, promise."

The dog didn't look happy, but settled down.

"You sure you don't want to give her a little brother?"

"Tonica, puppies chew, and terriers chew more than most. Even as it is now I'm probably going to go home and discover my apartment's been turned into a war zone. So, no. I really don't want another dog."

He lifted his hands in a sign of surrender, then gestured for her to go ahead of him.

The gym wasn't as busy as it had been during his last visit, or maybe he was better prepared for the sounds of gloves hitting bags, the low, repeating grunts and slaps that bounced off the walls, and the low, rattling hum of an overstressed air-conditioning unit.

There was a young black kid at the front desk this time, and, leaning back in his chair like he owned the place, he watched them walk across the floor.

"May I help you?" There was just enough sarcasm under the polite tone to amuse Teddy. Anyone who used "may" instead of "can" in a place like this, and implied that they were beyond help, was his kind of hire. He wondered if the kid was over twenty-one, and if he'd like to consider a change of employment.

A polite cough brought him back to focus, and he turned

slightly to his left, indicating that Ginny was the person who would be talking.

"I was wondering if I might have a tour of the gym?" She reached into her bag and pulled out her business card case, handing one to the kid as though he were a suited CEO. "I am working for a client who is looking for a . . . particular sort of place to work out. He prefers one that knows how to keep its members off the radar—no flash, no publicity, just a good hard workout. You understand?"

"Ah. Yeah." Kid was well-spoken, sarcastic, *and* quick on the uptake, even if what he was taking up was an utter lie. Teddy was totally going to try to steal him. Unless he was involved with whatever was going on, of course.

"If you'll wait just a moment," the kid was saying to Ginny, "I can arrange that." He nodded toward the row of chairs against the far wall and put his hand on the phone on his desk, waiting for them to move away before he called the back office.

Teddy tensed: last time he'd just been waved on through to the back. Then again, last time he immediately established himself as one of the guys, with a connection to an old-timer. Ginny was going to get a different reception.

"Think they're going to check my bona fides?" Ginny sounded casually worried, like it was nothing more than waiting for a credit card to be authorized.

"Probably going to tell them they have a fresh, flush fish on the line," Teddy said just as quietly as they sat down where indicated. The chairs were metal, and uncomfortable, but he stretched his legs out in front of him, crossed his arms across his chest, and tried hard to look like a bored but professional driver/bodyguard/purse-holder. "This place may not be gentrifying, but they're not going to risk offending a possible high-interest member, not if it's their ticket to being trendy."

"Unless something really is going on here, and they don't want high interest."

"Then they'll say they don't have someone to show you around right now and put you off politely. Relax." That was easier to say than do: he could feel the strain in his shoulders as he tried to look casual.

"Uh-huh." But she looked a little more at ease. "So what are you going to do while I'm getting the Sucker's Tour?"

"Talk to some people," he said, letting his gaze rest on one person, then slip on to the next. He could tell who had something they didn't want anyone else to know. They were the ones really interested in the newcomers, while at the same time trying hard not to look interesting themselves. He'd already found a few of the gym's clientele that might fit that bill. "You know, schmoozing, the thing you haul me around for."

"Technically, you haul me. Although it's nice that you acknowledge who's the brains of this operation."

Teddy was trying to come up with a comeback when they were interrupted.

"Ms. Mallard?" The kid was standing now, and there was an older white guy next to him. He was wearing dress slacks and a button-down shirt with the sleeves rolled to his elbow, but somehow managed to look right at home in the gym atmosphere, like a boxer who'd gone into management rather than a manager who did some recreational boxing. Teddy was pretty sure the guy's nose had been broken at least once, and reset professionally. "This is Alan, head of our sales team. He'll show you around."

Ginny stood up and walked over to shake the man's hand. "Thank you for accommodating me on such short notice," she said.

"Not at all, my pleasure," Alan said. He took out a business card and presented it to her with both hands. She took it with both hands as well, bowing slightly as she did so. "Will your companion be joining us?"

"Nah, I'm good," Teddy said, waving at them without disturbing his slouch.

Alan gave him a once-over—a professional one, if Teddy was any judge—and nodded. "If you need anything, just ask Clarence."

Teddy nodded in return and watched them walk away, and then returned to idly observing the activity in the gym until the kid at the front desk—Clarence, he presumed—lost interest in him. It took about five minutes. Thank God for cell phones and texting, Teddy thought as he stretched his arms out in front of him, and then stood up. Clarence didn't even look up, having relegated Teddy to background noise. He suspected that the only thing that would make the kid look up would be a yell from the back office, or the front door opening. That was a point against him: working in a bar, you had to constantly be aware of what was going on around you, sensing problems before they happened, not after.

The gym seemed to fall into three sections. Up front, there were the guys jumping rope or doing floor work. It was serious stuff, requiring a lot of inward-focusing expressions. Teddy didn't bother to approach anyone there: interrupting one of them wouldn't be productive, and might get him punched. The other two areas were the raised rings, two small ones and a larger one in the center of the space, and the double rows of punching bags toward the back, their images reflected by a wall of mirrors.

He wandered around the raised rings, pausing to watch a trainer coaching two young fighters in one. Teddy had no interest in boxing as either a sport or a science, but he had to admit that they were definitely athletes: the teens were breaking enough sweat to make him feel like he needed a shower, too.

But the fighters in the ring weren't his target, either. Teddy kept moving, skirting the larger ring, toward the first individual he'd picked out, working one of the bags toward the back. As he did so, he caught sight of Ginny's curls across the gym, the blond noticeable where so many heads were either bald or wrapped in bandannas against the sweat. The guy she was with held open a door, and they disappeared behind it. The sign over the door said LOCKER ROOMS. Teddy assumed they were coed, since women were working out here, although not many, and if not, he hoped they knocked before poking their noses in. Guys caught with their shorts down could take crude shots, and Ginny wouldn't let that go unanswered.

He almost wished he'd gone with them, just for that. But he had his own job to do. "Hey."

"Hey," the other man grunted, catching the bag he'd been hitting and letting it still. The guy was built like a brick shithouse, square and ugly, and nothing you wanted to mess with, but the eyes that met Teddy's were filled with curiosity, not challenge. When you looked like you could take all comers, you probably didn't have to, so much. Even in testosterone palaces like this place.

"Got a question, and you seem like the guy who could answer it."

"Try and you'll get your ass thrown out."

"What?" He hadn't expected that, nor the matter-of-fact tone the warning was delivered in.

"This is a clean shop. Owners don't allow drugs. Only stuff here's the aspirin, and you gotta get that out of the medicine kit they keep in the back. He don't have no truck with drugs, and if he finds you with it you'll get your ass thrown out—and mine, too, for talking with you."

"Oh God, no, I wasn't . . . I have no interest in drugs." He could see where the guy had made that assumption: he didn't know much about gyms, being more of a runner for his exercise, but yeah, these places were sort of designed for a low-end trade in whatever they were trading these days. He'd seen enough of that happening in the skeevier bars he'd worked at to not be surprised it happened here, too.

"So?" The guy paused, one hand resting on the bag, keeping it in place, the other on his hip. The smell of sweat and stale smoke wafted off him, making Teddy's nose itch. He turned away, just a little, and something caught his eye: a younger man, not so heavily built, was watching them. Teddy let his gaze linger, challenging the kid to join the conversation. Instead he broke eye contact and turned away, picking up a jump rope as though that was what he'd been meaning to do all along.

Teddy turned back to the first guy. "Dogs."

"What?" And now they were even in the caught-off-guard sweepstakes.

"My question's about dogs. I'm looking for a dog to train for, you know," and Teddy moved his hand in what he hoped looked like a convincingly casual-secret-code manner. "Something reasonably fierce, that would make a good guard dog."

"And you thought I could help you with that?"

"I did." And Teddy waited. Finally, after a few deep breaths, the guy let go of the bag and started stripping off his gloves and unwrapping the tape, shaking his fingers out, not looking at Teddy.

"Clarence sent you?"

The kid was immediately knocked off Teddy's list of potential hires.

"Okay, yeah. I might know someone who knows something about dogs," he said, finally, when Teddy just looked at him. "What you looking for?"

Not why, Teddy noted, but what. "The woman I came

in with, she owns a shar-pei. I like the way it moves, but it's too . . . It's a really sweet dog. I don't want sweet."

"Huh." The fighter studied him, taking in Teddy's clothing, his military-style haircut, the paper-thin scars across his knuckles, old but not entirely faded. "Okay. Yeah. Gimme your number and I'll see what my friend has to offer. But his dogs don't come cheap."

"I understand." Teddy found a scrap of paper in his wallet that didn't have anything written on it, and jotted down the number for the phone behind the bar at Mary's. Anyone did any digging, they could connect him to Mary's and figure it out, but if they just looked it up in the directory, it would be reasonably anonymous. In that vein, he wrote "Theo" on the sheet, not Teddy.

"Great. Now beat it."

Teddy nodded, moving on as though he'd just stopped to pass the time with a random fighter, wending his way to the back wall. The guy who'd been watching them was jumping rope now, his attention focused on the wall of mirrors. He might have been watching his form—or watching Teddy without having to look directly at him.

Ironic, that the more threatening-looking fighter hadn't given him the creeps like this guy did.

The door he'd gone through in his last visit was on the far side of the building, the plate glass window between him and it. But he wasn't interested in the back offices right now. That was Ginny's job.

The other man he'd noted as a possible source had paused for a break. He was sitting on the bench with a woman who looked tiny in comparison, until you noticed that every inch of her sweat-covered skin was impressively muscled as well. Teddy normally had no complaints about his body: he was in good shape and everything worked. But this place could give him a complex if he wasn't careful.

"Hey," he said, figuring what worked once might work again.

The woman eyed him, then looked sideways at her companion, who rested his head against the wall behind them and didn't say anything.

Teddy started to think maybe he'd picked the wrong person.

Ginny had been on enough facility tours, often with jittery brides and grooms in tow, to know when she was being shined on, or redirected. So far, her guide—Alan Black, according to his business card—had seemed utterly on the up-and-up, answering every question without suspicious hesitation, and allowing her to poke her nose in anywhere she asked.

Every single alarm in her head was going off. Nobody, in her experience, was that open, especially not when they had city permits and inspectors to worry about. Especially-especially not when they were trying to hook new money.

"And you can see that our facilities are both clean and surprisingly private," Alan said now, showing off the shower stalls. "Our members are not bashful flowers, but there are times when you want a little privacy."

"But there are separate locker areas?" Because that was a lawsuit just *waiting* to happen.

"Oh yes. Although in practice they are mostly coed. . . ." He shrugged. "As I said, our members tend to be practical about exposed flesh. In all our time we've only had one locker room incident, and that was settled by the participants themselves before we had time to act on it." He smiled, warmer than the usual tour-guide professional-grade affability. "Creepers tend to back off when they realize their potential victim can land a solid punch. It makes us . . . self-regulating."

"I bet." Ginny thought about pursuing that, then decided that it was self-explanatory enough and instead made a show of looking around. "This is a conversion building? It must have cost a great deal to bring it up to code."

Alan took the bait, determined to prove that everything in the building was perfectly legal and acceptable. "The original owner had the structure gutted down to studs, and installed a state-of-the-art HEPA air filtration system."

"The original owner?"

"Yes, he renovated, and opened the gym, but sold it a few years later due to health issues. Ken, the current owner, bought it in 2007."

The year after the gym had been cited for the illegal fights, according to Tonica's contact. Health issues her sweet ass. "It seems like an odd thing to buy. Did he have a connection previously, or . . ."

"Yes, he was the night manager. We're lucky he decided to buy; otherwise, well, we might have been turned into a hipster yoga factory." Alan gave a delicate shudder, but it was, like his earlier smiles, too calculated. The guy was good, but there was definitely something under the surface, and she didn't think it was nervousness about screwing up his sales pitch.

"You certainly would be able to charge more, if that had happened. This may not be the most expensive piece of real estate in the city, but taxes aren't cheap, and then there's the maintenance, and, well, I'm a businesswoman. I understand how these things add up."

"We manage. It's important to us to keep things . . . accessible. You never know where the next hot contender will come from, after all. Plus, there are a number of people who enjoy the more blue-collar feel we offer, even as the neighborhood gentrifies around us."

"The lack of frills and publicity could certainly be a draw to a certain low-media type," Ginny agreed, reinforcing the idea that her client was someone who wanted to stay out of the spotlight and was willing to pay good money to ensure it. Although Alan's words implied that they had a respectable revenue stream going . . . at blue-collar-reasonable membership fees, she wasn't sure how that was working out. Were the backroom fights still going on? Was dogfighting that big—and steady—a moneymaker?

They didn't seem to care if her nonexistent client was a movie star or a crime lord, either. Ginny didn't want to judge people by looks, especially not when they were stripped down for sweating, but she'd bet her next retainer that there were more ex-cons than CEOs out front.

"I can only imagine that there have been people who thought that *blue-collar* meant," and she waved her hand airily, "not respectable?"

Alan's smile suddenly looked like it hurt. Good, now they were getting somewhere. "I assure you, this facility is clean. We have a zero-tolerance policy for drugs and harassment. Anyone caught violating the rules is evicted immediately."

"That is reassuring," Ginny said, with her best professional smile in return. "My client will be glad to hear it."

No drugs, no sexual harassment, but no disclaimer of any other illegal activity. The gym might be totally legit these days, and Alan might be the most honest man in Seattle, but after discovering embezzlement and murder in an animal shelter, of all places, Ginny was pretty sure she would assume there was at least an off-the-books poker game at a nunnery, especially if the nuns insisted everything was on the up-and-up.

"So there's never been any police difficulty?"

That smile of his definitely hurt now. "The previous owner . . . had been allowing private fights to occur in the back, after hours. Those involved were fired immediately, or lost their memberships, of course, once it was discovered, and that is now strictly forbidden."

All right, when pushed he came clean. Alan *was* an honest man, or at least playing one on TV. Ginny was almost impressed. Take that, Tonica, she thought, for all your snarks about how she couldn't schmooze!

"And that's the back-office tour. Let's move on to the

truly important area, the workout spaces, shall we?" Her host turned them around and ushered her through a side door into the main room again, his hand flat between her shoulder blades. It should have been an impartial, if unwanted touch; but Ginny felt her skin prickle uneasily under his palm.

Ginny had no interest in boxing, but she could see that yes, everything was in good repair, the floors were kept clear, the equipment maintained, the safety features all in place, including an upgraded sprinkler system.

"As you can see, even at peak hours we have capacity to handle everyone. In fact, our membership is capped to ensure that."

"So you know all of your members personally?"

"Not me, myself, no. But our managers make an effort to learn the names of our regulars. And the trainers, of course. We have four who work during the week, and another two come in on the weekends, when we're busiest. Although some members do without, or bring their own. We do not charge visitor fees for trainers; it's just a courtesy to our members."

"Of course." Her hopes—lifted when she heard the membership was capped—fell again. More people they'd have to consider. Although she supposed a visitor wouldn't have the same level of comfort with a place, that they'd use it to score illegal deals . . . right? Most likely they were looking for a regular—or an employee.

"Your trainers—they're all licensed, of course. I can imagine that liability insurance in a gym could become problematic, and the insurance companies bury you under paperwork in regard to that. Especially after the previous owner's . . . side venue."

He pressed his lips together, and a faint flush showed on his face, but other than that, he showed no sign of having heard her. "There are, occasionally, waits for the preferred rings, but no one is left without a station for their workout. If you would like to speak with any of our members, or examine the equipment yourself, please feel free. And if you have further questions, or wish to set up a member account, please contact me."

Ginny started to ask another question, but he looked at his watch with a practiced obviousness, and then said, "Good day, Ms. Mallard. I hope to hear from you soon."

Ginny chewed on her lip, going over the entire interview in her head. She'd screwed up at the end, she'd pushed too hard with the comment about the previous owner, but he hadn't thrown her out or asked why she was really there, so she was going to take it as a win. Her only question was if it was the insurance angle that had spooked him, or her circling around the previous owner. Or possibly both?

"Just once, I'd like to get a neon sign saying, 'Oh, hey, this is your smoking gun right here.' Only, not having it actually be a smoking gun."

Although she'd been given carte blanche to hang around and ask more questions, Ginny was pretty much done with the place, and worried about having left Georgie out in the car alone for too long. She glanced around, but Tonica was nowhere to be seen. She had a moment of panic, feeling like she'd been abandoned.

"Get a grip," she muttered, and went out the front door, breathing a sigh of relief as the fresh air hit her lungs. They might have an excellent ventilation system, but the air in there still smelled like . . . well, like an old gym.

Once her eyes adjusted to the sunlight, she saw Tonica leaning against the wall, nonchalant as though he were seventeen and ditching school.

"Enjoy your tour?"

"Oh, it was a blast," she said. "I was ready to lay down money for a membership then and there."

"Might not be such a bad idea," he said. "Not there, I mean, but learning how to throw a few punches . . . You're not always going to have Georgie around to protect you."

"So you admit now that she's good protection?"

"I'll grant her 'decent,' anyway." It was a running argument that even Georgie's taking down a thug who was trying to shoot them hadn't settled. Tonica still only saw the goofy, sweet-tempered side of the shar-pei. Ginny was thankful for that temperament, glad that her dog showed that side to most people, but under the loose fur and goofy face, there was solid muscle and sharp teeth, too. And, thanks to a year of training, excellent control that made her a potential badass, if Ginny were threatened.

But he was probably right, for reasons having nothing whatsoever to do with the cases. If mugged, she was willing to give up her wallet and jewelry, but there might come a time when she'd face something scarier, and Georgie wasn't always with her. She should know the best way to defend herself, rather than reacting on instinct that might get her killed.

But she wasn't going to admit that to him. Not when he was still dissing Georgie.

"Anyway, the only thing I got from Alan was a confirmation that there had been illegal fights run in the back, but he claims that was the fault of the previous owner, all that had been sorted, and they're clean, clean, clean now."

"Which of course makes you assume that they're not clean at all."

"It's like you know me." That, and the fact that the insurance question had made him run. Something was still off-kilter there.

"Wipe that smirk off your face," he said without looking at her as they started walking toward the car. "How someone as sheltered as you ever got so cynical . . ."

"You don't have to grow up on the street to get cynical," she responded, carefully *not* calling him on the fact that she knew he'd grown up protected by more family money and status than she'd ever see. "All you have to do is pay attention. Speaking of which, did you learn anything useful?"

"Maybe," he said. "It depends on if I get any callbacks, or if they were shining me on. One guy practically fell over himself to put me in touch with a guy who might know something about buying a dog that could fight."

"But?" she prompted, because she knew Tonica by now, too.

"But he was *too* eager. If he was involved in something illegal, he'd want to check my bona fides before he admitted to even maybe knowing a guy who might know a guy. I think he's a wannabe—knows about what's going on but isn't actually involved. Or he's a cop, working undercover. Or he's an idiot; that's also always possible. But hey, if he calls, that's a possible in. We'll play that one by ear."

Ginny made a face. She wasn't a big fan of improvisation.

"And then there were these other two," he went on. "Tight-lipped, butter wouldn't melt in their mouths, but they definitely knew something. They asked the questions I'd been expecting, what kind of dog I wanted, why I wasn't going through a shelter or a reputable breeder. They should've run when I told 'em shelters wouldn't let me adopt—I hinted around what Este'd said, about the do-not-adopt list, so if they know anything, they know I've abused an animal in the past. Allegedly."

"And you think they bit?"

"Maybe. They weren't promising anything, but I left them a phone number, in case they were willing to follow up. I'm betting we'll get something more useful from them than guy number one."

"We should set up an email drop for stuff like this," Ginny said thoughtfully. "And a dead-end voice mail. I could do that easy enough. . . ."

Tonica put his hand out in front of her, halting her midstep and midthought. A year ago she might have raised an eyebrow and asked what he was doing, but now she trusted his instincts enough that she tensed, alert for trouble. She scanned up and down the street, seeing the normal scattering of pedestrians, all minding their own business, two joggers, one with a German shepherd running alongside.

"What's wrong?"

"Dunno. Hang on." He started to turn around, as though expecting to catch someone following them. In that same instant, a solid, denim-clad arm grabbed Tonica by the arm from behind, pushing him against the wall.

Or trying to, anyway.

"The hell?" It came out a little strangled, because the jerk had his arm pressed up against his throat, but Teddy was sure he'd made his point. The guy—and it was the first guy from the gym, even though he was wearing a jacket and a ball cap now, Teddy could see enough of his face to recognize him, even if the stale smell of cigarettes wasn't enough to choke a horse—tried to force him harder against the wall, his other hand on Teddy's chest. Teddy gave a moment to weep for idiots who thought with their upper body, and not their lower.

And then he let his weight shift to his left leg, stabilizing his shoulders against the wall, and brought his right leg up, aiming not for the groin—a fighter should know enough to wear a cup—but the fold between thigh and groin. There wasn't enough room to get his foot there, but his knee worked almost as well, throwing his attacker off balance, if not quite enough for Teddy to break free.

He managed to look for Ginny, and saw that she was busy, his attacker's companion holding her by the arm in a grip that was going to leave bruises. But nobody'd pulled a gun yet, anyway, so maybe—

Ginny twisted in her attacker's hold and shouted. "Georgie! Help!"

And a forty-pound, fawn-colored bullet streaked out the open window of his coupe, down the sidewalk, and aimed directly at the guy holding Georgie's human. Ginny dropped to her knees and Georgie took the guy down onto the sidewalk, her paws planted firmly on his chest.

Teddy took advantage of the distraction, turning the tables on his attacker, grabbing the arm and twisting it back hard enough to not-quite-break. He'd learned that move from a bouncer in Chicago, and had hoped to never have to use it again. But it still worked.

"The hell?" he asked again, shoving his attacker onto his knees and checking to make sure that Ginny was all right. She looked pissier than a wet cat, but nothing was bleeding or otherwise busted. She rolled back onto her feet and ordered, "Georgie, hold!"

The dog lowered her head to the attacker's chest and sniffed: Teddy could see where if you didn't know Georgie, that could be deeply unnerving.

Teddy returned his attention to the guy who'd attacked him. "Dude, if you wanted to talk, you had my phone number."

The guy stared at him, then shook his head. "Boss says you're a cop."

Teddy almost laughed. So much for thinking this guy was undercover. If he was, he was doing a hell of an acting job. "Your boss is wrong." Teddy stepped back so he could keep both men in sight, but still within reach if either of them made a move. Not that Georgie's chew toy looked like he was moving anytime soon; Teddy knew for a fact that forty pounds of dog muscle was heavy, even if she wasn't leaning on your rib cage.

A couple walking down the street stopped and stared, one of them looking like he was going to intervene, but Teddy caught his companion's glance and shook his head. "These gentlemen are swearing off mugging for Lent," he said loudly enough to carry. "Aren't you, boys?"

That was enough to convince those would-be Good Samaritans that they didn't want to get involved. But they were going to attract more determined attention if this standoff lasted any longer.

"Get up," Teddy said. "Don't be stupid."

"Um?" The guy under Georgie made a weak noise but stayed where he was.

"Georgie, release." Ginny's command got Georgie off the guy's chest, but she only took a few steps back, and looked quite ready to tackle him again. Both assailants got up slowly, keeping their hands in clear sight at all times. Teddy suspected they'd been rousted by the cops more than once.

"I'm not a cop," he said again. "And neither is she."

"So why were you nosing around?" guy number two said. Teddy recognized him now—the rope-jumper who had been watching them while they talked.

"Teddy, what's going on?" Ginny had a hand on Georgie's head now, and looked prissy-pissed. It took him a second, then he remembered that she was still working another story, sort of, and was trying to keep that cover intact. He didn't think it would matter, but he'd follow her lead.

"While you were touring, I asked a few questions of this gentleman," he said, indicating thug number one. "Personal matter."

"I would appreciate your keeping your personal matters out of time that I am paying you for. Particularly when it involves violence."

"Yeah, all right, fine. It's not like I knew this guy was going to decide I was a cop! Jesus."

Number one widened his eyes. "You were serious? About wanting a dog?"

"No, I just randomly walk into skeevy gyms and ask strangers about random shit. Yeah, I was serious." Teddy was pretty sure he hadn't sounded so disgusted since six-year-old Annalee had tried to kiss his seven-year-old self back when. "But there's no way in hell I want to do business with you right now. Your boss thinks I'm a cop? Have *him* contact me, and we can talk. Otherwise, forget about it. Ms. Mallard, I apologize. Let's get you back to the car, and let these gentlemen sort themselves out."

"No, wait," thug number two called as they started to walk away. "Look, we're sorry. But the boss, he doesn't talk to anyone direct. You want a dog, just let us know. We've got a bunch of litters coming due; you can have your pick, fair price."

"Litters?" Ginny stopped and turned, looking at him. "You're breeding them?"

"Well, yeah." Thug number two sounded believably surprised. "Direct distribution, no middleman. We keep it on the quiet so we don't pay no fees, nobody poking around demanding their cut. You don't get papers or nothing but that's not what you're looking for, right?"

"You—you're running a puppy mill," Ginny said in disgust.

"Hey." Thug number one looked insulted. "Our dogs get good care."

"Yeah, that's why you sold my contact an animal that's badly socialized, and looks like it's been fed crap and not enough of even that for its entire life?" Teddy shook his head, aware that he was blowing his story to bits, but not caring anymore. "Give me the name of your boss, and I'll forget we ever had any of these conversations."

"Ah hell, you're from one of those animal activist groups, aren't you?" Thug number two scowled. "Screw you. We're not doing anything wrong."

"The emotional swings in this are giving me a headache," Ginny said, her voice crisp. "Whatever you're doing, it's illegal. You know that; otherwise you wouldn't have been worried if my friend here was a cop or not. This little conversation alone is enough to get you into unpleasantly hot water with the officials, if we were to report it—and at the very least, enough to get you both kicked out of this gym, permanently, as I'm told that they're most concerned with keeping their noses clean."

That made thug number two snort with bitter amusement, and Ginny turned to him. "Excuse me, did you want to say something?"

In another life, Virginia Mallard had been the strictest librarian to ever rock a cliché, because that voice made Teddy stiffen his spine and feel the urge to say "no, ma'am."

"Management in there only knows one kind of clean and that's cleaning up. You buying their holier-than-thou crap?"

Ginny leaned in. "You saying something's going on there?"

"Maybe I am, maybe I'm not."

Teddy laughed. "Dude, yank my chain all you want, I don't care, I'll just walk away. But do not annoy the lady. Her client list would make you piss yourself."

Not entirely untrue: he'd heard some of the stories about some of her jobs, all with names withheld but enough detail to understand why Ginny was able to afford a nice apartment and fancy tech on a select client list. Not that she could ever call on them for a favor, probably. But maybe, if it was important enough . . . or she was angry enough, yeah.

Thug number one was made of lesser stuff than his partner. "The place is clean enough. Manager keeps a tight ship now. Like I said, they don't allow nothing to go down on the floor, and freelancing gets you kicked right out. But they've got their own action going on. I don't ask, so I can't tell. It's smarter that way."

Teddy doubted this guy had ever done anything smart in his life. But he could see where the self-preservation instinct would kick in.

"Something connected to the fights they used to hold in the back room?" he asked. "Only not with fighters anymore, because they got busted, and they don't want to risk anyone who might talk if they thought they weren't getting a large enough cut of the action? Maybe something with more bark than bite?"

Thug number one nodded his head, repeating, "I don't know anything, I can't tell anything. And you ain't got the chops to get invited in, neither of you."

"Let us worry about that," Teddy said, crossing his arms across his chest and smiling, his best "I'm the House and you're gonna get bounced" smirk. "Give us a name."

Seth walked out of the back rooms at Mary's and glared at the woman behind the bar. "Who let the rat in again?"

"Oh hush," Stacy said, gathering the puppy in her arms defensively. "You're the one who got them involved in this; it's your own fault Parsifal's got nowhere to live."

"How'n hell is that my fault?" Seth didn't bother to wait for an answer, stomping back into the kitchen and making as much noise as he possibly could to show how annoyed he was. Stacy shook her head, giving the puppy another kiss between his oversized ears before putting him back down on the bar. He sprawled there contentedly, watching her set up the cash register. Jon had called in sick—likely story, she thought with a sniff—so she got to fill in. She didn't mind: Mondays were slow days, so she was able to combine this with agreeing to puppy-sit, swinging by Ginny's apartment to gather Parsifal—and a handful of wee pads—before she came in.

"You think he's cute, don't you?" Stacy asked Penny, who was perched on one of the bar stools, washing her paw with immense concentration. One pointed ear flicked in the human's direction, but otherwise Penny declined to respond. "Well, I think you're cute, Parsi," she said, and the puppy reached up to cover her face with kisses, making Stacy scrunch her face away in disgust even as she giggled.

"All right, be good now while I work, okay? Ginny promised you knew how to behave, wouldn't be any trouble at all. You're not going to make her into a liar, are you?"

That earned her another face kiss. "Oh, yuck, dog—really?"

The phone behind the bar rang and she pushed the puppy down before twisting around to answer it. "Mary's Bar, Stacy speaking."

She frowned. "No, I'm sorry, he's not working this afternoon. Would you like to leave a message? Oh, you're calling about Parsifal? The puppy? Yes, he's here. Oh, sure, we'll be open; come on by and meet him!"

She hung up the phone and smiled down at Parsifal, who was now chewing on his hind leg. "Looks like we may've found you a forever home!"

12

After getting to knock someone down, Georgie's normally placid blood had been riled. She braced her stocky body on the pavement and resisted leaving the scene of the party, even though the two thugs had long since skedaddled, not risking their would-be targets changing their minds and calling the cops on them after all. Not even a handful of treats could convince her to get in the car, not when evildoers might come around the corner and need to be knocked down *again*.

"Damn it, dog." Ginny finally lost her temper. "Get in there *right* now."

Georgie made a surprised half hop into the car and squirmed her way into the backseat, turning around once and settling herself without further ado.

"Huh." Ginny made note of the tone she'd used, and wondered if it would work on people, too. Probably not, but she made another mental note to try it at some point.

It took a few minutes more for the humans to get in the car and settled, and by then she'd let go of dog-training worries and gotten back to the question at hand. Only they'd just been given so much information, she wasn't quite sure what the question *was,* anymore.

Tonica sat in the driver's seat, waiting, as though he could tell she was trying to sort through her thoughts. Maybe he could: they'd been working together long enough, and he was good at that kind of thing.

"Yeah?" he asked finally.

She focused on what seemed to her to be the most important thing.

"Do you think, maybe, we got pointed in the wrong direction? I mean, the landlord said dogfighting and we took after that like . . . well, like a dog with a bone, but maybe the dogs in Deke's basement were from a puppy mill, not a fight club? It would make more sense—the coming and going, the lack of space. Maybe they were using Deke's house as, I don't know, some kind of halfway house from breeder to buyers? Take the puppies, leave the mommas?"

Tonica considered the question. "Yeah. That would make sense. And . . . it fits the players better—there's been a sense of casualness to all this that didn't *feel* right, if we were talking about something so violent. It also explains why we got mugged by the loser twins back there, instead of getting an actual beat-down, or being shot." He paused. "Are puppy mills even illegal?"

Ginny had already gotten her tablet out, and was looking up the local regs on breeding facilities. "Washington has laws on the books regulating any place with more than ten dogs. How many dogs would you guess were down there?"

"I'd have said no more than ten, assuming the cages were

large enough to turn around in, and they weren't packing in any golden retrievers. So say nine, to keep them legal . . . Nasty, but legal."

Ginny harumphed. "You can't make a lot of money selling nine dogs at a time, not enough to justify the cost, I wouldn't think. Not for dogs without papers. But if you had a couple of these places, maybe five?" The number of houses Deke's landlord had on the books.

"Or more," Tonica said. "That's one landlord—it could be a franchise."

Ginny pressed her eyelids shut against the tears. Basement after basement of puppies like Parsifal, like the dog they saw on the street . . .

"How many of them do you think die, Teddy? How many of the puppies . . . ?"

"I don't know. A lot, probably. That wasn't a sterile environment down there, and they weren't getting the best of care." Tonica shook his head. "It doesn't matter, though." His hands were resting on the steering wheel, his fingers slowly curling and uncurling as though he were regretting not hitting Goons One and Two when he had the chance. "There's regulation, yeah, but it sounds like they're not doing anything illegal. We can't call the cops, because nobody was breaking any laws—they were just being scummy. And we have no proof of animal abuse to nail them on."

"So we've got nothing. Maybe . . . maybe it's time to let go."

In the seat behind them, Georgie let out a sigh, clearly

tired after all the excitement. Tonica's sigh almost echoed hers. "Mallard." She could hear the frustration in that one word.

"Look," Ginny said, "you're the one who's always reminding me that we're not pros, that we're going to get ourselves killed doing this, right? Well, Deke almost *did* get killed, and Shana, too—somebody I dragged into this. And we just got jumped, even if they didn't have guns—*this time*. And Deke's *still* going to be homeless at the end of the day. Literally, since his house isn't habitable right now. Oh, and remember, we got *fired*. So why not just cut our losses and walk away, let Deke take his lumps like an adult? Like we said we would, if he was actually guilty?" She stopped more because she'd run out of breath than because she'd run out of words.

"Because if we did that, we'd hate ourselves." Tonica glanced sideways at her, then he started the car, and pulled away from the curb and into traffic.

"So what, then?" she asked, frustrated, but unable to argue the point because yeah, he was right.

"So we keep going. And I can't believe I'm the one giving rah-rah pep talks this time."

That almost made Ginny laugh. True, they'd totally switched their usual positions on this.

"We know what we know . . . what *don't* we know yet?" he asked.

Ginny thought.

"We don't know who set fire to the house, and why—or

even if it was arson at all. We don't know who the loser twins' boss is, although I'll lay money on it being the cold-eyed podiatrist, what's his name."

"Hollins," Tonica supplied.

"Right. Hollins, who we know is linked to the gym, if not directly with Deke. We don't know if the two things—dogs and fire—are connected, or if the fire was the land-lord trying to clear the decks so he could upgrade." She reached back and rubbed the side of Georgie's head. "We don't know a lot. I don't know how any of it can help us, though."

"Start with the fire. If it was arson, if the landlord was behind it, or if we can even *suggest* that the landlord was behind it . . ."

"If the landlord was responsible, or he knew anything about what was going on, we can use that as leverage to get Deke good references, get him housed again. Yeah. Yes. All right." He knew her too well: the moment they had a plan, even the baby germ of a plan, her mind seized on it, focusing all the tension and stress into something she could *do*. "I should be pissed at how well you know how to manipulate me."

"It's called partnership, not manipulation," he said. "So, talk to me. What else do we have, what else do we need, to nail the landlord to the wall?"

"We need eyewitnesses. Deke's useless, and I'm pretty sure Shana told me everything she knew, but there was someone else there—the maintenance guy who called the fire department. The cops had to have talked to him already."

"But there's no way he'll talk to us, not if the cops have put the fear of being accused into him, and I'll bet they have, even if only by implication. So we're back to needing the accident reports, and the insurance forms. Because otherwise right now all we've got is a burnt-out boxer, and a burned-down house."

"And a tiny puppy. Pretty much, yeah," she said. She leaned her head against the back of the seat and closed her eyes. Somehow, this case seemed so much harder than their others. Maybe because they knew their client, maybe because Deke was so . . . hopeless, on his own. *Hapless,* was the word that came to her. She'd never understood what it meant before, not really.

"Huh."

She opened her eyes. "What?"

"Probably nothing."

"You don't say 'huh' when it's probably nothing, Tonica. What?"

His gaze strayed to the rearview mirror, and he frowned. "I think we're being followed."

"What?" She quashed the urge to turn around and look—not cool, if they were being followed—and stared out the windshield instead, as though the car in front of them might have an answer. "Why? I mean, why do you think that?"

"I've seen the car behind us before. I didn't think anything of it because hey, lots of cars in Seattle. But not so many black sedans, like a livery car."

"You think someone hired a livery car to follow us?"

Tonica changed lanes, then looked in the rearview mirror again. "Yeah, no, but I'm pretty sure they're following us. There was no reason for them to change lanes when I did, but they did and stayed a car behind. I think the guy's a pro."

"How do you know how a professional follows someone, Tonica?"

"I watch a lot of television."

She knew for a fact that he didn't even own a television.

"Seriously?"

"There's one way to find out." He changed lanes again, and took the next exit before the bridge, heading for Queen Anne. It took them out of their way back to Ballard, but Ginny didn't question him, and she didn't turn to see if anyone—specifically a black sedan—followed them off the exit ramp.

Tonica took them down side streets, staying just at the speed limit, driving as though he knew where he was going. For all she knew, he did. Ginny waited, her fingers pressed into her palms. Behind her, Georgie stirred restlessly, picking up on her unease.

"Damn," Tonica said.

"Still with us?"

"Yeah. No, wait." He looked in the mirror again. "I don't know." They came to a corner with a red light, and paused, waiting. The tension in the car was high, both of them staring straight ahead, Tonica occasionally glancing into the rearview mirror without turning his head.

"Is he behind us?"

"No."

"Yay?" she ventured cautiously.

"Yay, I guess," he agreed. "I was so damned sure. . . ."

A car pulled up at the other corner of the intersection, and Tonica cursed. Ginny was able to see that it was a black sedan, just as the light changed and the sedan turned on yellow and cruised past them—too slowly to mistake the considering look the driver gave them, as though he were inspecting the interior of their car. The other windows were tinted, dark enough to hide anyone who might be in the backseat.

"Teddy . . ." Ginny's fingernails dug into the flesh of her palm, which was suddenly slick with sweat.

And then the sedan and its driver were gone, speeding away.

Ginny exhaled, unclenching her fingers slowly. "What the hell was that all about?"

"Damned if I know," he said. "But that wasn't casual interest."

"No kidding," she said. "And it wasn't friendly interest, either. I've been checked out before and it doesn't look like that."

In the back, Georgie whined, and Ginny turned around to look at her. "What's wrong, baby? Did the weird man upset you, too?"

"It was like he was looking for something," Tonica said. "Something in the car. I—you had Stacy pick up Parsifal, right?" he asked, and his voice was a little too calm, a little too tight for comfort.

Ginny just looked at him, her hazel eyes wide. "Yeah."

Normally Stacy preferred the endless restless chaos of a night shift, where she had to think fast and be quick on her feet to keep orders moving and the patrons happy. But she had to admit that there was something nice about a slow afternoon shift, too. Especially when she had good company.

"Oh, puppy! A tiny puppy! Is he yours, Stace?"

"Nah. He is a cutie, though, isn't he?" Stacy smiled at Gwen, who was offering her hand for Parsifal to sniff, and then lick. "And I'm pretty sure that you've grown overnight, Parsi. Not that you're not still a tiny thing." The puppy looked up at her, all floppy ears and oversized eyes under a fringe of brown fur. "Better behave, or Penny will beat you up."

The cat was in her usual spot on top of the shelves now, looking down at the activity with the air of a mostly benevolent despot. Once she'd realized that her human wasn't coming in any time soon, she had retreated with a sniff, but not left entirely.

"How are they getting along?" Gwen asked. "Any chance we can keep him for the bar? Make it a cat-and-dog matched set?" Gwen was a regular, who had voted "yea" to making Penny the official bar cat several years ago—not that Stacy thought there had been any question in the matter. Once Penny decided, it had been a done deal.

"No," Seth said, walking past with a scowl on his face.

Gwen laughed, harder when Stacy stuck her tongue out at the older man's back. Seth's dislike of animals in the bar was well-known. Even though he tolerated Penny for being a good mouser, and had learned to grumble mostly silently about Georgie's free run of the bar, he'd still rather they were all banished to the sidewalk.

Then again, Stacy thought sometimes he'd prefer if they were *all* banished to the sidewalk.

"I doubt it," Stacy said to Gwen, serious again. "Penny pretty much runs her own life, but a dog you have to, you know, take *care* of. We'd end up arguing over who took him home every night, and who had to walk him. . . . It'd be like being married, only without the sex. Anyway, Penny already has a dog, Ginny's Georgie."

Penny's tail flicked against the cabinet, thumping once, and she yawned, showing all her teeth and curling tongue, as though to say that there, the discussion was settled.

"All right, fine. You still serving beer here?"

"That I can do. Whacha want?"

"A Bock, please."

Stacy pulled the beer and was making change from a twenty when the door opened again and someone came in, closing the door carefully behind them. She looked up and, when she realized he was a stranger, gave him a once-over the way Seth had been training her, trying to decide how she'd handle him if he became a problem. The guy was taller than her, broad-shouldered but not bulked up with visible muscle. A hit to the knees, then, while staying out of range if he tried to grab her, until she could grab the bat behind the bar or yell for help.

Professional security taken care of, she offered him a smile when he sat down at the bar. "Hi there. What can I get ya?"

"I, um, I called? About—" He spotted Parsifal sitting on the counter a few seats down, and an awkward smile crossed his face. "Is that the dog?"

"Oh, oh! Hi, yeah. This is Parsifal. Parsi, c'mere, baby."

The puppy tilted his head and looked at Stacy, then took a step forward, looked at the stranger, and stopped.

"Huh. That's weird." Stacy tilted her head as well, looking at the dog. "Parsi, sweetie, what's wrong?" She went to pick up the puppy, scooping him into the crook of her arm and turning back to the man who was waiting. "He's very young," she said, rumpling the silky ears. "So you need to move slowly, so's not to spook him, I guess."

"Hi there," the guy said, but he didn't reach out to pet the dog. Stacy frowned. Maybe he was observing her personal space or something, but she'd noticed that pretty much *everyone* reached out to pet Parsifal: he just had that kind of adorableness. Especially someone who had an interest in maybe taking him home.

Well, maybe the guy was scared of hurting him, or putting his hand too close to her chest. That would be a nice change, if so.

"Here you go," she said, putting the puppy back down on the counter. "He's really not supposed to be up here when we're open, but he's so little I'm afraid I'll lose him if he's down on the ground. I'm Stacy, by the way."

"Rick."

"Hi, Rick. So." She paused, eyeing the man, and decided to trust her instincts. "Why don't you see if you and Parsifal are suited? Just put your hand out and let him smell you, let him make up his own mind."

"Oh, um, yeah, okay. Hi, um, Parsifal, you called him?"

"You can rename him anything you want," she said. "It was just a name my boss stuck on him, I don't know why. He's not exactly the knight gallant type, is he?" She smiled, but her gaze was cold, watching as Rick lifted a hand and then shoved it toward the puppy. Parsifal didn't exactly cringe, but he showed none of his usual enthusiasm for affection, either.

"You're not used to dogs, are you?"

"What?" Rick looked at her, and then pushed his hand forward a little more, curling his fingers as he touched the top of Parsifal's head. "No, I—" And he yelped as Parsifal twisted his head and sank tiny needle teeth into his hand. "Damn it," he cursed, and backhanded the puppy, sending it skittering down the bar, yelping in surprise and pain.

"Hey!" Stacy cried, instinctively reaching her left hand below the bar for the panic button, and instead closing her fingers on a familiar wooden shape. "Back the hell off!"

* * *

After their detour, the drive back to Ballard, and Mary's, seemed endless, thanks to the usual afternoon traffic, and construction. For the first time ever, Teddy wished he'd left the radio in the car, because the silence was making him tense up even more. Ginny had tried to start a conversation a few times, but they were both caught up in a vague but real sense of worry that didn't lead to idle conversation, and there wasn't anything new and relevant to talk about that didn't just feed their worry.

Once the traffic cleared, Teddy started driving just above the speed limit, constantly checking the speedometer to make sure he wasn't turning into cop bait. Part of him wanted to call the bar and make sure everything was all right, but he didn't want to panic Stacy if nothing was wrong. And if anything had happened, they'd call him first.

He took his phone out and propped it on his leg, just in case.

Meanwhile, Ginny had pulled out her own phone and was dialing a number, waiting for someone to pick up.

"Hey, hey, it's Ginny. Have you been able to get anywhere on the thing I asked you about?"

Teddy glanced sideways at her, and decided that the expression on her face wasn't good news. Pity: they could have used some about now.

"What? No, no, I understand . . . yeah. No, I get it. I'm sorry. Yeah." She ended the call and shook her head.

"Bad news?"

"No news. Luce, my friend down at City Hall, got her hand slapped one time too many for sneaking looks at reports she wasn't supposed to care about. Who knew the fire department's records were so hush-hush?"

"You never know when a fire is going to become front-page political news," Teddy said. "So we're going to have to rely on my contacts to find out what really happened, and that's . . . going to be slow." They were good guys, mostly, but checking out paperwork on a fire they hadn't had anything to do with was not going to be a priority for them. He made a sound of exasperation that made Georgie lift her head with a what's-up grunt.

Ginny was still staring out the window. "Too slow. We're going to have to go on gut this time." She sounded disgusted; Ginny trusted her gut, but she hated having to rely on it. "Do you think the fire was accidental?"

He shook his head. "No."

And there it was, the question neither of them asked, but both were thinking: if it was deliberately set, had it been arson, a way to get rid of a now-unwanted house . . . or attempted murder of a potential witness?

By the time they pulled into the lot next to Mary's, his usual slot thankfully still open, the tension had settled into Teddy's bones, thrumming in the back of his head like a headache about to appear.

They went in through the back door, bypassing the storeroom and tiny kitchen. Everything seemed in order, but the usual low hum of noise he'd expect from the bar in late afternoon was missing. If Teddy hadn't already been tense, that would have triggered it. Then there was a yell, and a crash, and he was through the connecting door that led to the front bar, wishing like hell the baseball bat they kept behind the bar was in his hands.

Then he pulled up hard, feeling Ginny nearly crash into him, because Stacy had the bat in her hands, standing over a prone body, with Seth on his knees next to the guy; Seth was breathing hard and swearing, the same four-syllable word over and over again.

Penny, her tail flicking back and forth in irritation, was sitting on the bar and staring down in disgust at all the humans. Parsifal was curled up next to her, his entire body shaking, but his eyes bright as he watched the activity around him.

Only after he'd taken in that his people—and the animals—were safe did Teddy realize that there were other people in the bar. He identified most of the patrons as regulars, shoved up against the far wall with expressions that ranged from terrified to outright amused.

"Everyone okay?" he asked, his gaze including everyone in the question.

"We got this, boss," Stacy said, her cheerful tone at odds with the way the bat was shaking in her hands, now that the adrenaline rush seemed to be wearing off. The figure at her feet stirred, as though to object, and she dropped the bat point-down to poke him in the shoulder. "Don't you move, you ass."

"Seth?"

"Yeah, boss." The old man sounded winded, and

pissed-off. "I'm getting too old for this shit. This used to be a quiet joint."

That earned him a snicker from someone. The last time they'd had trouble at Mary's, Seth hadn't stopped grumbling for a week because he'd missed all the action.

"What happened?" Ginny kept Georgie on the leash, rather than letting her roam the way the dog usually did inside Mary's, and started walking a careful half circle around Seth and the stranger until she reached the bar and was able to reach out a hand to Parsifal. The dog uncurled himself enough to sniff at her, then scrambled along the bar, almost knocking Penny over in his eagerness to be picked up and cuddled.

"Fuck you," the guy on the floor mumbled.

Stacy glared at him, and gripped the bat more securely. "This guy called, said he'd heard we had a dog that was looking for a home. He used your name. I thought you'd sent him."

"No."

"Well, I know that *now*. He didn't seem to have a clue about dogs at all, acting weird, and Parsifal didn't like him, did you, baby?"

"So you clubbed him?"

"Bitch is crazy," the guy on the floor moaned, and Seth, who had just gotten to his feet, kicked him in the ribs. "Respect for the girl who just whupped your ass," the boxer advised.

"Parsi bit him, but only 'cause he was spooked, and he

hit Parsifal—hard! Then Penny jumped on his head." Stacy was indignant, but proud. "And then I hit him."

"And Seth, being the only practical one around here, tied him up," Teddy said, finally noting that the guy's feet and hands were bound with what looked like . . . "Seriously, duct tape?"

Seth shrugged. "He tried to hit Stacy."

"I ducked," she said proudly, and the old man shook his head, his earlier praise set aside in favor of scolding. "Not fast enough. You haven't been practicing."

"I've been busy!"

"Yes, and you get busy and you get sloppy. I—"

"Guys? Not now." Teddy reached down and hauled the guy up by the collar. It was a showboaty move, but one that usually impressed idiots. The guy was in his early twenties, muscular but wiry, his facial hair straggly, the skin around his watery blue eyes unwrinkled. His gaze skittered away from Teddy's, then came back, reluctantly. Defiant but not stupid: he knew he was screwed.

"Normally I'm a mellow kind of guy," Teddy said conversationally. "But you came into my bar, and you were a jerk. You hit a puppy, man. Seriously? I'm not even a dog person and that pisses me off."

The guy opened his mouth, but Teddy shook his head, stopping whatever he was about to say. "Nuh-uh. Now, I have a couple of options. I can call the cops, and file a complaint. Or we can have a nice little conversation about who sent you, and why, after which I will just throw your ass to the curb and warn you against ever coming near this place or these people again. Your call."

He let the guy's feet touch ground, but kept hold of his collar, just in case the guy decided to make a run for it. Georgie could probably take him down before he reached the door, and if not, then Stacy looked more than ready to do it, but Teddy'd rather this was settled in a less messy manner. They'd already had quite enough fuss for the day.

"You came here about the dog. Why?"

"Look, man, I was just hired to do a job, okay?"

"Okay," Teddy said agreeably. "What job?"

"To get the dog. I was going to pay for it, I swear. Money's in my pocket."

"And then what were you supposed to do with the dog?"

Silence.

Teddy tugged at the collar, just enough to get his attention.

"Put it down," the guy mumbled, obviously aware that the answer wasn't going to win him any fans.

"Why?"

"Man, I don't know! All right? Some guy calls me, offers me cash money to get rid of a dog. What do I care?"

"Some guy you've never heard from before offers you money and you take it?"

"Okay, so yeah, I've maybe seen him 'round before, you know? A few times. At the gym, talkin' to people."

Teddy lifted his head and met Ginny's look across the bar. Odds of it being a different gym than the one they'd just come from were, he suspected, ridiculously low.

"Describe this guy."

That seemed to be another breaking point. "Man, I . . ."

"I will call the cops," Teddy said, his words bitten off with boarding-school-taught enunciation. "And I bet that everyone in here—being of the dog-loving persuasion— will swear that you assaulted that young lady when she tried to defend the puppy. Hitting a dog, hitting a girl . . . you think that gets you cred in jail?"

When in doubt, hit their machismo. "Fuck, man. I don't know. He was short, blond, pale. Maybe in his forties? Starting to go bald. Cold eyes, you didn't ask questions or give him grief, you just took what he was offering and said 'yes, sir,' you know what I mean?"

Yeah. Teddy knew.

Ginny nodded once when he looked at her again, then shook her head. He took that to mean that she didn't have any other questions he should ask. He pulled the guy up by the collar again, his other hand grabbing the back of his jeans, and hauled him out the door, which a customer cheerfully held open for them. The urge to actually toss him was there, but instead Teddy set him on his feet, if ungently, and let go.

"Take your money and if the guy asks, the deed is done. I see you again, here or anywhere else in the city, and I will break both of your arms, got it?"

Teddy didn't wait for an answer, but went back inside, closing the door firmly behind him. The moment it clicked shut, he got a round of applause.

"Yeah, yeah, save it. Everyone okay? Stace, next round's on the house."

That got another round of applause from the patrons, who seemed to think that the entire event had been for their entertainment. Teddy shook his head. No matter where you worked, some things stayed the same.

"Why didn't you call the cops?" Stacy demanded. "He should go to jail!"

"Because this is related to the case, to what's going on with Deke," Teddy told her. "If he's arrested, whoever's behind this might close up shop and disappear. We can't risk that, not yet. Anyway, they weren't going to arrest him just for hitting a dog. Sorry, Stace."

Stacy wasn't pleased, but she nodded reluctantly and went off to collect orders for the house's round.

"If they wanted to get rid of the dog badly enough to try this, odds just went up that the fire was deliberate, too. Not to get rid of Deke, but any evidence they might have left behind." That also meant that the other dogs were probably dead, too, or already sold. And any other dogs in other houses? Probably. He said as much to Ginny, quietly.

"Something spooked them enough to make them close up shop. This kind of a breeding mill may not be illegal, but I'll bet there's something on the wrong side of borderline going on, so they're not going to take a chance on getting caught."

"Taxes, maybe," Ginny said. "I bet the dogs are all bought for cash. And . . . they might be selling some of them to the dogfighters?"

"Maybe. Probably. Christ, what a mess."

"The guy you let go, he's not going to tell whoever hired him what happened?"

"No. If he gets asked at all he's going to say it all went according to plan. He doesn't want trouble, and he sure as hell doesn't want to risk the money being taken back. So we've got some breathing room."

"Hang on, I'm confused," Seth said, breaking into their conversation. "He came here for the dog? They're willing to do all this for a *dog*? *For* that *dog*?" Seth's face wrinkled in worry, making him bear a disturbing resemblance to Georgie. "What about Deke, if these people are that crazy, is Deke gonna be okay?"

"He should be," Ginny said, which probably wasn't entirely comforting. "But let's just leave him where he is for now, out of sight and safe, okay?"

"You might want to check up and make sure everything's good on that end, though," Teddy suggested.

Ginny considered that. "Yeah, when she finishes up for the day—she turns off her phone when she's painting. You think I should tell them? About all this?"

He shrugged, then nodded. "She's your friend, you know her better, but it sounds like she's got a solid head on. But we should probably keep Deke out of the loop."

"Ya think?" she muttered in a nearly perfect imitation of Seth, and it made the man in question snort in amusement.

"So, we re-hired?" she asked him.

"Idiots," Seth muttered, and stalked back into the kitchen.

"Not that I should be asking this, after the crap I've seen

already, but what are you guys into?" Stacy asked when she came back, ducking under the bar to start filling orders. "Is it dangerous? I mean—obviously. But should we call the cops?" Her earlier bravado had muted.

Ginny picked Parsifal up and cradled the puppy in her arms, resting her chin on the top of his head, and didn't answer. Teddy looked down and saw Georgie was leaning against Ginny's legs, while Penny had reclaimed her position on the top shelf of the bar, staring down at him with wide green eyes. He wondered if all of this made any more sense from up there.

"Something we're going to get out of," he said, answering her first question first. "As soon as we make sure Deke's in the clear. If you want to take the rest of the night off . . . and why the hell are you here, anyway? Jon was on schedule."

She drew herself up and glared at him. "He called in sick, so Seth called me because you were, and I quote, 'off doin' damn fool things.' And tell me you did not just suggest I should run home and hide under the sofa."

"I did not just suggest that you run home and hide under the sofa," he said obediently. "But I am going to ask that you stay behind the bar the rest of the night, okay? Anyone else comes in, let me handle it."

She chewed on her lip, then nodded. "Yeah, you can get the next one, that's fair."

13

The black sedan pulled to the curb a few feet away from Mary's entrance, the driver putting the car in neutral while his passenger got out, removing his suit jacket and placing it carefully back in the car.

"It's all right, Stephen," the man said, not looking back. "I'll call you when I wish to return."

The driver was clearly unhappy, but nodded and rolled up his window, driving away. His former passenger studied the renovated storefront for a moment, taking in the relative quiet of the side street. Most of the stores were closed for the evening now, another establishment down the street emitting a welcoming glow to match that from the bar in front of him, with patrons occasionally coming in and out, singly or in small groups.

"Excellent location. Nicely peaceful atmosphere, removed enough from the hustle and bustle that you can relax without feeling isolated or off the grid, upscale but not ritzy or overtly trendy. Good demographics." He turned and studied the rest of the street, taking in the mature trees along the curb, the quiet sounds of traffic from the main avenue, the lights coming on in the apartments above some of the storefronts. "I really should come down here more often."

But first, there was business to conduct.

"I'm looking for Theodore Tonica?"

The bartender, a young woman who looked too skinny to be healthy, gave him a deadpan stare and hooked her head downward, as though to say she'd never heard the name, but her eyes flicked to the left and downward, a sure giveaway. He smiled and accepted his seltzer and lime, leaving a tip that was too large for the charge, but not so much as to be offensive, and then turned in the direction she had unwittingly indicated.

The bar was reasonably busy for early on a Monday evening, confirming his original valuation, but the prime table by the window held only two people, despite there being room for more. A shift of shadows at their feet drew his attention, and he saw the dog lying at the woman's feet, apparently sound asleep.

The same dog that had been described to him as entering the vet's office, with the purloined puppy.

That confirmed his suspicion, and he walked toward them with a conscious grace, pausing when he reached a polite distance from the table. "Mr. Tonica. And Ms. Mallard, I presume?"

They both gave him a once-over. They didn't speak, but he could practically feel the exchange flash between them before the man turned his body so that he faced him—giving the woman room to pull back, out of the conversational spotlight.

"And you are?"

"My name is Lewis Hollins." He was gratified to see a reaction. He so disliked dealing with people who did not do their homework. "I would like to discuss a matter of interest to all three of us, if I may join you?"

Ginny made it a matter of pride that she wasn't often creeped out. She could be disturbed by something, or upset, and she was often angered, but there wasn't much in her daily life that creeped her. But this guy? Was way up on the creep-o-meter.

On the surface, he looked perfectly respectable. He was wearing a white dress shirt, properly buttoned and unstained, with a solid blue tie that was loosened at the neck but still showing a properly tied knot, plus he had a steady gaze that kept to their faces, never dropping below her neckline. There was nothing to set off a warning note, no reason she felt creeper vibes crawling up the back of her neck.

Except that his gaze was cold, assessing, and matched too perfectly a description she'd heard only a few hours before. And oh, yeah, she thought, he was in the puppy mill business.

"Please." She forced her tone into equal civility. "Do sit down."

Across the table from her, Tonica let a startled glance

reach her before he looked down again, getting control of his features. She tried to reassure him that she knew what she was doing, but the truth was that she was winging it, utterly. Still, if the guy who might be behind their current problems came down here to talk to them, who were they to refuse? Better on their own turf than somewhere else, especially with Stacy—and the baseball bat—behind the bar. There was also a gun in a lockbox, but she didn't think that would be needed. She hoped to hell it wouldn't be needed.

"I believe that we have a mutual interest in a situation that should be resolved before things, well, devolve."

Hollins smiled, and Ginny recognized a predator when she saw one. She let her mouth curve up in what she hoped was an answering, equally predatory smile. Tonica might be good at talking to people, but she spent most of her time negotiating, one way or the other. She had this.

"If by *situation* you mean where a friend of ours has been taken advantage of, and entangled in something he should not have been—and suffered for it? Then I'm afraid that your definition of *devolve* is rather different than mine. Because it's already well past that point."

She let the smile drop, but kept her gaze locked with his, refusing to look away.

Hollins's eyes tightened slightly, but his pleasant expression did not otherwise change. Challenge accepted. "Yes, I heard about the fire. Regrettable. I was relieved to hear that no one had been harmed."

Ginny tilted her head, as though she wasn't sure that she

had heard him correctly. "Homeless, and losing all his possessions, you don't consider that harm?"

"Homes and possessions may be replaced, Ms. Mallard."

And there was the real opening salvo. Ginny leaned in slightly, keeping her weight off her elbows, and shook her head. "And what about a man's reputation? Can that be replaced, too?"

She risked a glance at Tonica, whose eyes had gotten a little wide, but who otherwise seemed content to sit there and let them bat the verbal volleys back and forth. A familiar tension filled her gut, but it was a more useful one than the directionless unease they'd been dealing with before.

Hollins did not smile, which might have been showmanship, but she respected his effort to not try to patronize or downplay her comment. "It is . . . regrettable that his landlord jumped to certain assumptions, when he became aware of the source of your client's revenue stream. The houses we use were selected with an eye toward their owners' . . . benign negligence. We did not anticipate his becoming a proactive landlord. That was our mistake."

Ginny didn't do anything as inelegant as snort, but it floated, unvoiced, between them.

"Sadly," Hollins went on, "the damage has been done. I am prepared to offer suitable compensation for the inconvenience. And, perhaps, do you a good turn, as well."

"You're trying to buy us off?" Tonica sounded less outraged and more amused. She remembered again that he'd come from money—come from it, and walked away. Yeah, probably not going to be enough money to buy his silence, not unless he'd already decided to be silent and then he was too much a Boy Scout to accept the money.

Was she? Ginny honestly didn't know. Probably. If only because it would be hard to look Tonica in the eye after. Or Georgie. Dogs believed that their humans were perfect. . . .

"I find that money is a preferable solution to most problems," Hollins said calmly. "It gives people what they want and what they need, all in one simple package, without need for violence." He looked at them both carefully. "I am a businessman. I invest in opportunities that profit me, and my associates. Particularly opportunities that may not be particularly lucrative in and of themselves, but where the large-scale franchise possibilities intrigue me."

Hollins's words were matter-of-fact, not creepy at all, but *what* he was talking about made it downright ick. He didn't seem to notice Ginny's shiver of distaste. She was a businesswoman, sure, but there were *limits*.

"And when I see something that is being done well, with room for expansion or franchise," he continued, "I follow up on it. Like breeding dogs. Or providing social outlets."

"And you think, what, Mary's should be a franchise?" Ginny's gaze narrowed, and then she smiled. "Too late for that, the owner's already doing things his way."

"It had been my intention, originally, to offer to invest in this bar, yes, or perhaps to fund Mr. Tonica's own venture, if he were so inclined. Also, to invest in your business, which I have determined will stagnate if it remains a one-person operation."

Ginny opened her mouth to tell him thanks but no thanks, when he continued. "But, in observing and speaking with the two of you, another option has occurred to me. Your little sideline of untangling knots, or cutting them. 'Private Research and Investigations,' your website calls it? The service is hardly unique, but you bring a nice frisson of ingenuity and outside-the-box thinking. I appreciate that, even when it is interfering in my own work. I could see supporting an expansion of that."

"So long as we butt out of your business interests?" The smoother he got, the blunter Ginny felt.

He smiled, and calling it a shark's smile would be an insult to fish everywhere. "There are two sides to every agreement, yes. Each party puts something on the table."

Teddy hadn't been enjoying the back-and-forth going on in front of him, even though he knew Ginny had it reasonably well in hand. This sort of high-stakes negotiation, with hidden meanings in almost every word, was the kind of thing he'd grown up with, the kind of thing he'd intentionally left, and the pit-of-his-stomach ache was too familiar. He would stay and listen, be his partner's backup and witness, but he couldn't help but wish for a distraction, something he needed to go and deal with directly, to get away from the table.

Guilt for wanting to run away made him pay closer attention to the back-and-forth, especially when he heard Ginny mention Mary's. He almost laughed at the idea of him opening his own place—he never wanted to work that hard *ever*—but Hollins was probably right about Ginny's business needing to hire someone, at least a part-time assistant.

And money *would* solve Deke's housing problem, in the short run, at least. But the old man would still be on the hook for arson, especially if it *was* just a craptastically timed coincidence, and the landlord had set it himself and was looking for a stooge. Hush money could buy a lot, but Ginny was right—not a reputation. And that was assuming Deke would be willing to accept the money in the first place. Teddy had gotten a firsthand taste of how stubborn the old man could be. . . .

He felt something warm and heavy bump against his leg, and he reached down automatically, to reassure Georgie. But the dog didn't settle down again, and when he glanced under the table to see what was going on, her attention was focused on something at the other end of the bar. No, Teddy realized, following her line of sight: not some *thing*, some*one*.

"Excuse me," he said, when there was a pause in the conversation. "I need to take care of something at the bar."

When he got up, Georgie hesitated, whining, as though unsure if she should go with him, or stay with her mistress.

"Georgie, stay," he said, hoping that she'd accept the command from him. She sighed heavily but settled back under the table, her gaze still on the bar.

He got halfway there before everything went to hell.

★ ★ ★

He saw it happen in that weird slow-motion-but-speeded-up sensation that came every time he was in a fight, where he could almost predict each move before it happened, although he knew there was no way he could get there in time to do anything.

The woman—Teddy recognized her even from the side view: it was the quiet woman from the gym, the one who'd asked all the right questions—reached across the bar and grabbed Stacy by the hair at the back of her head, yanking her forward just enough that Stacy looked like she was leaning in over the bar to hear better.

Her companion, the same guy who'd been with her at the gym, was a few paces away, watching his partner while still keeping an eye on the rest of the bar's patrons. There was a kind of coiled stillness in the guy that Teddy's years of bartending told him to keep an eye on. The odds were depressingly good the guy was carrying. But he wasn't waving a weapon around, which meant that whatever they were here about, they didn't want to cause a panic.

Stacy was in trouble, but not immediate danger.

Teddy's gaze flicked up to where Penny usually rested, but he didn't see ears or tail dangling over the side of the top shelf. He didn't see Parsifal, either. Good. The last thing they needed right now was a puppy suddenly under-foot.

In the corner of his eye, he saw Seth moving, his shoulders forward, chin down, ready for a fight. Teddy moved a hand back at hip level, warning the older man away. Seth's face shifted in a grimace, but he paused.

They'd already been assaulted by low-end hoods, and propositioned by a high-end corporate criminal—he hoped things were only coming in threes today, not fours.

"Excuse me," Teddy said, projecting just enough to be heard by the woman, without breaking into the overall crowd noise and drawing more attention.

"There you are," the woman said, letting go of Stacy's hair. Stacy fell back a little, her eyes wide against tears, and he saw her reach for the baseball bat she'd replaced below the counter. He shook his head at her, too, and then tilted his head to the left. She nodded, about as happy as Seth to be told to hold on and stay calm.

If things got ugly, she was within reach of the panic button, but he really hoped they didn't have to use that, either.

"Here I am," Teddy said to the woman. "You had my contact info, you could have called."

"We felt that a personal visit would be more conducive to resolution."

"MBA talk. So not just a goon, then." Okay, so he warned the others off escalating things and then he went and taunted the bear. They could bitch at him later: right now he wanted her focused on him.

The woman didn't take the bait, though. "You've been nosing around in things that don't concern you, and do concern us. That's not wise. We're here to teach you some wisdom."

Teddy would have rolled his eyes in exasperation in any other situation. "Let me guess. There really is a dogfighting ring in the back room at Sammy's. And you think we were investigating that?" He remembered how much money Ginny had said was involved in dogfighting. Of course they'd react to someone poking around and asking about dogs. Damn it. Because God forbid this actually could have been an easily resolved job. "So what now?" he asked.

"Now you learn better."

There was a crash behind him, and Teddy swore, not wanting to take his eyes off the woman but needing to know what her companion was doing. From the sounds of it, breaking a table. And—there was the slam of something softer, heavier, against a hard surface—maybe people, too. He took a step forward, already calculating the odds, when the woman produced a Bowie knife and someone grabbed him from behind.

Penny had been dozing, one eye on the people below her, half that attention focused on Georgie, who was just out of sight under a table. Penny would have preferred the dog stay closer, but she was with Ginny, so that was all right.

The puppy was with the girl who worked with Theodore. That was all right, too. The puppy needed a person, and the way the girl's hand kept reaching out to touch his fur, the girl needed a dog, too.

The sounds and smells here-and-now were normal, familiar, soothing, and Penny had drifted into her thinking-space, mulling over the smells and sounds she'd been collecting, the things she'd overheard and nosed out for herself. None of it made sense to her, even for people, and that worried her. Humans often did things for strange reasons, but normally she could piece together what

Theodore and Ginny said, add them with what they'd learned, and find the cause. Not this time.

Penny blamed that deep-thinking, or the soothing familiarity of her surroundings, for how she was caught off guard, letting trouble come without her seeing it. The first she knew something was wrong was when the girl let out a frightened cry, and the puppy echoed it with a pained yip, as though someone had yanked its tail. Penny instinctively slipped down off the shelf, hiding herself behind the rows of bottles, tail bristling and whiskers outstretched, trying to find the danger.

On the floor behind the bar, the puppy whined at her, and she shushed it irritably with an ear twitch and a flick of whiskers. He hunched down and quieted, watching her intently.

Maybe there was hope for the thing yet.

Penny turned her head and took in the scene below her, her eyes widening and her ears going flat. A low rumble started in her throat.

This was her *place. Her* people.

Ginny had tried to keep her attention on the discussion with Hollins, trusting Tonica to deal with whatever was going on at the bar—it had to be serious for him to leave, but that was his job, after all, as manager. She could slog on without him, especially knowing that there was a bar full of backup, if she needed it.

"This is a business," Hollins was saying again, and Ginny was *so* tired of that word already. "I see no reason why everyone should not benefit from it, if we all do our jobs properly. Your side venture has shown that you have initiative, and potential. I am a patron of potential. Can we not consider all this a job interview?"

The worst thing was, he was totally serious. She was about to lay out the reasons why she wouldn't take a job with him if he were the last paycheck in the Pacific Northwest, when a loud cry and the sound of something breaking grabbed their attention.

Ginny was out of her seat in an instant, Georgie at her heels. She didn't know what Hollins thought of her behavior, didn't care, because the sound of splintering furniture was not a sound she should be hearing at Mary's, not now and not ever.

There was too much of a crowd gathering around the bar, blocking her view. She shoved impatiently at a shoulder until someone moved, and she could see Stacy, glaring over the bar at a woman, tall and strongly built, wearing a baseball cap, dark jeans, and a dark blue windbreaker. The woman was facing the bar but half turned, looking at Tonica like she was daring him to move. Someone else shoved one of the patrons aside and stepped forward, coming up behind Tonica. A man, holding the broken-off leg of one of the chairs, which he brought around Tonica's neck and used to yank him back so hard Teddy's head jerked back and stayed there. Ginny felt the command for Georgie to attack rise in her throat, and then choked it off, not sure if that would only make things worse.

"Shit," Ginny whispered into the sudden silence in the bar. She could almost feel the piece of wood pressed against her own neck, her mouth dry and her pulse too fast. Her phone was on the table; there was no way she could call the cops. Had someone else called the cops? Her gaze went to Stacy, who was looking from Tonica to the woman, who was now holding a knife, a big-ass one with a blade that caught the bar light but didn't reflect it back. "Shit," Ginny said again, louder this time. No way the cops would get here in time.

A hand came down on her shoulder, gently. It was Hollins standing beside her. His gaze was focused on the scene in front of them, the same as everyone else, but somehow the expression on his face was different. Not concern, not fear or even shock, but an intense . . . *study.*

Keep her talking. Keep her talking. Teddy swallowed against the weight across his throat, tried to relax a little rather than resisting, hoping that the hold would loosen. No such luck. He tried to talk, and felt the rough wood press more firmly against his Adam's apple, making him cough. At a signal from the woman, the wood eased a little. He swallowed, trying to get some moisture back into his mouth, then got the words out.

"You're here to tell me to back down from asking questions, and walk away?"

The woman shook her head, smiling slightly under the bill of her cap. She was weirdly relaxed, as though they were just shooting the breeze over a few beers, not in a standoff in front of nearly twenty people. "That would presume that our boss gives warnings. He doesn't. He takes care of problems."

"Seriously?" His voice, annoyingly, cracked on the word, and he felt the man holding him huff with laughter. That—more than anything else—pissed him off. "You come here, in the middle of a crowd, and threaten to carve my face up, and think the cops won't notice?"

The woman smiled at him again, unfussed, and stepped up closer, letting the knife's edge curl down the side of his face gently, not quite cutting skin. She didn't have cold eyes, he realized. She had dead eyes. There was someone home back there, but they weren't taking calls.

Great. He was about to get carved up by a professional sociopath.

"I really wouldn't advise that," a new voice said.

The woman was clearly not pleased with whoever had interrupted what was probably going to be a fabulous "As you know, Mr. Bond" speech. "Excuse me?"

"I said, I really wouldn't advise that." Lewis Hollins was standing next to Ginny, who was wide-eyed, one hand resting on the top of Georgie's head, keeping the dog still. He walked past them as calmly as though he were heading to the bathroom, and stopped barely a foot away from the woman, well within reach, if she decided to lunge for him.

"I've been hearing rumors about your employer for a while. Nasty work, that. None of my business, of course, except as it touched my people. I gave them orders not to sell to him, and presumed that would be the end of that. It appears not.

"Now, I realize that you are following orders—or perhaps elaborating on them, as you seem the type to do that. But even if your employer has not realized that this sort of behavior is bad for continued business, I'm afraid your too-high profile has cut into *my* business. And I can't allow that."

"You . . ." Her laughter was derisive, raking him from head to foot. Even to Teddy, who knew who he was, the guy didn't look very impressive, shirtsleeves and dress shoes, against a sociopath with a knife and the muscle-bound fighter who was armed, at the very least, with a wooden club. "How are you going to stop me?"

Hollins didn't posture, didn't make a witty comeback. He merely lifted his left hand and shot her with the pistol he held there.

The wooden club dug deep into Teddy's throat again, and he felt his abdomen clench as the air was yanked out of his lungs. Everything else went bright, and then dark as he fell to his knees, the last thing he heard a high-pitched screaming that might have been a cat's battle cry. . . .

"You need to let go."

Penny hissed, her claws still deep in soft, satisfying flesh. She had no intention of letting go.

"C'mon, Penny. You have to let go." Georgie was nose-to-nose with her, big brown eyes mournful, and she felt the urge to hiss, to scratch at her friend's muzzle, to make the dog back off, go away. But then she'd have to let go, and she wasn't angry at Georgie, anyway.

"Penny?"

Georgie's human knelt down beside her, eyes wide, a dark mark on her face and blood on her lip. She had gotten into the fight, too. Penny approved.

"Penny, sweetie, come on. The cops are here, and if you don't let go they can't take him into custody." She lifted a hand, wisely not touching Penny's fur: instead she let her hand drop into the folds of Georgie's pelt. "If you don't let go, they might think you're vicious, and . . . if they take you away, if they call animal services about you, who's going to look after Teddy?"

Penny's tail lashed, and she flexed her claws into skin, the man underneath her moaning slightly.

"He hurt Theodore," she said to Georgie.

"And you hurt him," the dog said.

That was true. He wouldn't be hitting anyone anytime soon, not after what she had done. She sighed and flexed her paws, releasing claws. Ginny scooped her, hands delicately under her belly, and lifted her up, holding her against her chest.

Penny permitted the indignity because this was Georgie's human.

"Were these the bad guys, Penny? Were these the ones who took the little man's home?"

Penny didn't know. But she wasn't going to admit to Georgie that she didn't know.

And then there were two men in uniform standing behind her, smelling of bitter smoke and cold metal, and the rest of the humans had backed away.

"Sir," one of them said, kneeling by the man, but not touching him. "Sir, can you?"

The man surged up, and the uniformed human grabbed him by one arm, twisting it behind his back and snapping a metal collar around his wrist. "I guess he's not too badly injured, after all," the uniformed human said to his companion, and hauled the man to his feet. "Better get the medics to look at his face, though. God, what a mess."

"Just get him out of here," Ginny said. "Get them both out of here. Please."

The crisis sorted, Penny leaped out of Ginny's arms, crossing the floor to where another human was inspecting Theodore's throat. Her human looked up and saw her there.

"Hey, you." His voice sounded strange, but he was smiling. Penny's tail lashed one more time, even as she purred her pleasure that he was all right. Not even the sight of the puppy on his knee, his hand stroking its fur, could ruin her good mood.

14

The cops weren't the same ones who'd come out the last time someone came into Mary's looking to do damage, but they'd obviously heard about Georgie.

"Looks like your dog's been teaching that cat some lessons about being badass," the younger of them said to Ginny, eyeing all three animals clustered by the door as though expecting Parsifal to suddenly sprout fangs.

The gunshot woman had been loaded into the first ambulance, and taken off, while statements were taken from everyone in the bar. The injured man—still moaning about his face—was being packed into a smaller emergency vehicle that had been called once the situation had been assessed. The other cop said something to the paramedic, and then stepped back, the doors closing just as the vehicle took off down the street.

"I think Penny was born badass," Ginny said after a moment, when the noise of the sirens died down. The cop smiled politely, made his excuses, and joined his partner outside on the street, where they seemed to be comparing notes.

"They've suggested that we hire a private security

guard," Teddy said glumly, watching them through the window. "Because yeah, that's the rep we want, exactly."

Ginny patting him on the arm. "Still. Nobody seems too traumatized, and only the bad guys got hurt. That's good, right?"

"Excuse me?" Stacy raised her hand, dragging their attention back to the others. "I haven't had my hair pulled that hard since I was in fourth grade."

"You got close enough to get grabbed," Seth said. "You haven't been listening to a thing I been teaching you?"

"I was serving customers! How was I supposed to know that she was going to go all psycho hair-pulling on me?"

Ginny tapped Teddy on the arm and tilted her head, indicating Hollins, who had calmly given his statement to the cops first, and was now waiting off to the side, near the table they'd been sitting at originally. A quick look at him, you'd never think he'd walked up to a knife-wielding sociopath and shot her in cold blood. Or maybe that was exactly what he looked like.

He'd had a permit for the pistol, fortunately. And since there were witnesses galore that the woman intended to do significant harm . . .

"It seems fair to expect that those individuals will roll over on their employer, yes?" he said to them now.

"Maybe," Teddy said. "Depends on if they were paid enough to ensure their loyalty. But the cops have enough to charge them, and if they're smart they'll make a bargain." He didn't think they were very smart in that regard. "Either way, their boss knows that officials are watching, so I suspect he's going to close up shop, at least for a while."

"Good." He must have seen surprise on their faces, because he looked exasperated. "I told you, as I told that female. I did not like their methods, and will be pleased to see them shut down."

"And it doesn't bother you that you're going to be called to testify?"

"I'm a respectable businessman," Hollins said. "Here to meet with potential business partners, who are entirely on the side of good, if not always the letter of the law. Why should I be worried?"

Since they didn't actually have any evidence against him, Teddy had to, reluctantly, give him that.

"And he will certainly have more pressing matters now than coming after two reasonably intelligent but relatively powerless amateur investigators," Hollins added.

"That helps us, but it still doesn't help Deke," Ginny said. "He's still homeless, and the cops still want to talk to him. And the moment they do that, the minute he gets flustered, he's toast."

Hollins made a coughing noise, stage-perfect faux-concern. "I take it, from your comments, that this individual is not one who wishes close contact with the police?"

"You know that already," Teddy said. "You do your homework."

"As I was saying before our discussions were so rudely interrupted, it was because he worked for me, however indirectly, that your friend got into this bind," he said. "Therefore, I will make reparations."

"Not a deal? Why the change in tone from earlier?" Teddy didn't want to look a gift horse in the mouth, but this had the look of a Trojan horse more than a pet pony.

"I have already determined that neither of you is interested in a continuing association. And if this bar has already developed a reputation among the local police, then it would not suit my needs, either."

"Well, there's a silver lining," Ginny said, quietly snarky, and Teddy grinned at her. If she was back to snarking, then everything was under control. Or nearly, anyway.

He turned back to Hollins. "Reparations how?"

"So we just let the bastard go?" Seth sounded like he was a hundred percent done with everything.

"It's not like we actually have anything we could nail him on," Ginny said reasonably. "His concealed carry was in order, by the cops' standards he did the righteous thing in shooting that crazy woman, and like he said, far as anyone knows for certain he's a respectable podiatrist who happened to be in the wrong place at the right time, or something."

It was a few minutes after midnight, and Tonica had finally kicked everyone out, claiming they'd had their fun earlier, leaving the four of them leaning against the bar in various poses of exhaustion. This was also the first chance they'd had to fill Seth and Stacy in on the discussion they'd had with Hollins.

"So we keep quiet about what little we know about the

puppy mill, don't give his people any grief, and he makes all this go away?" Tonica was still having trouble swallowing that, too, even though he'd agreed to it.

"It's . . . not a bad plan, actually. He pins all the blame on the maintenance guy—turns out, he's the guy who came around every month to check on the dogs, at all the houses, not just Deke's. Hollins is pretty sure he's the one who actually did set the fire—that's why he was there in time to 'rescue'"—Ginny used air quotes—"Shana and Deke in the first place. Said he's the kind of guy who'd do pretty much anything for a hundred. So Hollins will just pay him a little extra to take the fall. Cost of doing business."

"We just have to say he was the one who had the dogs in the basement and Deke, being hard of hearing, never realized it," Tonica added. "Since that's more or less the line Deke was taking, anyway . . ."

"And the maintenance guy will go along with this?" Stacy was frowning, too. She had really wanted *everyone* to go to jail.

"He's going to get nailed for the fire, one way or the other," Tonica said. "Better to get paid for it, too, I guess. Nobody died in the fire, and an unregistered puppy mill isn't illegal, just skeevy. And it's not like the people he works for are all that concerned about clean references. His willingness to take a fall might actually make him *more* employable."

Ginny glared at her ginger ale, wishing it was something stronger but not trusting herself with booze, this late at night. Georgie might be able to sleep comfortably in the storeroom, but she couldn't. Then again, she wasn't sure even booze would help her sleep well tonight.

"He's a bit player, Stacy," Seth said. "Long as those goons turn on their boss, the fights at Sammy's are over, and from what these two say, Hollins sounds like the kind of guy who, when he cleans his house, cleans the entire neighborhood, if you know what I mean. Even if the cops drop the ball on their end."

"Good," Stacy said, and knocked back the last of her beer, slamming the glass onto the counter with a little too much emphasis.

"It's not perfect," Ginny went on, "but this way Deke gets people to leave him alone, which was pretty much all he wanted, anyway."

He still didn't have a place to live, but being homeless because of fire was a lot better than because you were evicted—especially when nobody was claiming that the fire was your fault.

Hollins had also offered Deke a job—a legitimate one—but neither of them had felt like they could accept on Deke's behalf. Whatever those two agreed to, Ginny and Tonica had decided the less they knew, the better.

Teddy noted that Seth still wasn't looking happy. "Who twisted your shorts, old man? We did what you asked."

"Yeah, mebbe. But seems like that Hollins guy solved most of the problems, means what you did was just a whole lot of running around and shouting. So much for your vaunted investigative skills."

"Excuse you?" Both Ginny and Penny's hackles rose at that, Teddy was amused to note.

"You fell over the answer, and somebody else solved the problem, Blondie. That ain't what I was paying you for."

"You fired us," Tonica replied.

"And you never actually paid us our retainer, either," Ginny pointed out.

"Well, that's convenient, innit?"

And there was the next round of Old Coot vs. Mouthy Dame, off and running. Teddy was about to pour himself another beer and watch the show when his phone vibrated at his hip. He looked at the display, and stepped away from his friends to answer it.

"I'm busy."

"No you're not," his oldest sister said, sounding far too alert considering it had to be 3 a.m., her time. "You don't work on Mondays. I'm tired of you ducking your shit."

Teddy raised his eyebrows at that, but trying to interrupt his sister when she was in flow was pointless.

"There's a conference call on Wednesday and you will get your ass on it, all right? Nobody's going to make you come back to the East Coast if you don't want to, but you are going to own up to your damned responsibilities this once, Theo."

"Yeah. All right."

There was silence on the other end of the phone. Clearly, she had expected more of a fight. Equally clearly, his cousin hadn't told the others that he'd already given in. He sighed. The politics of family was *much* harder than the politics of the bar.

"All right, then. Eight p.m. Be there, Theo!" And then she ended the call, as abrupt as ever. No doubt there was a senator or a diplomat who needed handling more than her baby brother.

"Tonica!" Ginny was calling him over. Apparently he was needed to cast the deciding snark. Maybe he hadn't fallen so far from the family career-tree as everyone thought. For once, the thought amused rather than depressed him.

As he passed by the bar, he lifted his arm, and Penny leaped onto it, walking up to his shoulder, where she draped herself comfortably, her claws digging in just enough to make themselves known.

"That's twice now you've helped out," he said to her. "Maybe we should make you and Georgie official members of the team, hmmm?"

Penny purred in his ear, and flexed her claws in satisfaction, as though to say *what took you so long to figure that out?*

ACKNOWLEDGMENTS

This book owes a great deal to Barbara Caridad Ferrer (again), for above-and-beyond, the Tenants Union of Washington State, for answering oh so many odd questions, and the ASPCA, for everything they do.